Praise for *Waiting for Bones*

"A taut thriller that mixes detailed survivalist fare and character study with aplomb, expertly framed by a vibrant setting."

—*Kirkus Reviews*

"*Cousins* begins with a mystery and ends with—I won't tell! In between, the book is just plain hard to put down."

—John Lionberger, author of *Renewal in the Wilderness*

"Four American tourists in the wilds of Africa ... learn their limitations and their strengths after their guide vanishes. Every step brings perilous confrontations with fierce animals, malevolent plants, and—most dangerous—their own assumptions."

—Jane S. Smith, author of *The Garden of Invention*

"A gifted storyteller whose skills are apparent on every page."

—Joyce Lain Kennedy, syndicated columnist

"The writing ... is considered and memorable."

—*ForeWord Reviews*

Praise for *Landscape*

"The fifty-page climax of the book is one of the most exhilarating stretches of suspense writing I've read in ages."

—John Lehman, *BookReview.com*

"Absorbing reading. Fast-paced and intense, a fascinating window into the world of medical technology and the environment."

—Judith Michael, *New York Times* best-selling author

"If you can put this book down before you find out what happens next, you have a tighter rein on your curiosity than most people."

—*New Mystery Reader*

"It's a choice between family lives and wider community safety that keeps this novel riveting."

—*Midwest Book Review*

Novels by Donna Cousins

Landscape

Waiting for Bones

The Story of Bones

THE STORY OF BONES

DONNA COUSINS

iUniverse

THE STORY OF BONES

Copyright © 2018 Donna Cousins.

All rights reserved. No part of this book may be used or reproduced by any means, graphic, electronic, or mechanical, including photocopying, recording, taping or by any information storage retrieval system without the written permission of the author except in the case of brief quotations embodied in critical articles and reviews.

This is a work of fiction. All of the characters, names, incidents, organizations, and dialogue in this novel are either the products of the author's imagination or are used fictitiously.

iUniverse books may be ordered through booksellers or by contacting:

iUniverse
1663 Liberty Drive
Bloomington, IN 47403
www.iuniverse.com
1-800-Authors (1-800-288-4677)

Because of the dynamic nature of the Internet, any web addresses or links contained in this book may have changed since publication and may no longer be valid. The views expressed in this work are solely those of the author and do not necessarily reflect the views of the publisher, and the publisher hereby disclaims any responsibility for them.

Any people depicted in stock imagery provided by Thinkstock are models, and such images are being used for illustrative purposes only.
Certain stock imagery © Thinkstock.

ISBN: 978-1-5320-3544-9 (sc)
ISBN: 978-1-5320-3545-6 (e)

Library of Congress Control Number: 2017917092

Print information available on the last page.

iUniverse rev. date: 12/21/2017

For Harper, Dotch, and Alex

Happiness requires something to do,

someone to love,

and something to hope for.

African proverb

Until the elephants tell their story,

the tale of the hunt

will always glorify the hunter.

—African proverb

1

I was ten years old the day Skinner taught me that a person could be the most dangerous creature in Africa. It was a valuable lesson for a boy raised with a deep respect for living things. I was learning to coexist with the natural world, yet I remained ignorant of the many ways human beings can inflict misery. Fortunately, I didn't know that Skinner's life and mine would become as interlocked and tangled as an old osprey nest. All I hoped for then was to be rid of him.

On that awful day, the cobra that lived in the ditch beside our house decided to coil itself in the grass next to my bicycle. I didn't see it until I had tied my books onto the rebar welded over the back wheel and undone the chain. By then I was standing in the narrow space between the bike and the splintered boards that held up our front porch. Through the rusted metal frame I saw the pointy reptilian head rise and sway, hood flared to full effect, and I found myself staring into the blunt-eyed gaze of one of the world's deadliest snakes.

I knew it was "our" cobra because of the mark on its back where my father previously whacked it with a hoe before flinging it off the porch. "A Mozambique spitting cobra," he had announced, always wanting to teach me something. "Unless it tries to come into the house, we let it be."

I stood as still as I could. I wasn't a meal for this animal, and once it decided I posed no threat, it would calm down and slither away. I had learned enough about the creatures that shared our acre of the African bush not to try anything fancy. "Kill a fly, and a thousand come to its funeral," my father had said. "Wild animals aren't much interested in people unless we get in their way. Just let them be."

My father was a decent hunter who helped feed our family by shooting game, usually an impala, bushbuck, or other species of antelope that thrived in the bushveld where we lived. Although he said he liked hunting—the focus it required and the way tracking and aiming heightened every sense—he killed only for the pot, to feed our family. He detested ornamental kills and, worse, the slaughter of animals for ivory or horn. He told me about poachers who massacred with automatic weapons, leaving the landscape strewn with the hacked and bloody corpses of elephants and rhinos. I had never seen such evidence, and I hoped I never would.

So far, snake meat hadn't turned up on our dinner table, not even during the long, dry season when we ate little but the cassava we grew and whatever game hadn't migrated to wetter territory. The muscular cobra whipping its tongue in my direction could have fed our whole family. Uncoiled, it was longer than my bicycle. Fat too—good at catching mice and rats, which was why Mama had tolerated it in the yard for so long.

The fixed line of the up-curved mouth formed a frightful smile. My heart was racing, but I stood my ground. I knew cobras had weak vision and struck at movement. If I blinked too much, it could spit in my eyes. I squeezed them closed and stared into blackness. A warbler chirped. A fly whined past. Zola, my older sister, had already left for school, so the usual girlie chatter and *thwack-thwack-thwack* of flip-flops on the floorboards had ended. I could hear my mother inside trying to soothe the wailing baby. My father—Baba, we called him—was probably still in bed.

With my eyes closed I sensed rather than saw the cobra, not two feet away, holding itself erect, trying to figure out whether I was there. I had on the gray Fightin' Irish T-shirt I had found in the trove of used clothing at the Sisters of Charity, so long it almost covered my blue shorts, and the sandals Baba had made from the tread of a tire. I remember how vulnerable I felt, standing there bare skinned and tender. The slightest current of air rifled my body. Goose bumps rose on my arms. Baba had once watched a viper slide across his naked feet while he stood quietly, waiting for it to leave. I tried not to move my toes. The only thing to do was wait, the way Baba had done. *Just wait until the cobra settles and decides to go.*

Even with my eyes shut tight, I knew Skinner was coming down the road. When Skinner was in a hurry, his gait combined a skip and a sidle, his long body turning left and right as he rabbited along. I was familiar with the sound he made because he passed our house often, looking for my sister Zola. I had seen him turn his oily charm on her and other girls too. He would look them straight in the eye while he lied about having a job or boasted that he had killed a hyrax with his bare hands. He was a shameless girl chaser, as far as I could tell. I was glad Zola avoided him most of the time.

The double crunch, double crunch of his sneakers grinding against the dirt abruptly stopped, and with a stab of fear I realized he was taking in my predicament. When he hollered, "Don't move! I'll get him," fresh dread speared through me. "Getting" a cobra was far more dangerous than simply letting it go its own way.

Skinner wasn't known for good deeds or sound judgment. He came from a nasty background that had done nothing to improve his character—a brutal, felonious father and a trodden, defeated mother who died of abuse. Already Skinner's reputation for lying, delinquency, and bullying suggested a familial pattern. I swallowed hard and felt a trickle of sweat course down my back. This could go wrong, very wrong. I wished Skinner would just disappear.

I heard him run onto our porch, stepping lightly now, and down again. I wanted to know what he was up to, so I cracked open my eyelids. Through thickets of lashes I saw him creep forward, toward the snake and me, holding aloft Mama's round tin washtub. *The washtub?* I considered making a run for it, but first I would have to sidestep around the bike, a reckless move with a nervous cobra flipping its tongue an arm's length away. My stomach contracted as I watched Skinner pause to consider the angles and then snatch another look toward the house. I gathered that this was a show he hoped Zola would see.

Wearing a look of utter concentration now, he took aim. The tension in his body resembled the stillness of a wild creature preparing to strike, every nerve and muscle connected directly to his will. We both knew our lives were at stake—mine, in the direct line of fire, for sure. Venom from this snake could cause a person to seize up like a stone, become paralyzed, and suffocate within minutes.

What happened next is a big blur, but it must have gone like this: Skinner threw himself down on the overturned washtub, trapping the cobra, or most of it. The bike knocked into me so hard that I tipped backward against the rough boards and sank to the ground. I was only vaguely aware of the splinters clawing through the back of my T-shirt. All my attention was focused on the mayhem inside the tub, where the enraged snake unleashed a power so mighty that I couldn't believe it was the work of one small creature. The cobra thrashed and banged, making a horrible racket against the metal and bucking Skinner, who had laid his entire body across the top of the jerking, bouncing platform. He had captured all but about ten centimeters of tail. The protruding length whipped back and forth with terrifying force, kicking up a mess of dust that got in our eyes and noses and made Skinner cough.

Still sprawled on the ground, I sat almost eye level with the slashing, lashing section of manic snake flesh. The edge of the tub hadn't cut into or even deeply dented the tail, as far as I could tell. The ropey muscle swiped and pounded the earth, whipping up gobs of grass and dirt. I felt sure the snake was capable of beating its way out and attacking both Skinner and me. But with every thrust and buck, the edge of the tub sank further into the cobra's battered back. I both hoped for and dreaded the moment when living tissue would finally give way to unyielding metal. The maiming of animals went against everything I had taken to heart about life in the African bush. To cut apart a living creature was unthinkable to me. But then, I had never been forced to defend myself against an animal that wanted me dead.

I blinked away the grit in my eyes, scrambled to my feet, and stepped over the bike to fall on top of Skinner. I was a few years younger and many pounds lighter than he, but I guessed our combined weights would be sufficient to inflict a mortal wound. Beneath me, Skinner's chest pressed down so hard he gasped for air. The load of us suppressed the tub's herking and jerking but did nothing to reduce the frenetic pounding within. We endured the terrible commotion for what seemed forever. Then, at last, the thumping slowed. Skinner pointed to a thread of fluid winding into the depression formed by the thrashing tail. We watched the dark, wet pool enlarge as though our lives depended on it, which they did. The noise gradually diminished to a listless, hollowed rap, then stopped.

Skinner listened for a minute or two. "It's dead. Get off me."

He tried to throw me over, but I kept my arms tight around him with my hands gripping the sides of the tub. "How can you be sure?" My voice against the back of his head sounded small and weak. I knew the cobra could still be alive, lying in wait for a glimpse of daylight and the chance to nose out and sink its fangs in the nearest available flesh. "It might be faking."

"When it looks dead, sounds dead, and feels dead—it's dead. Now let me up, dung beetle. I have places to go."

I doubted that. Skinner had quit school years earlier to spend his days getting into trouble with a rough bunch of teenagers who swore, stole, and terrorized the smaller kids. Skinner wasn't one to keep appointments or, I was about to learn, finish what he had started.

He wriggled out from under me, cursing. When he had freed himself, he stood and brushed the dust from his shirt, eyeing the porch, still hoping to see my sister. I rolled over, taking care to keep my weight centered on the tub, and sat up, cross-legged, gripping my knees. A faint thump sounded below.

"Where's your uniform, Fightin' Irish?" he sneered, looking at my T-shirt.

"In the wash," I lied.

He eyed the washtub under me and snickered. "I hope not."

Our school principal, Mr. Kitwick, encouraged uniformity in students' clothing—blue and gray, at least. He was a tall, bony man who reminded me of a stick insect, an effect heightened by the long, sharp creases in his trousers. The gray suit he wore every day was shiny from pressing, and the knot in his blue necktie pressed against a mighty Adam's apple. Beneath the buttoned-up exterior, though, Mr. Kitwick was a practical man who understood the realities of his threadbare district. He usually looked the other way when our school clothes strayed from the standard uniform, and he was quick to make exceptions for financial hardship.

The burden of poverty was something I had learned to endure and even overcome from time to time by wearing to school a particularly choice, preworn T-shirt. I prized the swagger in my Fightin' Irish tee, although the words were risky around kids who actually liked to fight. The problem of dressing appropriately for school was even harder for my sister Zola. Her ill-fitting skirts and tops compounded the embarrassment of a budding body that drew unwanted attention from the boys. She had started cutting class days in a row, a secret she had sworn me to keep.

Now, leaning over me as I sat on the washtub, Skinner waggled a finger in my face. "You owe me, you little runt. I saved your life. Be sure to tell Zola."

"You did not. That snake would have gone away if you hadn't trapped it.

You made it angry, and it's still alive." My voice rose in pitch. Under me I felt the presence of the living, breathing reptile as surely as I felt my own pulse.

Skinner stared at me as if measuring the exact depth of my stupidity. "That snake is as dead as dead can be. You're lucky I'm letting you keep it. The skin will make a nice belt." He turned toward the road. "Be sure to tell Zola."

"It's still alive!" I shouted at his receding backside, feeling tears leak from my eyes. The vibrations in the metal had started up again, urgent and threatening. I was terrified and, at the same time, heartsick that we had treated the cobra so brutishly and wanted it to die. I felt ashamed to be sitting on Mama's slimed and bent washtub, not knowing what to do. I despised hearing my sister's name on those sneering lips. I didn't like missing school. And most of all, I hated Skinner.

I didn't move from my seat on the washtub, and I didn't call for help. In minutes Skinner had turned an almost normal school day into unthinkable torment. The rapid turn of events had left me hollowed out and dazed. I sat stiff-backed, frozen with fear of the creature trapped under me. Inside the house the baby had stopped crying, but I was too embarrassed by my predicament to summon Mama and too hungry for Baba's approval to admit I couldn't fix this myself.

My father encouraged self-sufficiency, an expedient attitude for a man with three children, an overburdened wife, and a weakness for drink. In spite of Baba's late, boozy nights and long, quiet mornings, he was a hero to me. I thought he knew everything worth knowing, and I never doubted he loved us. I had come to see his intemperance as a cruel foe that came knocking unbidden, like a recurring case of malaria. He would awaken soon, take a long drink from the pump, and without saying a word to anyone, lift a rake or watering can and retreat as if to do penance among the jagged rows of corn, potatoes, and cassava he managed to keep alive most of the time. I recoiled at the thought of him finding me helpless, sitting like an imbecile on Mama's overturned washtub.

The sun was clearing the treetops. Heat pressed down on my head, arms, and legs. Under me, the tub was warming up too. Before long the metal would feel like a griddle. I shifted my weight and considered how much heat a reptile could endure. The cobra hadn't moved in a while, as far as I could tell. The protruding length looked limp and lifeless. I was unsure whether the tail had been severed or was still attached by a flattened shred of tissue. Blood had drained into the soil, leaving a glistening black circle. I tapped my knuckles against the metal, braced for a furious explosion. No response. I knocked again, louder.

In the distance a dog barked. A squadron of insects buzzed in for a look at the bloody mess on the dirt. I heard nothing from the cobra, and for some time I hadn't detected the slightest quiver in the metal surface touching my skin. The snake was dead, playing dead, or catatonic from heat and exhaustion.

Hyunk-hyunk-hyunk. Rooper Nobbs, my best friend from school, was coming up the road with some other kids. Roop's distinctive laugh rang out over the shouts of the rest. *Hyunk-hyunk.* They were kicking a ball made of knotted plastic bags, too absorbed in their game to look in my direction. As they came nearer, I considered calling to Roop for help, but how, exactly, could he help? The lot of them would rush over and create a big scene. I could not imagine a happy outcome. I sat very still, eyeing the commotion beyond the scrappy hedgerow. The boys were clustered around the ball, yelling and laughing. Was this what they did when they skipped school? I wouldn't know because I had never skipped. Although I liked Roop, cutting class to play in the street seemed stupid to me.

The barking dog nosed through the churning mass of legs. The boys' cries rose as the mutt snatched the ball between its teeth and loped away, leading the whole pack on a rowdy chase. They disappeared down the road. Roop's laughter melted into the suffocating air.

I used a knuckle to wipe the sweat from my eyes. Flies circled my head. My mouth felt like cotton, and my legs tingled with cramps. Worse, I felt like an idiot, perched on a washtub in plain sight of anyone who cared to look. I was lucky the boys hadn't taken notice. What if Skinner came back? He would howl with derision.

The flat shag of our yard stretched before me. I considered the odds of a long jump and a clean getaway. More than once, I had seen this cobra winding its way through the scrub, and I knew it could move at impressive speed. Unless the snake was good and dead, I would have to clear the tub by a sizable distance to make a safe escape. I gulped in air, gathering courage.

As slowly as I could manage, I altered the angle of my folded legs until my feet sat flat on the tub, snug against my butt. I took great care to keep my weight centered, to prevent the slightest tilt from opening an exit at ground level. Now my chin rested on my knees, and my arms were tight at my sides, braced on fisted knuckles against the tin. I took a breath and pushed myself up.

My legs felt wobbly. I windmilled my arms for balance as I rose, rocking forward and back, terrified of tipping over. Once I had straightened up to stand on the flat surface, I felt a little calmer, more in charge. The treads of my sandals formed a barrier against the thin, hot metal and its unnerving vibrations. I bounced on the foot closest to the exposed tail. The tip moved up and down counter to the pressure—not the cobra's doing but what looked like the reaction of a rubbery dead weight. Dead or alive? *Cobra, are you dead or alive?* I bent my knees and swung my arms a few times, warming up for the longest jump of my life. *Steady, steady.* I eyed a spot in the middle distance, willing myself to land there. I flexed my knees, took another deep breath, and pushed off.

My heels landed about a meter and a half from the washtub. The rest of me tipped back, and I came to rest with my hands splayed against the ground behind me. If the snake had gotten loose, this would be its moment to strike. I remained in that vulnerable position about one one-hundredth of a second. Springing to my feet, I ran as fast as I could across the yard to the far corner of the house. I stopped there, breathing hard, and ventured a look back. The washtub was just as I had left it, upside down next to my bicycle.

My relief was sweet but replaced almost immediately by worry about what to do next. I couldn't leave the cobra, dead or alive, hidden under Mama's washtub for her or someone else to discover. The porch door was open. Baba hadn't appeared yet. I heard Mama singing to the baby. Both of my parents thought I had left some time ago. If I knocked over the tub and freed the cobra or removed its corpse without bothering them, I could still ride to school and avoid a big commotion—and avoid fingering Skinner too.

The decision to carry on without help from anyone came naturally to me. I was a resourceful, peaceable boy who shied from turmoil and liked order and routine—conditions difficult enough to achieve in our teeming household. I enjoyed solving problems, and I would rather try to fix something than stir up a hornet's nest of blame. Skinner, I just wanted to forget.

Thinking up a plan as I went, I ran to the stream that coursed past our square of farmland. The water was just a trickle then. During the rainy season, the stream and the river it fed rose and rushed, a thoroughfare for travelers paddling dugout *mokoros*. The water then churned with tilapia and catfish and the crocodiles that arrived to feed on them.

The fishing pole I had made from a slender branch still rested in its hiding place among the bushes. The pole was longer than I was tall and awkward to carry. I gripped it in both hands and ran as fast as I could back to my viewing spot by the corner of the house. What I saw from there changed everything.

Mama was striding across the grass. The thin line of her mouth and the parallel creases between her eyebrows told me she wasn't at all pleased about the current location of her washtub. Panic seized the back of my throat. I managed to yell, "Stop!" but my voice sounded strangled and weak.

In a hurry, she only glanced at me. "What are you doing home?"

Before my lips could shape another word, she leaned over the tub. The world went silent and slow. I watched her fingers curl under the metal rim. My mouth froze in a horrified O. She swung the tub up on its side, and a dark length of enraged cobra rocketed from the grass. With a dart of its head, the snake spit a volume of venom so great that I could see the fluid fly through the air. The spray sparkled in the sunlight, a silvery arrow shot from the gaping jaw straight into my mother's wide, surprised eyes.

She dropped the tub and cried out, turning away with both hands pressed against her face. Cobra venom in the eye burns and can blind but seldom kills. The pain, however, creates a gasping, flailing target that tells the snake where to land the fatal bite. I had seen this very cobra spit at a gecko that turned and bolted to safety. That memory gave me hope.

"Run, Mama, run!" I shouted, finding my voice at last.

But the enflamed cobra wasn't finished yet. The swaying, slithering body followed my mother's movements—the swing of her skirt, the bend of her knees. With terrifying precision, it lunged for the soft flesh on the back of her leg. The fangs gripped and held even as she staggered away. She cried out again, a keening wail, and stumbled forward, dragging the snake behind her. Finally, the creature unhooked its jaw and sank into the grass.

Baba appeared at the door looking sleepy-eyed and disheveled. He took in the scene—Mama, the cobra, me—and went rigid with understanding. He bolted down the steps faster than I had seen him move in a long time. When he lifted Mama in his arms, his face had gone gray. "Stay away,

Bonesy," he said, not looking at me. I didn't know if he meant from him and Mama or from the mangled snake winding its way toward the ditch.

I watched him carry her up the stairs and across the porch. The whites of her eyes had turned a ghastly, livid red. Her face was shiny with tears. As they disappeared through the front door, I heard her raspy breathing and a sob that must have come from him. I collapsed in the grass and stayed there, slack with shock and grief and a crushing sense of shame.

We buried Mama on the crest of a hill stalky with sunflowers. Zola quit school to take care of the baby. Baba succumbed with increasing frequency to drink, and at ten years old, I felt responsible for all of us. I practiced tracking and hunting small game for our dinner, worked hard in school, and marked off the days of each term on the wall calendars I got free from Ruby's Amazing Safaris. No one asked why I had been home on the day Mama died or how the washtub had come to be in the yard. The cobra turned up dead in the ditch. And for a while, Skinner kept his distance.

2

Zola was inconsolable for months after Mama died, but she was not unhappy to leave school. At thirteen, my sister was taller than average, shy, and too womanly in appearance to go unnoticed by the older boys. She would slope her shoulders and cross her arms over her chest to flatten her rounded breasts. She wore her tops untucked and unbelted to hide the gentle curve between waist and hips. With no money for new school clothes, she did her best to put together suitable outfits from the castoffs available to her, but fit was always a problem. The buttons on her blouses strained and popped. Her skirts either stretched tight across her hips or hung shapeless and bothersome, catching at her calves. At school I could do little to protect her. Trying to stop whistles and jeers was like trying to stop the wind. Her decision to stay home came as a relief to both of us.

I watched her take on Mama's household chores without complaint. At first she moved mournfully through the work, silent and downcast, finding in every pot and pan a sad reminder of our dead mother. She handled the wooden spoons, the straw broom, even the old scrub brush with a reverence that made me ache. She showed special tenderness for the baby, Hannie, who was generous with her smiles and smitten by the sudden intensity of her sister's affection. Zola herself—her willowy movements, the line of her back as she bent over the cradle, the soft notes she sang—so vividly recalled our mother that I often had to turn away and blink back my tears.

Zola's talent for the home arts surprised me. I realized I hadn't paid attention earlier when she was helping Mama. Now I saw her move among her everyday tasks with a calm efficiency that both relieved and saddened me. My sister's girlhood had ended. The trill of her laughter was rare, but she possessed a knack for creating warmth and comfort in our shabby surroundings—wildflowers in a jar, a polished window that let in the sunlight. I helped as much as she would allow, but she didn't pile on chores. "Your job is to study," she said, sounding ever more like Mama. "Study and make something of yourself."

School was free through the tenth grade, when we became eligible to take the all-important Junior Secondary Certificate Examination. Passing the test opened the door to two more years of high school for students who could afford to pay. For boys like me who couldn't pay yet hoped to escape a life at the barest edge of subsistence, the certificate stood as a passport to a better future—a respected marker of diligence and promise. In my small village, a JSC counted almost as much as a twelfth-grade diploma.

Neither of my parents had gotten past primary school. "My family showed little interest in book learning," Baba once told me. "They wanted help in the field, and that was fine with me because I preferred the outdoors." Then he looked me in the eye as if to clear up any misunderstanding. "A man can learn a lot on his own, you know."

He had learned a lot about farming and hunting, and his knowledge of the bush was undisputed. But as I grew older, it became clear to me that those skills hadn't gotten him very far. I loved the outdoors as much as he, yet I saw a cruel trap in the exhausting, uncertain work of subsistence farming. Drink had become my father's avenue of escape. Mine, I believed, would be through the bright portal of a Junior Secondary Certificate.

As the most difficult months of bereavement passed, Baba became a benign though increasingly undependable presence in our household. On his good days, he worked in the field, even selling a few extra bushels at the market. But we couldn't count on him to rise from bed before noon or to get much done at all. "I'm not quite awake today, Zo," he would murmur, shuffling out of his dark, rank bedroom for water or a hunk of bread. "Sorry, Bonesy. We'll go hunting next weekend." Many evenings, he drank out on the porch while he rolled and smoked the cigarettes that Mama, and now Zola, wouldn't let him smoke inside. Some nights he went to Captain Biggie's Tavern in the village. Some nights he didn't come home.

Early one Saturday he knocked on my bedroom door, clear-eyed and sober. "Wake up, Bonesy. Get your gun."

We set out on foot while the air held a cold, clean nip, and the first spill of light marked our path through the bush. The thought of fresh game on the table cheered me almost as much as a day out hunting with Baba. My pack contained two squares of corn bread and two twists of biltong Zola had wrapped in paper and tied with a string. We had eaten thinly for weeks. I was pretty sure the dried meat was the last of our supply.

My father went in front, resting his shotgun on his left shoulder. I walked behind with my shotgun resting on my left shoulder. Baba didn't own a rifle. He said I didn't need one either because I mostly shot birds and hares. The biggest game he hunted was impala, a species so plentiful on the open plain we called them "bush groceries." Baba could take down an impala with a single, well-placed slug fired at close range. I hoped he would get one today.

We said little. He had taught me to move quietly, placing one foot down before lifting the other, avoiding dry foliage, toeing each stick and root with snake sense. I watched his broad shoulders dip under branches and the way his head turned right and left, wary, as he monitored our surroundings. Hunting heightened the importance of everything. The slightest rustle drew our attention. A wisp of wind determined success or failure. My heart beat fast as we walked along. I was very happy.

Mama's death had not warped my interest in the natural world or in any of the life-forms that thrived near our home. I did not see evil in venomous snakes or poisonous plants, and I wasn't ruined for excitement and adventure. Although Zola seemed prematurely somber, almost fully grown overnight, I kept my boyish enthusiasms, including a love of the outdoors in all its messy, elegant, endlessly captivating variety. I was learning that grief was a season that changed over time, like the rains and the drought. My memories of Mama occupied a sweet and achy chamber in my heart, a place where she would remain for the rest of my days. But for me, the dark sadness of her death had given way to acceptance and a heightened respect for the survival instinct so devastatingly unleashed in the cobra that had killed her.

On this Saturday morning, Baba and I had been on the move for more than an hour when we came to a circular midden of black pellets, dung that marked impala territory. He stopped and glassed the open plain. A herd of twenty or more impalas was spread out, grazing. The animals closest to us stood with their necks stretched tall to look in our direction. "They know we're here," he said in a low voice. "Let's go downwind and find a place to settle."

I followed him in a wide circle around the herd. Another midden indicated we remained on promising turf. Baba pointed to a fallen log, and we stopped there, shielded from the impalas by a thicket of bush. I rotated my stiffened gun shoulder before sitting down next to him, quiet and still. He turned to me and smiled. A current passed between us that swelled me with love and pride. I was only a boy, but already I felt the bone-deep camaraderie that forms among men on the hunt, as ancient and enduring as survival itself.

For many minutes we sat motionless but present, sensitive to the air feathering our skin, the faint creak of branches, the earthy smell of trampled vegetation and dust. I imitated Baba's posture, relaxed and stooping, a pose that declared with every angle of his limbs an infinite willingness to wait. Small creatures alert to our arrival soon got used to our presence. A mouse darted into the underbrush near my foot. A dragonfly landed on Baba's shoulder, dipped its wings, and flew off.

An uptick in the ambient chatter of birds and squirrels signaled a new arrival. Baba raised his head. We both knew the intruder could be anything, including a predator stalking us. Quietly, we took our shotguns in hand and rose from the log. For several minutes we stood in a state of acute awareness, open to every whisper and scurry. When the sound we were waiting for finally broke the air, the crackle of footfall seemed unnaturally loud. My heart was thumping so hard I was sure Baba could hear it. He had directed his attention to the thicket of bush in front of us. I peered through the branches. Four slender legs and the elegant flank of a young male impala stood well within the range of our guns.

Baba lowered his shotgun and turned to me. My eyes widened as I realized he meant for me to take the shot. The biggest game I had ever brought down was a two-kilo hare. A miss now would end the best hope of meat we'd had in a long time. I swallowed hard and nodded.

The impala stood about fifteen meters away. He was a handsome young buck with a glossy coat and midsized, S-shaped horns. I raised my gun and flicked the safety, slipping into the calculating, impersonal zone that enabled me to aim, shoot, and kill. I knew a lung shot would spoil the least amount of meat, so I aimed up the foreleg about a third, then a little to the rear. I settled there, calm, and squeezed the trigger.

The bush is never silent except in the stunned moment following a gunshot, when even the insects cease their whining. In that noiseless instant the impala shuddered, pronked, and bolted out of view. I wasn't sure whether I had hit my target or missed completely. The confidence I had felt moments earlier vanished. Had I failed to hold my breath? Did my hand shake at a crucial moment? Was the wind playing tricks? What I dreaded most was the shame of inflicting a wound that doomed a creature to a prolonged and senseless death, even as it escaped. The sour taste of panic rose in my throat.

"You first," Baba said, stepping aside.

I ran around the thicket and into the open, where a splotch of blood darkened the leaves. I saw more blood a few meters away and followed the trail up a gentle rise into a stand of trees. Looking around, I feared the worst: that I had destroyed a beautiful animal that had vanished and would die for nothing. Baba stood beside me, scanning the ground but not taking the lead. After a moment, he cleared his throat and dipped his head in the direction of a medallion of blood I had overlooked. Not far beyond the blood, I spotted the impala lying dead in a clutter of yellow leaves.

I was familiar with the emotions that whipsawed through me then, feelings unrelated to the size or stature of the animal I had killed: elation and remorse, pride and humility, respect for the game I had brought to ground, and relief that my family would soon eat well. The act of killing a blameless creature, big or small, never felt quite right or truly wrong either.

I knelt down and stroked the impala's still-warm, golden flank. One dark hole indicated the path of the slug. It was as neat and humane a kill as I could ever hope to make. "Your body will feed my family," I whispered.

"That was a fine shot," Baba said.

His opinion mattered to me, but killing was not an experience we celebrated or even shared. I felt a little quiet inside as we repositioned the animal with his head uphill. Baba made quick work of gutting and dressing out the carcass, letting gravity send the fluids and offal downhill, out of our way. He showed me how to turn the stomach inside out and sew it into a tidy sack for holding the still-warm heart, liver, and kidneys—delicacies Zola would cook with special care. We did our work respectfully, without saying much. Baba sliced the meat and handed pieces to me to stow in a canvas bag. He had large hands and knuckles like walnut shells, yet he wielded the blade with delicacy, making neat cuts close to the bone to minimize waste.

When we had finished, he tested the weight of the bag and said we would leave the head and bones for the hyenas.

I cut a pole and hung the tripe sack on the end for carrying over my shoulder. The sun had almost reached its zenith.

"Let's go clean up. Then lunch," Baba said, knowing food was never far from my mind. He hoisted the bag of meat onto his back and set out for the river.

For a moment I stood beside the scant remains laid out on their golden cape. The wide brown eyes stared at me, glossy and lifeless. "Thank you," I murmured and turned away.

* * *

Baba and I walked faster then, unworried about scaring away game but still alert to our surroundings. The habit of vigilance in the bush had become second nature to me, both for safety reasons and because there was so much to capture my attention. A clutter of spiders clinging to a web held as much fascination as a herd of elephants. I was learning to identify birds by the sound of their calls and to notice small details, like a tuft of lion mane caught on a thorn. I was always on the lookout for lucky bean seeds, the glossy red kernels with a single black dot that Zola strung into necklaces and bracelets. The seeds were supposed to bring luck in love and work. They possessed the added glamour of being deadly poisonous. Exactly what love and work were going to look like for my older sister, I couldn't have said. At the time, I didn't see beyond her affection for our family and all she did to care for us. I was still a boy who relied on the order and certainty she provided at home. I never considered that she might have a different future in mind or what that future might be.

Baba strode ahead of me at a determined clip, causing the sack of impala meat to bounce against his back. I kept an eye on him because from time to time he would uncurl a finger or tilt his head toward an attraction I might overlook: a lizard on a branch or a frog the size of my fingernail. We were always watching for lions and leopards, of course. Although the cats were nocturnal and usually hunted in the cool, dark hours, they were not immune to the scent of fresh meat or the allure of an easy strike in daylight.

The day before, Baba had pointed out a cloud of vultures circling not far from where we were walking now. The cloud had funneled down to a single location, a sure sign lions had killed and eaten well. That night, I noticed my father drank only water. I guessed he wanted to stay sharp so we could hunt early in the morning when the pride was sated and lazy. At present, the big cats were probably resting their swollen guts nearby, nearly senseless with the effort of digestion. We had come upon lions in this condition before—adults and their offspring sprawled in the grass, panting, with blood-reddened faces and huge, distended bellies. They had barely raised their heads to look at us.

At the moment, I was most concerned about the hunger sinking its jaws into my stomach. A scrim of green marked the river ahead. Baba quickened his pace. I knew we would make our way to a shallow runnel where the water ran clear. There we would wade in to rinse the blood, dust, and sweat from our feet, hands, and faces before eating lunch. Baba was a meticulous hunter for whom every ritual signaled a category of respect—for the game he shot, for the animal's fragile habitat, even for the person who would have to wash his bloodied shirt and pants. He always cleaned himself before coming home, plunging into the river fully dressed if necessary to spare Zola an unpleasant job of laundering. Today, I was glad we needed only a quick splash that wouldn't delay our meal.

As we neared the river, however, I felt a change in the atmosphere, a troubling new sensation without apparent cause. My footsteps slowed. The air seemed heavy, suggestive, freighted with a meaning I couldn't grasp. It was oddly quiet. The sense of sunny peace had drained away, and the tiny hairs on my arms began to bristle.

Baba stopped in the shade of a marula tree. "Smell anything?"

He had cautioned me never to copy his smoking habit if I valued my keen sense of smell. So far, I had taken his warning to heart. I hadn't tried even a puff with Rooper Nobbs or the other boys who smoked behind the schoolhouse.

I raised my chin and whiffed the air. Making a face, I put down the pole attached to the tripe and stepped upwind of Baba's sack of meat. He was watching me, waiting for my report. I took my time, partly to prolong my standing as the authority and partly because what I smelled made me uneasy. I sniffed again. If anything, the stench was stronger from this position. It rode up my nostrils like an assault, overpowering the sweet fragrance of the marula tree and the usual swirl of dirt and vegetable scents that enriched the African air. I knew this smell: the stink of death. But my excellent nose had never encountered a stench so pungent that it seemed to possess weight, a sticky materiality so dense and bottom-heavy it made me want to puke.

The look on Baba's face told me he had smelled enough not to wait for my opinion. He lifted the binoculars and glassed the riverine woodland.

"It's a kill," I said, needlessly.

"We saw the vultures circling. This must be it."

"But the stink ..." My eyes had begun to water. I was trying not to breathe.

"It may be more than a day old. The lions are well fed by now." He paused. "Let's go upwind and keep our distance." He sounded calm enough, but I heard tension in his voice. He pointed a finger in the direction we would head, and off we went.

We walked with the breeze on our faces until the stink subsided. Upwind, the change in air quality refreshed and energized me. My thoughts had already returned to corn bread and biltong when the river came into view.

The first thing I saw was a herd of elephants, cows and their calves, oddly reclined in the muddy flats as for a nap. The second thing I saw was that all the elephants were dead. Bullet wounds riddled their collapsed carcasses. Several of the great gray bellies yawned open to expose shredded entrails and arcs of dripping bone. Most horribly, all the slaughtered elephants bore deep, bloody gouges where the killers had hacked away their tusks—their entire faces.

Saliva pooled in my mouth. I closed my eyes, swallowed, and managed not to barf. Baba placed a steadying hand on my back. When he found his voice, it was low and pinched. "Ivory poachers, Bonesy. This is what they do."

"Are they still around here?" I managed to whisper.

"No. They're far away by now. They have trucks and helicopters." He kept his eyes on the atrocity, taking in every detail.

I swallowed again and made myself look. The condition of the carcasses and the remains strewn across the dirt said everything. The poachers had not been interested in food for the table. Tusks were all they had taken, and to get the tusks they had destroyed and mutilated an entire breeding herd of elephants. I counted fourteen adult females, five juveniles, and three small calves too young to have sprouted more than an inch or two of ivory, yet their fuzzy cheeks had been cut to pieces.

The earth between the bodies was littered with bullet casings and claw-torn flesh. Feeding by opportunistic carnivores had been underway for at least a day or two and might have started even before the poachers loaded the last of the ivory into their vehicles and fled. I knew the natural order: the king of beasts, first in line, would have arrived to chase away interlopers, rip open the kill, and claim the most tender morsels. After several hours of feasting, the lions, exhausted and hypermetabolic, gave way to the dozen or so hyenas currently on the scene. Two of the hyenas turned reddened muzzles toward Baba and me and then went back to their meal. I noticed movement at one gaping carcass and realized I was looking at the backside of a hyena that had waded all the way in to sample the deepest core of musculature.

After the hyenas would come the wild dogs, then the leopards and cheetahs, then the jackals. The vultures currently perched thick in the treetops. And finally, the beetles, ants, and worms. It would take months for even the mightiest appetites in the African bush to erase this wholesale slaughter.

Just when I thought the sight before me couldn't get any worse, it did. A feeble toot sounded among the bodies. I spotted a calf so small that its tusks looked like aspirin tablets glued to its face. The tiny creature stood next to the mauled remains of a large female. With its miniature trunk, the newborn traced random, awkward loops through the air, touching down here and there on the cow's putrefying flesh. The calf tooted again, and one of the hyenas lifted its head to cast a predatory eye.

"Baba, look."

He didn't answer, but he put his arm around me and pulled me closer. We both knew the orphan wouldn't last another day.

"Can't we do something?"

"I'm sorry, Bonesy. This is beyond us."

I had known the words "ivory poaching." But knowing the words had been nothing compared to the experience of standing there, taking in the true dimensions of the cruelty committed in the lust for ivory. Now I saw, heard, smelled, and felt what ivory poaching really meant. I registered a pressure in my chest, a painful contraction. I took several shallow breaths and leaned into Baba.

I had grown up with the sound of elephants' trumpets, in a world where sightings of closely bonded breeding herds were routine. I knew the herds so well that I could identify individual animals by the tears in their hide, the color and curvature of their tusks, the scars on their wrinkled bodies. I knew the matriarch with a pear-shaped hole in her ear, her sister with one tusk striped yellow, the juvenile with a checkmark scratched into its side. The corpses before me now were so mutilated that I doubted anyone could tell for sure which elephants they were.

I couldn't imagine the terror these animals had felt as their mothers, sisters, aunts, cousins, and offspring fell one by one in the barrage of bullets. The colossal waste and the utter savagery of the humans who killed in this way were almost unbelievable to me.

Even as I swiped at the tears pooling in my eyes, something inside me hardened. I felt bitter, older, like a distant relative of the boy I had been only a few minutes earlier.

"Let's go," Baba said, turning away.

We had not walked far when the frantic, high-pitched cry of the newborn calf tore through the air. We kept going and did not look back.

3

Displays of joy by Zola were rare in those days, but when something lifted her from the tedium of domestic life, her smile could outshine the sun. Baba and I returned from our hunt to find her sitting on the top step of the porch peeling potatoes. Hannie sat in the grass below, banging on a pie plate with a spoon. The transformation in Zola's face when she saw us carrying fresh game was sweet to behold, and her smile raised the corners of my lips too.

That sacks of meat could trigger such a welcome told me something new about my sister's state of mind. Since Mama died, Zola had become increasingly difficult to read, as though a protective layer had filmed over her. Fortunately for the rest of us, she complied willingly enough with the expected routines of the household. Seeing her go about her work with wordless efficiency had come as a relief to my boyish self because it meant my life would continue almost as before. Although I wasn't insensitive to her new duties or her early acquaintance with the cares of adulthood, I hadn't guessed the worry she must have felt about putting enough food on the table, day after day. Her elation at the sight of meat to feed our family scared me a little. Was real, gut-wrenching hunger so close to our door?

"I shot it." I tried to sound offhand, as though killing a prime antelope was nothing out of the ordinary. I watched her face, alert to hidden inner workings. "One slug."

"Good for you." Her lips formed a kiss aimed at my forehead, but she didn't actually touch me. Her gaze was fixed on the bag of innards hanging from the stick. In one quick motion she freed it and turned to go inside. "I'll soak these and fix some tonight. Will you watch Hannie?" Without waiting for an answer, she hurried through the door.

I let my shoulders slump a little. Her praise for the man of the hour hadn't been the gusher I had hoped for. I thought about the fine young buck that had met his match in me, Bonesy. Then I thought about my clean lung shot and the prospect of eating well, at least for a while, and my disappointment shifted to something more heartening. At the time I couldn't have formed the words, but I was coming to understand that my self-worth did not depend on praise from Zola or anyone else—a consoling thought for a boy with a small, distractible circle of supporters.

Baba and I had washed in the river after leaving the elephants, but the stink of the killing field still clung to my nostrils. I wondered if Hannie would notice as I lifted her high in the air. She laughed and waved her spoon in my face, so apparently not.

"Bobo, Bobo," she said, spitting a little. "Bobo."

To Hannie, Baba and I were one vowel apart. I put my nose close to her cheek and breathed in her sweet baby scent. "A BB, like you, baby. *Bbbbbbb.*" When I fluttered my lips against her skin, she shrieked with delight.

I carried her around to the back of the house and sat her down near the workbench. Baba stood over the contents of the sack, which he had emptied onto the wooden surface. He was sharpening a knife—quick, hard strokes on a stone. We needed to move fast while the meat was very fresh. Biltong, correctly made, would supply our family with a prized delicacy for many weeks.

Baba got to work cutting the meat into strips. My job was to rub the strips with salt, lay the salted pieces in a flat container, and sprinkle vinegar on each layer. To me, the pungent odor of vinegar had come to signal this very curing process and something more: good food ahead. As the smell wafted up my nose, I felt cleansed and optimistic. Flies delirious with indecision zoomed toward the meat and back again, repelled by the salt and vinegar. I ignored them, knowing they would lose interest altogether once we had brined the meat and scoured the table.

"Dinner tonight will be good," Baba said, casting a glance at me. On the way home he had made a quick detour to Captain Biggie's. A bottle of beer from the six-pack he had bought sat empty on the ground.

I nodded. Already my stomach pulsed and growled in anticipation of the meal ahead. It was important for me to eat well because for one thing, I was famished, and for another, I faced a ration of work. The raw cuts of meat could sit in the brine only a few hours. If we let them soak until morning, they would be oversalted and ruined. I eyed my father, who was relaxing toward stupor. I knew I couldn't count on his help later that night.

All the stages Baba went through when he drank were familiar to me. Currently, he was in the genial, conversant zone he occupied after his first beer or two, a precious and fleeting time that fostered intimacy between us. During this particular phase, I always paid close attention and usually learned something new and remarkable—who had left our village for jail or junior college, for example, or how to make a bottle-cap whistle. In one startling, long-ago revelation before I had connected animal and human behaviors, he had told me how a man uses his penis to start a baby.

Instead of resenting Baba's slow, steady slide into the fog of alcohol, I noted his decline like a nurse tracking the onset of fever, hoping to make the lucid period last as long as possible. Only years later would I fully realize how much my sisters and I had sacrificed to Baba's drinking. Even then, my love for him would eclipse my anger.

"I wish you hadn't seen what we saw at the river," he said now, eyeing me. "Are you holding up?" He studied my face as though he was the one searching for signs of illness.

I nodded. Silence hung between us while I tried to gauge whether or not this was true. The question itself alerted me to the possibility that I was not holding up. I rotated my shoulders elaborately, testing for aches, and wagged my head right and left as I had seen the older boys do before games of soccer. Baba looked away because of course he wasn't asking about physical pain.

I took a breath. My voice came out shaky. "Will the poachers kill all the elephants?"

He sliced a few strips before answering. "Ivory's called 'white gold,' Bonesy. Actually, it's worth more than gold." He wiped the blade with a cloth and ran the steel over the sharpening stone a few more times. "Poaching was once a crime of opportunity carried out by locals looking to support their families. Now it's orchestrated—militarized and transnational. Heavily armed networks use poaching to fund drug selling and big-league crimes of all sorts. Every year the poachers are more ruthless and better-armed. The elephant population is heading toward zero."

"Zero?" I felt a thud in my heart. A world without elephants seemed impossible.

"We lose tens of thousands of elephants a year to ivory hunters. The stress of the gunfire and killing can cause surviving herds to stop breeding altogether."

"Isn't *anyone* fighting the poachers?" The question came out sharpish. I couldn't believe the extermination of elephants would go unchallenged.

"Game rangers do their best, but they're outmanned and outgunned. They walk into the bush, land they've lived on and loved all their lives, and come face-to-face with hardened fighters—soldiers, really, who will not hesitate to shoot. Rangers can make arrests, but they're not allowed to fire except in self-defense. The two sides operate under entirely different, unfair rules."

How my father had come upon this information, I didn't know. He must have read my mind because he looked up from the slab of meat and said, "A few rangers live in the village. They keep quiet to avoid becoming targets." His face was as expressionless as a lid. But his eyes locked on mine in a way that told me more.

"You help them, don't you?" My voice came out a whisper while something like relief flooded through me. My father had never truly believed the atrocities were "beyond us."

He looked down, considering. "When I can. I've alerted rangers to tire tracks and fresh graves. I do this quietly, you understand."

I nodded, both afraid for him and swelled by the confidence he had shown in me. "Graves?"

"Poachers try to hide actual murder."

When I found my voice, I said, "Did you tell the rangers about the elephants today?" I guessed he had completed more than one errand at Captain Biggie's.

He nodded. "They already knew." He paused and shook his head. "They saw the vultures too. But they got there too late to do anything except file a report."

Almost involuntarily, I raised my eyes and scanned the sky. From that moment forward, every funnel of vultures I saw spiraling toward earth would carry a new and troubling possibility.

* * *

We finished the brining in time for me to hang around the kitchen and help Zola cook. "We're having the heart for dinner," she said when she saw me, flashing a tender look so like Mama's that I forgave her for her abrupt dismissal earlier. She had already sliced the kidneys and liver and put them to soak in water mixed with lemon juice. I knew she would make a delicious kidney scramble in the morning and liver and onions tomorrow night.

"I'm following Mama's recipes. At least I think this is how she did it."

We fell silent for a moment at the mention of our dead mother. From her little chair in the corner, Hannie called, "Mama, Mama." Hannie knew the word but not the heartache.

I stood close to Zola, admiring her long, tapering fingers and the easy way she handled the knife. She applied the slender blade to the thickest part of the muscle, telling me about each part as she cut it away—the ventricles, the valve openings.

"This is a lot like hollowing out a bell pepper after you've sliced off the stem and cap," she informed me.

I had never hollowed out a bell pepper, but I nodded, fine with her assumption that I knew more than I did. Like Baba, Zola liked to teach me things. I had learned a lot about anatomy from watching her clean game in the kitchen. Now, as the trimmed heart flesh fell neatly away, the image of the eviscerated elephants flashed before me, and my mood darkened.

"We saw dead elephants," I said all at once. I hadn't planned to tell her; the words simply escaped. "A whole herd of them."

She held the knife midair, looking at me. "Dead elephants? Today?"

"Poachers cut out their tusks."

"That must have been a terrible thing to see."

"It was." Having gained her full attention, I stood a little taller, manning up to the trauma in a way I thought fitting for a triumphal impala hunter. Nonetheless, my chin trembled. "It was terrible."

I waited, hoping for more sympathy. But Zola had turned away. She took up the trimmed heart, cupping it in her hands as gently as she would a baby. She held the heart under running water for a moment and then laid the rinsed muscle on the cutting board.

"Beautiful, isn't it? So hardworking, and now it feeds us too." She paused, looking at me. "You did well today. You can be proud of your hunting. Poachers have to run and hide."

I nodded, not trusting my voice. I had never attached the word "beautiful" to an organ cut from an animal. I watched the moist cutlets tip from Zola's knife and found solace in the reminder that "my" impala's recently beating heart would nourish five people. The pride I had felt at my clean shot resided somewhere beneath the boulder in my chest. As much as I loved hunting, mixed feelings like these had become a familiar aftereffect of taking the life of an innocent creature. I wondered whether poachers who slaughtered elephants for ivory felt even a twinge of remorse. The likelihood that they did not gave me a chill.

We sat down for our meal of fried heart and potatoes. Zola cut Hannie's portion into tiny bits. I liked mine with ketchup, even though Baba said anything other than salt and pepper was sacrilegious. When we finished, Baba retired to the front porch to smoke a cigarette and finish his six-pack. Zola freed me from cleanup to tend the brined meat that sat waiting on the workbench outside.

We had eaten early, but already the sun was sinking. I pumped fresh water into a pail and added a splash of vinegar, hurrying to make the most of the remaining light. On the workbench I lined up the container of brined meat, the pail of vinegar water, and the lengths of string we boiled and reused for hanging game. At the end of this row, next to the workbench, sat the drying rack with four horizontal rods spaced a hand's width apart.

The sharp bark of a baboon pierced the air, calling a troop to its evening roost. The air simmered with mosquitoes. I rubbed vinegar on my skin to discourage them from biting me. I felt belly-full and grown-up, an essential cog in the welfare of my family. Rinsing, tying, and hanging each strip of meat was tedious work, but this night I welcomed the job. I liked the prospect of biltong in our pantry made from game I had bagged, cured, and hung myself. I still felt pleased that Baba had trusted me to take the shot. Even now, as he sat useless on the porch, peering out through the amber lens of his fifth or sixth beer, I didn't resent him for abandoning me after dinner or judge him harshly for his bad habits.

I suppose my forbearance, no matter how much Baba drank or disappointed, sprang in part from my guilt about Mama's death. I knew I could have done things differently: yelled for help or screamed at Mama about the snake under the washtub. To my relief, Baba never associated me with the horror of that day. I don't think he even remembered I had been at home. For weeks his grief was a frightful, crushing thing so all-consuming that he forgot to eat and wash and even misplaced our names. He would stumble out of his dark room and stare at Zola, Hannie, and me as if taken aback by the strangers in his kitchen. He lost weight, grew an untidy beard, and sprouted silvery threads in his hair. We feared he might never recover until one day he stepped through the door and said, "Good morning, Bonesy, Zola. What's for breakfast?"

If he had been an abusive drunk, like another father or two in the village whose sons came to school marked with ugly purple bruises, things would have been very different. But alcohol made our father quiet and dreamy. He could go for days, even weeks, between binges. During the sober periods, he was capable of impressive spurts of energy. He would be up at sunrise to hoe, weed, and water. He repaired the fence, the pump, Hannie's broken doll, anything that needed fixing. He sold surplus vegetables at the market; he bought supplies for Zola. He took me fishing and hunting. He did all of this with the urgency of a family man preparing for disaster—a loving father who knew his sobriety wouldn't last.

A bright, gibbous moon appeared just as I got to work. Soon I found a rhythm. Rinse, tie, hang. Rinse, tie, hang. I was careful to space the strips of meat evenly so that each one hung free, not touching another. The rack could hold about fifty strips per pole—two hundred total. I kept count, and as the number grew, so did my gratitude to the animal whose life I had taken.

Every household in our village claimed to have the best biltong recipe. Some families rubbed the flesh with spices or sugar. Some liked it soft and fatty; others preferred it hard and dry. Rooper Nobbs said his grandmother added coriander, aniseed, and garlic to her brine. Now *that* sounded sacrilegious. Our method required only salt and vinegar, one day of drying in the sun, and about four days in the shade. This produced biltong with a clean, meaty flavor and a nice chew, not too soft and not too hard. Stored in tight containers, our biltong lasted for months.

By the time I finished, I had hung ninety-nine strips, and the moon shone bright as a lantern. A light breeze had come up that would broadcast the scent of meat to every nocturnal scavenger within miles. I ran to my room and snatched the mosquito netting from my bed. Good people waging war on blood parasites that spread malaria, encephalitis, West Nile virus, and dengue and yellow fevers frowned on the removal of bed nets from beds. Even so, repurposing was common in our village, particularly among fishermen wanting nets and brides needing veils. By the light of the moon, I arranged the diaphanous material over the drying racks and gathered stones to place at close intervals around the perimeter. Finally, I dragged my mattress and a blanket to a spot nearby, lay down with my shotgun by my side, and fell asleep.

Some time later, the crackle of footfalls woke me. I gripped my gun and sprang to a crouch with my back against the netting. Moon shadow spilled over me. I peered through the blackness, searching for a shape out of sync, a pair of shining amber eyes, or worse, several pairs of shining amber eyes signaling a pride or a pack. The slightest sound caused me to brace and aim. Although the night air felt sharp in my lungs, a bead of sweat rolled down my neck. Another faint crunch told me the intruder was approaching from the other side of the rack. The footfall of a man? I turned, steadied the gun against my shoulder, and rose.

"Whoa, Bonesy. Don't shoot."

"Zola?" She looked ghostly in a pale shawl wrapped over her white cotton nightdress. My hands shook as I lowered the gun. "What are you doing out here?"

"Restless." She walked around the rack and held out a cup. "I warmed some milk to help us sleep."

I didn't point out that I had been sleeping just fine before she turned up. "Uh, thanks. I'm glad I didn't shoot you and spill the milk."

Thin moon glow lit her fleeting smile. "Baba went to Captain Biggie's. He's still not back."

I sipped the warm liquid, stalling, while I thought this over. Baba's visits to the tavern weren't always about drink; I knew that now. Helping rangers fight poachers was a dangerous business, yet he had done this for … how long? For the first time, the news that our father had gone to the tavern filled me with cautious pride.

"That's nothing new." I tried to sound nonchalant even as I pictured Baba conferring secretly with rangers, maybe over a map or a cache of high-powered rifles. "He'll be back."

She hugged herself against the cold night air. "Do you think he has a girlfriend?"

I had never considered the possibility. "No way." I found the notion offensive and mildly shocking. "He likes his bottle." This was true but a tad disloyal considering I believed I knew the real reason he might be out late. At the moment I preferred to think of Baba with almost any companion other than a woman who was not our mother. I swallowed the rest of the milk and handed back the cup. "Thanks."

"He will eventually, you know."

"I know. Just not yet."

After Zola left, I stayed awake thinking about Baba and the secret we shared. I couldn't explain how I knew he wasn't seeing a girlfriend, even though his trips to the village easily could have included more than one stop. I had seen his shock and grief, the way his face had collapsed, and how tenderly he had carried Mama into the house on the day she died, only a few months earlier. I supposed he would find someone eventually, but this was way too soon.

I drifted off and slept through the rest of the night. When I awoke, Baba was standing over me, holding a bowl of steaming oatmeal. I sat up and eyed him over the spoonfuls I shoveled into my mouth. He looked too fresh and clear-headed for the morning after a binge. I didn't ask about his nighttime visit to Captain Biggie's, and he didn't offer a report.

All day Sunday I stood guard while the hot sun did its work. My shotgun came in handy for waving away birds that flew in for a look at the meat, but I never had to shoot. At dusk, Baba and I relocated the rack to the porch, where he kept watch for the next four days while I was at school. Near the end of the week, we got our first taste.

Baba, Zola, and I each chose a strip from the rack. Standing shoulder-to-shoulder, we held, flexed, and sniffed the dried delicacy before taking the first, crucial bite. Too salty? Too dry? I closed my eyes and worked my jaws, thinking, *Man oh man, it's perfect.* I raised one eyelid to spy on Baba. He had closed his eyes too and was chewing, intent as a ruminant. It didn't take long for him to grin and say, "This is the best biltong I've ever eaten." Zola was too busy chewing to speak, but she nodded and looked pleased enough.

Afterward, she and I emptied the racks. We worked silently, untying the string and laying the biltong in a flat container, our movements fluid and sure. I handled each piece with care, placing it parallel to the others in a tidy row, adding up the numbers. Zola moved faster, building haphazard piles that stuck out every which way and made me lose count. What looked like disrespect for the food I had shot, cured, hung, guarded, and dried for days chafed me like a rope on a goat. I reached over and straightened her mess, getting in her way.

"They're not bars of gold, Bonesy," she said, swatting away my hands.

"They are when you're hungry." Even as I said the words, I knew they didn't make sense. Nonetheless, I eyed her with a stern expression.

A small smile played on her face. "Let's hope not."

4

My uncle Stash gave me the name Bonesy. He was fond of nicknames, and I had been a skinny, angular, rib-chested tot. Uncle Stash's real name was Stanley. As a young man he had worn a moustache, but my father said the stash of money he made working as a carpenter was more to the point. Baba asserted his older brother's financial advantage without rancor or jealousy, which told me something good about their relationship.

Stash had a gimpy leg from falling out of a tree when he was a boy. The accident had left him unfit for working in the field with Baba and their father, so instead he had become the family handyman, starting with only a hammer, a saw, and a bucket of nails. He had made it far enough in school to decipher the carpentry book he found on a shelf at the Sisters of Charity, and he could read the manuals that came with the tools and shop equipment he gradually acquired. Like Baba, Stash had learned a lot on his own.

Now, his woodworking shop occupied a ramshackle shed behind the house where he and Aunt Letty lived, just down the road from us. A thick electrical wire running from a pole to the roof was all that distinguished the shop from the other patched and rickety structures on the lane. But the inside was rich and magical: a jungle of half-built tables and chairs, exotic tools, and winking piles of metal and glass.

As a gift to my parents, Uncle Stash had built a cradle when Zola was born. It was a beautiful thing, crafted of mahogany with heart-shaped dovetails at the corners and rockers cut for gentle movement without tipping. The cradle later held me and, subsequently, Hannie. It would last for generations. Cradles became one of Uncle Stash's specialties, along with household furniture and cabinets that he sent on trucks to bigger markets in the cities. Our school principal, Mr. Kitwick, even hired him to build and repair the desks and benches that saw hard duty in our classrooms.

Uncle Stash and Aunt Letty's son, Squeak, and I were born the same year. We became close pals, like brothers. As young children Squeak and I were frequent visitors to the carpentry shop, where Aunt Letty's home-baked cookies greeted us on most days after school. When we weren't in the shop or at school, we ran around outdoors, playing kickball in the road, climbing trees, fishing, or swimming in the river with other kids from the village. Often there were as many as a dozen of us, a pack of laughing, shouting, howling boys our mothers were glad to keep outside.

One hot afternoon when Squeak and I were still in grade school, ten of us went for a swim. I knew we had ten because we had just played Capture the Flag with five on each side. The game had ended when Skinner and his pack of low-life followers showed up to snatch away the flour sacks we used for flags. We had come to expect trouble from those boys. The mere sight of Skinner triggered fear and loathing in me even then, years before the cobra killed Mama. He had at various times pushed me down, stolen my fishing pole, thrown my bike into the river, made rude remarks about my sister, and told Roop not to play with me because I was a dweeb. I was not Skinner's only victim, but that was small consolation.

On this day, when he and his cobullies grabbed the flags, our enthusiasm for the game had already dwindled. We were hot and sweaty, and there was strength in our number. When Squeak yelled, "Beat you to the river!" we raced after him, happy to leave the older boys behind.

None of us owned swimming trunks. We pulled off our T-shirts, stepped out of our flip-flops, squelched through the mud, and plunged in. On the hottest days it wasn't unusual for us to cool off like this two or three times. Between dips, our shorts dried fast in the breeze. I often found mud in my pockets and, one time, a leech.

The river was shallow during the dry season except for a dark channel that ran down the middle. Only four or five of us had learned to swim, so we mostly splashed and tumbled in the waist-deep water near the edge. On this day, I floated on my back, looking up at the sky and the fish eagle riding a thermal draft overhead. A gentle current stirred the water into whorls. Bugs danced on the surface. The sounds of laughter and splashing filled the air until the sun sat low in the sky and the temperature began to drop.

We scrambled up the riverbank, shivering, and shrugged into our shirts, eager to reach home before dark. In twos and threes, heading in different directions, we called goodbye. It was then I realized only nine of us had emerged from the river.

"Squeak!" I shouted, a sense of crisis already scything through me. Squeak was the strongest swimmer among us. I had last seen him doing a smooth crawl out in the main channel. Frantic, I scanned the water. The river slid languidly along its course, glassy and silver in the waning light. The only signs of my cousin were the T-shirt and flip-flops he had flung on the grass. Roop and a few other boys stood next to me, silent. Tears filled my eyes. I sank to my knees. Like every kid raised in the African bush, I recognized the work of a crocodile.

Few creatures are as still and well camouflaged as a crocodile sunning itself in the mud. None of us had spotted the one that must have taken Squeak. We had gotten lazy about checking because we hadn't seen a croc near our swimming spot for many months. Undetected, a crocodile simply waits for an opportunity, slips noiselessly into the water, clamps its jaws on its prey, and pulls it under. The capture happens quickly, almost silently, without a trace left behind. Any one of us could have been the victim.

Uncle Stash and Aunt Letty kept to themselves for a while after that. Death was never far from our world—it snatched the unfit and the unlucky with grim regularity but the loss of a child meant special grief. Squeak had been a late baby, arriving more than a decade after the youngest of his three sisters. My girl cousins were all grown and married, and for weeks after Squeak's death, the house and workshop down the lane sat quiet and dark.

Baba led a hunting party to track and shoot the crocodile. No person wading in the river, fetching water, or even fishing from the shore near our village would be safe with a crocodile in the vicinity that had tasted easy human prey. I wanted to help, but Baba made me stay inside with Mama and Zola. I heard him telling Uncle Stash to stay home too. "You don't want to be there, Stash. You really don't."

The crocodile was likely to remain out of sight, near its sunken, ripening prey for at least a day or two. The men organized shifts of armed lookouts to patrol the river's edge until the killer reappeared. On the morning of the third day, Baba took first duty. Even before the sun had risen above the tall grass, he spotted the tracks—clawed footprints with a gutter down the middle carved by a heavily dragging tail. The prints were large and deep, indicating a weighty old male. They led from the water through the mud to a prime, north-faced sunning spot.

The kill was quick—two shots to the head. Baba told me later that the crocodile was almost twelve feet long. When he and the other men slit open the stomach, they found enough to know they had slain the killer of my cousin Squeak.

In time, I heard sounds coming from Uncle Stash's carpentry shop again. It took a day or two for me to raise the courage to venture down the path. The last time I had seen Uncle Stash, his face was so contorted with anguish that I had run and hidden behind a tree. Now, standing outside the shop door, I waited for a break in the buzz of the saw before knocking twice. When the door finally opened, my uncle stood before me, grayed by grief and sawdust. For a moment he remained expressionless. I wondered if I should back away and go. But then the kindly expression I remembered returned—the warm smile, the crinkly eyes. He wrapped me in a hug that smelled of fresh wood. His voice was hoarse when he said, "I've missed you, Bonesy."

My visits became frequent again, then daily after school. Uncle Stash let me sit on a barrel and read or do homework. More often, I watched as he worked, as the sawdust flew from grinders, routers, and sanders—thrillingly powerful tools so loud he made me wear earplugs. From time to time, he asked me to hand an item to him, and in that way I came to know the names of chisels, planes, clamps, and rasps. When I was a year or two older, I helped add up the numbers in the accounts. He even let me use the electric drill and my favorite, the nail gun. Watching me fire nails into a pair of offcut boards, he clucked, "A nail is a temporary thing, Bonesy. Screws hold the world together."

By the time Mama died, I knew my way around the shop pretty well. In the fragile years after her death, Uncle Stash's workroom became a refuge from both the bullies and the painful reminders of Mama at home. I learned to be alert for trouble on the way there in case I ran into Skinner and company. But I couldn't always avoid them.

One day as I was leaving the shop, they were right outside the door, making a game of tossing banana peels over the wire that powered the shop. Skinner had something new tucked under his belt—a switchblade. His cheek bulged with chewing tobacco.

"Well, hello, Sawdust-for-Brains," he said, spitting at my feet. "Did you have fun screwing today?" He closed in on me, pumping a banana against his crotch.

The other boys bent over with laughter. Skinner had emerged as the undisputed alpha bully. He was tall and handsome in a rugged way, with formidable muscles he had developed along with his talent for cruelty. His nose had been broken in a fight. A jagged red scar trailed down to the bump an inch or two above his nostrils. These deformities only added to his dangerous, tough-guy image. Stories circulated about how he shot stray dogs for fun and how, when angered, his fury and the violence that came with it could last for days. Roop had seen him throw a kitten against the wall of the school, and once, he had kicked a chicken to death after it pecked at his ankle.

"Which do you like better, screwing or nailing?" He reached out and pinched my cheek, hard. "I'd guess you're a pretty good screwer, for a feeb."

Another kid the size of a refrigerator added, "Planning to fill all those cradles yourself, Sawdust-for-Brains?" Laughter erupted again.

I broke from Skinner's grasp and walked fast, pretending to ignore them while heat rushed to my face. The jeering voices stayed close behind. I was still small for my age, and the sheer size of my tormentors scared me almost as much as their taunts.

"Is your uncle teaching you how to screw?"

"Does your aunt come in to help? Show you those big tits?"

They were howling now, circling around me. "How about the lovely Zola?" Skinner sneered. "Is she a good teacher too?"

My hands formed fists at my sides. Anger almost trumped my fear. I was about to do something stupid when a group of girls rounded the corner ahead of us, coming our way. As if snapped to attention, the boys turned toward the girls.

"Well, hello, lovelies," Skinner said, slicking back his hair.

The girls passed us, giggling. Fortunately for me, gnats had greater powers of focus and concentration than Skinner and his pals. The boy swarm turned as one to follow and tease the girls, forgetting all about me. I hurried the other way and was well out of sight before the lovelies lost their charm.

Even with the risk of harassment on the walk there and back, Stash's shop became a place of contentment. My uncle proved a thoughtful, curious man. He encouraged me in my studies, and he liked to pose questions that tested theories he had come across, as if he trusted me to know the answers.

Gazing at my faded Manchester United T-shirt, he once asked, "Do all people see the same colors, Bonesy? Is my red the same as your red?" Sometimes he would state an unusual fact while looking at me hard, waiting for my reaction. "A watermelon is really a berry, you know." "Some turtles breathe through their butts."

We could be quiet too, working silently side by side for hours at a stretch. Once in a while, Baba or Zola poked in to summon me to a meal, but neither stayed long. More often, Aunt Letty stopped by carrying a tray of lemonade and cookies or a container of soup or stew for my family.

Aunt Letty was a large, good-hearted woman who found solace in food. Since the day Squeak vanished, her ample body had inflated even more, and now, five years later, her bosom preceded her like the prow of a barge. She walked as if leaning into a gale. At thirteen, I was acutely aware of female anatomy, but I tried not to stare. I had recently glimpsed Zola in the shower (before she yelled and threw a bar of soap at me), yet I found it hard to imagine the enormous breasts that heaved and bobbed under Letty's flowered dresses.

One day, I was sitting on my barrel, sorting through a box of bolts, when I heard a perfunctory knock at the door and looked up, hoping to see my aunt. Instead, my school principal, Mr. Kitwick, ducked through the door, lustrous in his shiny gray suit. His hair was parted in the usual strict line. The dust raised by his stroll to the shop had only lightly dulled the gloss on his shoes.

"Hello, Stash," he said, greeting my uncle. Then he spotted me. "Well, hi, Bonesy."

Without even thinking, I stood, the way we did in school whenever Mr. Kitwick walked in. He looked too tall and polished for the cramped and grimy workshop. I was struck by the oddity of him looming above a thicket of dismembered chairs. His long, lean appendages suggested a kinship with the missing furniture parts, as if he had stopped by for a new arm or leg.

"I didn't know you worked here," he said, using his pleasant voice instead of the stern one he saved for expulsions and intolerable violations of the dress code. "Are you your uncle's apprentice?"

I felt myself blush with pleasure at the notion that I actually worked. "Uncle Stash lets me use some of the tools. Mostly I just watch." My teenage voice swooped up and down.

"Nonsense." Uncle Stash stuck a pencil behind his ear. "Bonesy's a big help, and he's better with numbers than me. But I never keep him from his schoolwork." He shook his forefinger as if the very idea needed chiding. "He has to pass that exam, you know."

"He does." Mr. Kitwick nodded in approval, looking at me. "Certification is the ticket to a bright future." His big Adam's apple leapt like a toad trapped in his throat. He stepped forward to hand Uncle Stash a pair of crisp bills, careful not to brush his coat or pants against a surface furred in wood dust. "I think we're even now?"

"Yes. Thanks." Uncle Stash took the money and limped to the cash box that sat on a shelf above the workbench. His gimpy leg seemed worse, somehow, in the presence of my unfailingly upright principal.

"The new chairs are very fine—almost too good for the rascals," Mr. Kitwick said, winking at me. Then he pinched in his shoulders to avoid touching anything and made his way back through the maze of dusty furniture. As he stepped outside, he called over his shoulder, "See you in school, Bonesy."

Once he was gone, I turned to my uncle. "What's an apprentice?"

* * *

I liked the suspense of not knowing what animal would appear next on my wall calendar from Ruby's Amazing Safaris, so I never looked ahead. Zola called the big, glossy photos "Bonesy's latest crush," which was pretty close to the truth. I could stand and gaze at the creature of the month for minutes at a time, memorizing every wart and whisker. I could almost hear the relevant snorts and whinnies, and I had no trouble imagining my pinups in motion: the hippo's jouncy trot or the lions, all muscle and glide. Every year the front of the calendar featured a dark green Range Rover and four new, smiling passengers—safari guests so wholesome and spotless in their earth-toned attire that I imagined they were royals flown in from a distant kingdom.

Adding to my fascination was the mystery of who took the photographs. Ruby herself? I had never seen the titular head of Ruby's Amazing Safaris, but in my feverish fantasies she embodied everything a boy could love and fear. As shapely as Aunt Letty but more rugged and brazen, Ruby was, in my mind, as enchanting and awesome as the word "safari" itself. Her calendars, stacked free every January on the stoop at Captain Biggie's, had captured my imagination as long as I could remember. Though I admired every photograph, I felt something close to adulation for their semilegendary source—Ruby and her amazing safaris.

Our village was far removed from the reserves and private concessions that hosted tourists. No one I knew claimed much knowledge of the safari business. But one day a Range Rover carrying four Europeans and a driver stopped at my school. The visitors, pale as codfish, wore khaki shirts and floppy hats. Mr. Kitwick introduced them. He told us they were en route to a photographic safari some distance away. They had taken a wide detour because they wanted an "authentic local experience."

The four travelers filed into our classroom, waving and smiling. Three of them gripped water bottles, as though crossing our schoolyard required lifesaving measures. They eyed the cracked blackboard, the wide-open windows, the corrugated roof, and the swallow's nest plastered to the beam inside the door. It didn't seem like much of an "experience" to me, but we were happy to learn they had brought us boxes of chalk, several cartons of number 2 pencils, and a brand-new soccer ball.

The driver of the Range Rover was the true star of this unexpected visit. I got a good view of him through the open window near my desk—my first, riveting look at a real safari guide. Big-shouldered and unsmiling, he leaned his long body against the vehicle while his passengers dipped into the local scene. He appeared neat and professional in dark green shorts, a matching shirt with two breast pockets, and the finest pair of hiking boots I had ever seen. Dark, wire-rimmed glasses completed the ultra-cool masculine glamour. I was totally smitten.

Of course, the other kids had spotted him too. Roop kicked me under the desk we shared and whispered, "Check out that mofo." The contortions we all went through to remain technically in our places while we stretched and craned and raised our butts inches above our seats for a better look created a churning mass of child flesh that must have amused the visitors.

As we watched, our man-crush reached into the front seat and retrieved a small object that turned out to be a two-way radio. He held it close to his lips while he spoke and then waited for a reply. His deep voice wafted through the open window. I could hear the hollowed basso of the person at the other end, but what that person said, I couldn't tell. I imagined dramatic safari business involving rogue wildlife or misbehaving royalty.

Mr. Kitwick clapped his hands to refocus our attention. "Class, please sing a song for our guests."

We sprang to our feet. Our teacher led us in a loud, if not particularly melodious tune:

> *I flew to the animals' dance*
> *A skinny giraffe made all the birds laugh*
> *By dancing in elephant pants ...*

While we sang, I kept one eye fixed on the guide outside. Fortunately for me, he was forward of due left, so I had to turn my head only a little. He had lit a cigarette and was exhaling smoke in long, lazy streams. The way he held the cigarette, low, pinched between thumb and forefinger, struck me as dashing and manly. After seeing that vision of he-man sophistication, within a week I would take my first, wheezy puff behind the schoolhouse with Roop.

When the song was over, the four visitors clapped, grinning and nodding so enthusiastically that I wondered whether singing children might be new to them. They clucked and bobbed as Mr. Kitwick led them out of the classroom. In a moment, I saw them file back into the Range Rover. The guide crushed his cigarette under his boot. Then he picked up the flattened butt and put it somewhere inside the vehicle, a gesture that sealed him in my mind as a great champion of nature. Before he stepped into the driver's seat, he turned in my direction. The sun glinted off his dark glasses, but for one thrilling moment I was pretty sure he looked straight at me.

* * *

On the day before my final month in school, Baba stood next to me in front of my calendar from Ruby's Amazing Safaris. A warthog whose month-long reign was over stared back with burnt-umber eyes. I was about to learn what new species would turn up to preside over the critical weeks ahead, when tenth grade ended and I would sit for the all-important JSC exam. "My ticket to a bright future," I told anyone who cared to listen. If I passed, I would be the first in my family to do so—to be officially certified as a literate, numerate, educated tenth-grade graduate. For me, the end of free schooling meant the end of school, period. But I didn't mind because now I had other, better plans.

I bid a silent farewell to the month gone by and the impressively tusked warthog staring out above thirty-one squares marked off with neat red X's. To prolong the unveiling of my newest creature crush, I took my time raising the page. Baba shifted his weight and exhaled with more force than necessary. Undeterred, I lifted the calendar slowly, making one week at a time disappear while the photo on the opposite side curled into view—a ribbon of clear blue sky, dark ears shaped like calla lilies, the sharp points of two medial horns.

"A black rhino!" I raised the page all the way up and pegged the photo at the top. My new pinup peered into the distance with little piggy eyes. Its ponderous, square snout hung inches from the ground. Thick folds of body armor topped four stumpy legs. It was a fabulous, enormous black rhino.

"It's a white rhino, Bonesy."

I looked at Baba. "It's not white."

"The name's a mistranslation. Dutch settlers called it *wijd*, meaning 'wide'—to describe the broad mouth."

I had glimpsed a real rhino only once, on an expedition with Squeak to collect grasshoppers. The great, gray hulk had raised its weighty head to gaze myopically in our direction and then returned to mowing grass with wide, square lips. A *wijd* rhino.

"The name's a mistake?"

"A misunderstanding among the English. It stuck." Baba sank into a chair next to the kitchen table. He had gotten out of bed late that morning. I was pretty sure he was hungover and felt like shit.

Was there a better word than "shit" to describe how my father felt? Mama had said that using vulgar language showed ignorance—"proof of a limited vocabulary." The first time she had told me this, I was in the first grade and didn't know the meaning of "vulgar" or "vocabulary." I started avoiding all words beginning with "v." For years, the words "shit" and "fuck" never crossed my lips. But now that I was older and motherless, it occurred to me that those potent words actually expanded my vocabulary. I had started to use them sparingly, like hot pepper flakes, because really, in certain situations, no other words would do.

"Africa has black rhinos too," Baba said, rubbing his temples, "with pointed snouts. Black rhinos are the same color as white rhinos—gray."

I sighed. Human beings could foul up the simplest things. "People think the horn is medicine, don't they?" This was not a question. I knew that the same gangs that took ivory from elephants also hunted rhinos for their horns.

He nodded. "They think it cures hangovers." He managed a rueful smile. "Also fevers, nosebleeds, rashes, typhoid, strokes, cancer, comas, whatever. Poachers and their dealers can be very convincing. People who are sick want to believe what they say."

"They think a bone will cure them?"

"It's not bone. Horns are keratin, same as your hair and fingernails."

Almost reflexively, I curled my fingers until I felt my nails tucked safely against my palms. "What do they do with it?"

"I imagine they grind, shave, chop, boil, and swallow it. They might sniff or inject it. Maybe they wear rhino horn in lockets, massage it into their skin, or toss it over their left shoulder." His voice held both scorn and pity. "I really don't know. They do whatever they think brings a cure."

He rose from his chair and went to the sink, where Zola had placed a pitcher of water. She had gone shopping with Hannie, who was nearly five now and would start school soon after I finished. I cast a parting look at the possibly doomed, possibly already dead white rhino and, with a heavy heart, sat down at the table to study.

5

My friend Rooper Nobbs wasn't much of a student. He didn't plan to take the JSC exam but would gladly leave school, uncertified, at the end of the academic year. For Roop, simply sticking it out, more or less, for ten rocky grades of compulsory schooling was a magnificent achievement. I suspected our teachers agreed and wouldn't be too sad to see him go.

Roop lived with his grandmother in a tilting shack they called "Rotting House." When malaria took both of his parents within a week, his numerous siblings had gone to distant relatives who had the youth and stamina to foster them, while Roop, the oldest, had become the ward of his wizened, widowed grandmother. Granny Nobbs raised Ovambo chickens and was getting to the age when she could use some help.

Grandpa Nobbs had died not long before of a stab wound from a thief who robbed him of all the cash in his pockets. Cockfighting—or rather, betting on cockfights—was Grandpa Nobbs's favorite pastime. Roop told me that over the years his grandfather had lost a lot of money at the pits but on the last night of his life, he won big. His assailant nabbed him on a dark path not far from the fights. After the attack, Grandpa Nobbs lasted long enough to stagger home, penniless, and whisper to Granny not to worry—he had won more than enough, picked the best of the best, and loved her above all. Granny said he died in her arms with a smile on his face.

The best part about visiting Roop was seeing Granny Nobbs's wide, gap-toothed grin when I stepped up to her chair on the porch. "It's Bonesy!" she would exclaim, as though my arrival were a rare and delightful event. Her face was as pale and lined as crumpled paper. She smelled sweetly of Lifebuoy soap, a bath bar made of red carbolic and flowery perfume and sold in barrels at Swale's Grocery Store.

The worst part about visiting was getting past Granny's chickens.

Although she did not raise them to be fighters, her roosters and hens had plenty of spunk. Ovambos are a feisty, aggressive, dark-plumaged breed capable of catching and eating rodents, pecking insects from the backs of cattle, and flying up to roost in the tallest trees. Rather than scattering when I walked into the yard, Granny's Ovambos rushed toward me with the zeal of starving omnivores. *Anything worth pecking on here?* Watching me zig and zag my way forward, Roop would stand on the porch and laugh. *Hyunk-hyunk-hyunk.*

Granny Nobbs peddled chickens and eggs at the market. As she got older, she became known for the excellent walkies she made from boiled chicken feet and sold off the steps of Rotting House. Her walkies were the crunchiest, spiciest, most delicious snack I had ever tasted. Purchasing them took courage, though. The Ovambos, as if affronted by the delicacy on offer, harassed every customer who ventured across the yard. This was fine with Roop and me because it left more walkies for us. We were growing like stinkweed and almost always hungry.

One afternoon a week before the certification exam, Roop barreled into Uncle Stash's shop carrying a fishing pole and a net. "Tilapias, Bonesy! A big school spawning in the backwater. Oh, hi, Mr. Stash."

I was counting money from the cash box and checking it against the receipts we listed in a dusty ledger. Uncle Stash's bank visits were irregular, based more on when he felt like going into town than on the number of checks and bills straining the hinges on the tin box. I glanced at him.

"Go ahead when you're finished. I'll close up."

Roop stood in the doorway, impatient, jiggling a foot while he rolled a bread ball between his fingers. In truth, I was almost done when he arrived, but I took my time, showing off a little as I handled the stacks of cash. When I realized my friend truly wasn't interested, I returned the box to its shelf and bid Uncle Stash goodbye. In five minutes flat, Roop and I had fetched my fishing pole. In another five minutes, we stood on a grassy ledge, peering down at a fine mess of fish.

Tilapias prefer quiet, well-vegetated water free of currents and eddies. We knew their favorite location, near a deeply undercut bank in the shallow, sloping margin of the river. It was there Roop had spotted the mother lode. "See the spawning beds?" he said, pointing.

Round, bowl-like impressions as vivid as moon craters marked the bottom about two feet from shore. Swimming above the beds, keen-eyed and watchful, were a dozen or more tilapias the size of dinner plates.

I felt a rush, not unlike the heart flutter that preceded taking aim with a gun. Fishing and hunting were alike in this way. The great challenge of outsmarting a wild and wary creature never failed to stir the blood. What made this expedition especially thrilling was the catch we hoped to take home. Tilapias were the tastiest, most tender fish I had ever eaten.

"Oh boy, Roop. Dinner."

"Granny's favorite, with her gums and all." He cast a pointed glance upstream. Roop and I had not forgotten our early acquaintance with the river's cruel surprises.

Although the chance was slim that a crocodile would snatch a person fishing from the bank, Roop and I had learned to be cautious. A crocodile wouldn't prevent us from fishing, but if one happened to be in the neighborhood, we wanted to know where it was. "I'll check downstream," I said, turning to go.

While Roop scouted upstream, I turned and walked in the opposite direction, scanning the left and right banks as I stepped over the uneven terrain. Nuggets of rock gave way to slick green vegetation and dark tongues of mud. A flock of plovers pecked along the verge. A turtle nosed into a bed of algae bordering the opposite bank. Above the central channel, a few iridescent dragonflies swooped toward their own reflections. I inhaled the sweet scent of a flowering tree and felt the familiar sense of peace that comes with being outdoors on a fine afternoon.

"All clear down here," I called to Roop, retracing my steps.

"Dangerous chameleon roosting on a branch, *hyunk-hyunk*. Otherwise, all clear upstream." He dug in his pocket and handed me a chunk of bread. Bread balls were the bait of choice for spawning tilapias. The fish wouldn't tolerate anything floating above their nests, so they would likely push away, or better yet bite, whatever we tossed in.

I stood back from the overhang to avoid being seen by the fish while I worked a wad of bread into a ball. Roop, who had prerolled several rounds, threw his line in the water and almost immediately got a strike. The tilapia he pulled in was a beauty—dark olive-green fading to pale on the flanks and about twenty centimeters long. I guessed it weighed at least a kilo, enough to provide an excellent meal for him and Granny Nobbs.

"Nice catch, Roop."

"They're biting, all right."

The tilapia thrashed at the end of Roop's line. It took him a few tries to get a good grip on it. When he had removed the hook and let the fish flop into the net, we stood over it for a moment without saying a word. I wondered whether my friend felt the way I did while watching the life drain away from a wild creature. I never told Roop, but every fish I landed gave me a moment of contrition even as I rejoiced in the catch.

In no time, though, we had lowered our hooks again. I settled into the focused, almost meditative state that erases the boundary between fishing gear and flesh, as though the pole had become an extension of my body. I pictured the tilapias cruising around my bait, eyeing it, not liking the pale blob that had dropped in from nowhere. The slightest, most tentative tap on the bread ball felt like a message sent directly from a fish to me: a tremor pulsing up the line, through the pole, and into the sensory network poised at high alert in my hand, wrist, and arm. My concentration was intense. I willed that creature to bite. Only a person who has fished can understand the exquisite sensitivity between an angler and his catch, the intimacy of it.

Roop's pole jerked. In one swift motion he landed another tilapia, slightly smaller than the first but still a keeper. He looked a little sheepish as he unhooked and netted the fish, avoiding my eyes. Usually we came out even. In a moment he had caught yet another.

"Did you give me the voodoo bread?" I kidded, only half-joking.

"Here." He handed over one of his prerolled bread balls. "Let's trade."

Although I understood the element of luck in fishing and didn't really blame my bait, I decided a swap was worth a try. We made the trade and threw in our lines. I waited. Imagined. Willed. Then I felt it, a little nudge. And another. I held the pole steady. When it came, the strike was so sudden that I almost lost my footing on the grassy ledge.

"I got one!" Gripping the pole in both hands, I pulled up the biggest tilapia I had ever seen—two kilos at least. Handsome markings stood out like the illustration on a poster: greenish vertical stripes, a thin red margin above the dorsal fin, dark spots on the caudal fin. About thirty centimeters long, my fish was beautiful enough for a page in a calendar from Ruby's Amazing Safaris.

"That's a trophy, pal." Roop sounded relieved that I had finally caught one. I felt more than relieved. This minor goliath would feed my whole family.

As I swung the catch toward land, a dark shadow passed over Roop and me. A whoosh ruffled my hair. In a flash, an osprey swooped down and sank its talons in the tilapia at the end of my line. The bird flapped its great wings, trying to steal the prize.

What the fuck? I clutched the pole and tugged, fighting back. Ospreys can lift twice their weight. For a moment I was pulled up onto my toes.

"Holy moly!" Roop poked his pole at the bandit, trying to help. The bird flapped and jerked the line. I feared the thin strand might snap, or the hook might tear through the tilapia's lips. The pole felt rough and splintery in my grip. I staggered toward the edge, dangerously close to being yanked over. Then things took an even more terrifying turn.

A crocodile sprang up from under the cut bank beneath my feet. A gaping jaw, jagged with teeth, flashed before me. Like a spring-loaded trap, it snapped shut on the osprey and fell back into the river, taking with it the bird, the fish, the line, and my instantly surrendered fishing pole. While Roop and I stood open-mouthed, the giant reptile and its flailing captive disappeared in the undercut below us. We leapt back from the edge. For a heart-stopping moment the sound of the death struggle tore through the air. Then, as abruptly as it had begun, the splashing stopped. A few dark feathers floated into view.

I turned to Roop. He was pale, clutching his net full of fish.

My voice came out hoarse. "We missed a spot."

He stared at me. Then we burst out laughing.

Our laughter quickly sputtered and died. A brush with the same force of nature that had taken Squeak turned us inward, remembering. I felt a chill that had nothing to do with the late-day slant of the sun. I had stood an arm's length from a crocodile's wide-open jaw—the very thing my unlucky cousin might have seen in the final, horrifying seconds of his life.

Calm soon returned to the riverbed. The plovers called out: *tink-tink-tink.* The crocodile had crept back into its dark green realm. The silence troubled me almost as much as the violence that had preceded it. Who could have known a thousand-pound reptile lounged in the undercut a few feet below us? Not for the first time, I was struck by the genius of the natural world—its power and stealth.

Roop and I didn't need words to agree it was time to leave. We walked a while without speaking. Every now and then, one of the tilapias flopped in the net hanging behind his back.

"Good bait," I said.

He shrugged. "Bread and spit. Same as always."

"We almost caught a crocodile."

We shared a nervous laugh.

Roop turned serious. "Two of these fish are for you."

"No way."

"Granny and I can split the big one. She doesn't eat much."

I gave him a look.

"You need it more. Brain food."

My family would welcome the fish, of course. But from a boy who lived hand to mouth with a dependent grandmother in a truly rotting house? "Are you sure?"

"Yep. You'd do the same if you skunked me."

I supposed I would. "Well, thanks." This felt awkward, so I blinked and said, "Zola will thank you too."

I watched him blush. It never failed; my older sister had this effect on boys—even the polite ones like Roop, who really just wanted to give me the fish. Then I felt bad for creating a diversion at his expense.

"Let's go by your house so I can say hi to Granny."

On the porch of Rotting House, we made quick work of cleaning Roop's catch. Although I liked Granny Nobbs, my real reason for stopping by was to contribute the leavings from the fish Roop had given me. Ovambos could, and would, eat anything, including fish guts. We filleted the tilapias with care, collecting in a bucket every slimy, scaly bit that wasn't prime fish flesh. While we worked, Granny sat near us, shooing away chickens with a broom. When I told her about the osprey and the crocodile, she threw back her head and laughed, her merry grin checkered yellow and black with old and missing teeth.

"The crocodile did you a favor. You wouldn't have wanted to reel in that bird. Have you ever tasted osprey meat?"

I shook my head.

"Almost as bad as eagle. Any bird that eats fish and long-dead rot tastes like the bottom of a garbage pail."

"Ewwww!" Roop and I chorused, savoring the gross imagery.

I eyed a chicken that had slipped past Granny's broom and was investigating a splotch of fish blood on the floorboards. "The Ovambos eat rot, and they taste good."

"They also eat grain and real chicken feed when we have it. Scavenging makes them a little gamey is all."

I waved away a rooster circling the pail of offal. Like my uncle, Granny was a font of interesting information. Stash would appreciate the item about birds that tasted like the bottom of a garbage pail. I planned to tell him as soon as possible.

After we finished cleaning the fish, Roop placed four wrapped filets in my hands and shoved me toward the steps, preventing further awkwardness. The Ovambos chased me out of the yard, and as darkness fell, I ran all the way home.

* * *

I spent the last few days before the JSC exam with my nose in one book or another, brushing up on math, history, science, and English. Hannie had come down with something that made her nose run and her eyes water. From time to time, she would wander into the kitchen where I was studying and reach out with her sticky, virulent little hands for a hug or a lift up to my lap. Zola tried to keep her away, but increasingly, Zola's assistance included a poke at me.

"Get down, Hannie. Bonesy's studying for a ticket to a bright future." The words "ticket to a bright future" came out flat and mocking. For someone who once had encouraged me to study and make something of myself, Zola showed little enthusiasm for my actual success.

I gave her a look meant to say, *You got that right, sister,* but she was too busy wiping Hannie's nose to notice. Watching her tend the baby, I realized what my bright future must look like to her. She probably imagined me finding a good job, becoming successful, and leaving our threadbare existence—and her—far behind. I wasn't ashamed to admit that almost everything about that excited me.

A couple of days later, less than a week before the exam, Baba fell ill with symptoms similar to Hannie's. During the cool morning hours he managed a few chores outdoors, but he spent most of each day in bed, sniffling and coughing. When he passed me studying at the kitchen table, his eyes red and raw, he patted my back as if to say, *Go get 'em, Bonesy!* Or maybe, *I'm sorry I can't help you because I'm sick and I drink too much and I never went far in school.* Either way, I felt he was on my team.

Uncle Stash became my best champion. He set aside a table and chair in the shop where I could study in peace. He also gave me two new number 2 pencils.

"The average pencil can draw a line thirty-five miles long," he informed me.

"Really? Did someone do that?"

"Someone must have, or we wouldn't know, would we?" His tone suggested I wasn't as smart as he had previously thought. "Pencils can also write underwater."

"That would be easier to prove."

"Yes, it would. And be sure to use the same pencils you study with to take the exam because they'll remember the correct answers. That's Chinese."

I wasn't so sure about that. I eyed him. "I've been meaning to tell you something."

"What?"

"Osprey meat tastes like the bottom of a garbage pail."

"It does?"

"Yes."

On the morning of the test, I woke up half dead. I had a headache that felt like an invasion of brain termites, and my throat was raw, as if the termites had already been there and chewed their way north. I stumbled out of bed and into the clothes I had laid out the night before when I still felt okay. *Sick? Today of all days?*

My pencils rested on the kitchen table alongside a spoon and a bowl of oatmeal that Zola had prepared and sprinkled with brown sugar. She and Baba sat at the table staring at me as though I was going off to war and wouldn't be seen again for a long, long time. I did my best to act healthy so they wouldn't try to keep me home. I managed to eat most of the oatmeal even though it tasted like dirt, and for once I had zero appetite. I smiled a little and jiggled my eyebrows meaningfully so I wouldn't have to talk. I was pretty sure my voice had gone south.

A duet of "good lucks" and "do your bests" accompanied me to the door.

"Thanks," I rasped, hurrying out before either of them could realize I clung to life's ragged edge. Every step coincided with a hammer hitting my skull. My eyelids brought to mind sixty-grit sandpaper. I felt hot, cold, freaking haywire. But nothing was going to prevent me from taking the exam.

The sun had barely cracked the horizon when I walked past Uncle Stash's workshop. My uncle seldom came to work until later, yet the door to the shop stood wide-open. I noted this and kept going, fearful of being late. By then sheer momentum was allowing me to put one foot in front of the other. The complication of turning in a new direction seemed beyond my resources. I gripped the number 2 pencils as though they were lifesaving amulets. They felt slick in my palm.

Then, not with conscious intent but because I couldn't help myself, my feet changed direction. I turned around and retraced my steps. My woolly head prickled with questions. What if something was amiss? What if Stash was in trouble? How could I fail to check and, at the very least, close the door myself?

I was in a feverish stupor as I lurched down the path to the workshop. The door stood open. At the threshold I came to an abrupt halt because a person rushing out almost ran into me. "Skinner?" I croaked.

He straightened and stepped back as if called to attention by a superior officer. Sliding one hand behind his hip, he managed to look stern and put-upon at the same time. "Your uncle should not leave the door open. I went in to see if everything was okay."

"What?" I stared at him. My head felt ready to explode.

"To make sure everything was okay," he repeated, louder, enunciating to underscore my obvious mental deficiency.

"Including that cash you took?"

"What cash?" With the one arm available to him, he tried to shove me out of the way.

I had the presence of mind to notice I had grown nearly as tall as him. I grabbed the arm tucked behind his back and pulled it forward. He wound up, getting ready to slug me. A wave of dizziness tilted the ground beneath my feet, and in one mighty contraction, I booted the contents of my stomach onto his T-shirt, shoes, and the fist clutching a thick roll of bills.

His fingers sprang open so fast that they might as well have held burning coals. While I got another, wretched look at my breakfast, Skinner dropped the money to the ground. He unleashed an impressive string of expletives as he swiped at the pungent mess running down his shirt. Then he did a little dance, shifting his weight back and forth as he tried to knock the slime from his sneakers. But he succeeded only in smearing dust into the lumpy crud caked between the laces.

When he looked up at me, his face displayed such revulsion that you would think I was the one caught in a criminal act, with stolen cash in my hand. "You're disgusting."

"You stole from Uncle Stash."

"You can't prove anything, Sawdust-for-Brains. And you don't know squat."

"You're a loser, Skinner. That much I know."

"You don't know squat."

He shoved me aside and walked away, cursing. As I watched him go, I wiped my mouth on the hem of my shirt. My pencils remained miraculously clean and shiny. Except for the outermost bill, the roll of cash was in good shape too, scattered over dry land rather than in the puddle of worse-for-wear oatmeal. I returned the money to the metal box on the shelf and hurried out, pulling the door closed behind me. I was quite sure Skinner wouldn't be back anytime soon.

The vomiting must have released something nasty because I felt a little better then. It didn't hurt that I had given Skinner a good going-over. "Trying to help," he had said. Did he really think I would believe that? He had to be the dimmest bulb I had ever known. Also the meanest and most destructive. I was learning that the connections between stupidity and malice were tangled and dense. Exhibit A: Skinner.

When I started out again, the sun produced a dazzle that hurt my eyes. What time was it? The test would begin on the stroke of the hour, no exceptions. Panic squeezed my heaving chest.

I stepped up the pace until tortured breathing brought me to a halt. Gasping, I bent over, braced my hands on my knees, and sucked in air. I vowed that if Skinner had made me late for the exam, I would track him down and barf on him all over again. No, I would do worse. Murderous thoughts coursed through my mind. I gave them full rein until my breathing finally settled. Then, gripping the number 2 pencils, I made my way forward again, teetering and clenched with worry.

I skidded into the classroom at the very last moment, just before the proctor closed the door. I was sweaty and rank. In my ravaged shirt I must have appeared an unlikely candidate for a bright future. The proctor slid his eyes over me. I tried not to speak or wheeze. With as much dignity as I could muster, I squared my shoulders, croaked my name, and held up the shiny new pencils to prove I was an actual test-taker and not a rotter who had lost his way after a ruinous night at Captain Biggie's.

The proctor consulted a list and, frowning, waved me toward an empty desk. A minute later he gave some instructions and said, "Begin."

6

Aunt Letty brought homemade ice cream. Zola baked a chocolate cake. Baba poured coffee into mugs for Uncle Stash and Mr. Kitwick, the honored guest if you didn't count me. We were celebrating my tenth-grade graduation and the Junior Secondary Certificate I had earned with highest honors.

My father had invited Mr. Kitwick as a special surprise. When my school principal appeared on our doorstep, I stood up so fast I knocked over my chair. At first I thought he had come to inform me it was all a mistake—that I hadn't graduated or passed the exam after all. I barely took a breath until he shook my hand and said, "Congratulations, Bonesy." His long, thin fingers bunched in mine like a bundle of twigs. "You've made a good start down your path to the future."

The dirt lane to Uncle Stash's workshop came to mind before I took in the real significance of his words. I would understand his meaning better in the years ahead, when my path would split into forks that snaked farther away from the shop down the road. For now, my new occupation as Uncle Stash's apprentice led only a short distance to a place I already knew, yet I was giddy with anticipation. I felt my world expanding beyond the chokehold of the blighted field behind our house. Compared to an endless struggle for yield from the flinty earth, making fine and useful things out of wood seemed like a glorious occupation. Uncle Stash said my wages would grow along with my skill. Soon I would earn enough to support my family. I was a full-fledged, certified junior adult, heady with possibility and the admiration of everyone around me.

Baba gave me a leather carpenter's belt he had made from a kudu hide that he'd tanned himself. There were pockets for nails and loops to hold tools. When he handed the belt to me, he shook my hand, man to man, something he had never done before. "I'm proud of you," he said. I must have looked startled because then he let go and wrapped me in our normal hug.

Zola's gift was a bracelet of bright red lucky bean seeds she had strung on a fine black cord. "For luck in love and work," she said, tying the ends around my wrist. At least ten strands of lucky bean seeds circled her slender neck.

"Then *you* must be very lucky," I said, teasing.

She blushed while pretending to ignore me. "Don't let Hannie chew on them."

I stood eye-to-eye with Zola now and would soon grow even taller. My voice frequently betrayed me with sudden squeaks and boomlets. My wrists poked sticklike from my longest sleeves, and my feet were as big as Baba's. He had given me a razor and a lesson in shaving, although the hairs on my chin were still nearly invisible.

"I'm going to miss you telling me to study and make something of myself," I said with a smile, in a lighthearted way.

"You're *fifteen*," she replied, as though my age were a repulsive disease. "You have a long, long way to go." Her words flew out like darts, without regard for my feelings or our distinguished guest.

Stung, I felt heat rise in my cheeks.

Baba turned sharply to her, but his words came out gentle. "Learning is lifelong for all of us, Zola. Your mother didn't go as far in school as either of you, but she always read and learned new things."

"Mama had a big vocabulary," I added in a too-bright voice.

"Mama, Mama," Hannie echoed, smiling broadly. We had recovered from the flu or whatever we'd had. Baba still coughed a little, but Hannie looked as fit and plump as a peach. Chocolate frosting circled her mouth. The mess on her face gave Zola reason to turn away from a conversation that seemed to annoy her.

She moistened a towel and applied quick, efficient swipes that pushed Hannie's head right and left. Zola's features were slack with ... what? The tedium of a chore she had performed a thousand times? Watching her, I was struck by a new awareness—a vision of my sister's vulnerable, well-defended core. What surprised me was the unhappiness I saw there. She was not just unhappy today, about me, but with herself and her life. Circumstance had pinned her to a small, unchosen world of domestic duty. Who was encouraging *her* with a range of alternatives or a ticket to a bright future?

I felt a flare of shame for the success I had achieved at her expense. Of course she cultivated resentment as I started making my escape from the narrow life into which we had both been born. I was heady with my new status, eager to bid farewell to the remains of an unpromising childhood. Yet I felt powerless to make things better for her.

"I really like the bracelet, Zo," I said. It was all I could think to say.

Mr. Kitwick cleared his throat. He had brought a bag and had kept it stowed under his chair. Now he reached down and removed a parcel wrapped in paper and string. "For you," he said with a little bow, handing it to me.

Even though the gift was most certainly a book, the formality of the presentation and the way he had saved it until last lent a certain drama to the opening. I wondered what he expected me to study now. Everyone watched as I fumbled with the string. There would be no ignoring this book, whatever it was. I wondered if Mr. Kitwick planned to track me down and quiz me on the contents.

The volume that emerged from the wrapping was like nothing I had ever seen. The cover was made of smooth, burnished leather, so fine to the touch that I wanted to simply cradle it in my hands. I turned it over and saw that both the front and back were blank. No title, no author. Puzzled, I fanned open the thick, cream-colored pages and was startled to find the inside as blank as the cover.

"It's a journal, Bonesy," Mr. Kitwick explained, "where you can write whatever you wish."

"Me?" Defacing those immaculate pages seemed unthinkable. "Uh, what should I write?"

He sat back and made a nest of his folded hands. "Your thoughts, ideas, something you learned. Lists, drawings, doodles. Anything you want."

"Are you going to read it?"

He laughed, a throaty chuckle. "No. And no one else should either, unless you want them to. The journal is just for you."

Just for me? I touched the leather, as smooth as a baby's skin, and tried to imagine a thought worthy of expressing between those fine covers. My mind went as blank as the book in my lap. "Well, thank you."

"A cockroach can live for a week without its head," Uncle Stash said. "Write that down."

"Hey, this is just for me."

"It's something you learned, isn't it? How about this: the average ear of corn has eight hundred kernels, sixteen rows. Write that down."

"How about you stop talking?" Baba said. "You're not his boss today."

"That's right, Stash. Tomorrow morning will come soon enough." Aunt Letty stood and started collecting plates. When she got to me, she winked and said, "Better get a good night's sleep."

* * *

Not surprisingly, my first job as Stash's apprentice was to build a cash drawer that locked.

When I had told my uncle about Skinner's failed attempt at thievery, the day after it happened, he had tried to look stern but ended up laughing so heartily that sawdust shook from his overalls. "I guess we don't need to report Skinner to the authorities. A bath in puke is punishment enough."

"I heard he got pretty sick too."

"Hard not to when you're covered in it. We'll keep an eye on him and use his, um, visit as a warning to improve our security."

I remember how he had rubbed his graying head and admitted, "I might have left the door unlocked, now that I think about it—maybe ajar, for air—and then gone out the back way. From now on we'll both be more careful. That's a pretty good result right there."

I supposed it was, though I wouldn't have minded seeing Skinner locked up. At least Stash realized he had left the shop open without my having to point out the absence of damage to the door frame or any other sign of forced entry. It made sense Skinner would take advantage of an easy situation rather than execute a full-scale break-in. He was opportunistic to the core, a stinking hyena.

My uncle could be absentminded, but he proved an excellent and patient teacher. I appreciated this right away on the first day of my apprenticeship, because building a drawer was far more complicated than I had expected.

"A drawer is not merely a box without a lid," he said, reading my mind. "It receives more punishment than any other furniture part. We yank it open, slam it shut. Yank it open, slam it shut." He demonstrated this with arm movements resembling punches. "So a drawer must be sturdy and tight, not too heavy, and easy to slide open and closed. The wood can expand and contract. If you don't allow for that, the drawer will stick. The dovetails at the corners can be finicky to fit. The runners have to be cleanly set into dadoes and the kicker properly mounted to prevent the drawer from tipping down as it is opened."

"What's a dado?"

"A slot cut to receive a board. That's carpentry. In architecture a dado is the bottom of an interior wall."

My tenth-grade certificate hung above the workbench in a handsome, Stash-crafted wood frame. I couldn't help thinking that a tenth-grade certificate wasn't very useful at present. My admiration for my uncle, who had learned so much on his own, grew with every passing day. Through the drawer project alone, he introduced me to joinery, fastenings, and runner systems and taught me how to use a miter saw, router, and dovetail jig. Equally important, he taught me the importance of precision.

"Measure twice, cut once," he said so often that I came to anticipate the words and blurt them out before he did.

We set the drawer into a frame attached to the legs and underside of the workbench. Stash showed me how to add a plunger lock with two keys, one for him and one for me. The key to the cash drawer was the first one I had ever been responsible for. I threaded it onto a cord from Zola's beading basket and wore it like a necklace under my shirt.

When we transferred the money from the metal box to its new, more secure location, I opened and closed the drawer several times, proud of the snug fit and smooth glide. The drawer pull that I had made from a scrap of mahogany and sanded to a silky sheen felt solid and fine against my fingertips. The scent of cut wood wafting up from the drawer's interior seemed particularly fresh and workmanlike—a stark contrast to the dingy, crumpled cash we placed inside.

For a time, Uncle Stash made me the drawer specialist, starting with a single, center drawer in a simple desk and moving on to chests with three, four, or six drawers with flush, polished fronts. Soon he taught me to make chairs to go with the desks, bed frames to match the chests, and night stands to pair with the bed frames. He posted advertisements in several newspapers, and before long we were selling bedroom sets to a furniture store in a distant city. The store called them "suites" and sent a lorry as big as an elephant. The truck proved too wide for our lane, so the driver, a man of great weight named Chiddy, parked in the flats where our village gave way to bushveld and walked to the workroom. He used an ancient, squeaking dolly to push the pieces back to the truck one by one, past the neighbors, the shops, and Captain Biggie's.

Chiddy's face was as round and shiny as a kukui nut. In one earlobe he wore a sparkling diamond stud. His voice was a magnificent, trumpeting instrument. "Helloooooooo, Bonesy!" he would call as he walked up the path, a greeting that sounded like fanfare for a prince. "What beautiful furniture do you have for me today?"

We soon realized that Chiddy served as the quality control expert as well as the driver. He carefully inspected each piece for imperfections before taking custody. To my great satisfaction, he never found fault, not a single flaw. Instead, he exclaimed over the sturdy construction and smooth finishes, "Workmanship as fine, fine as any I have seen."

I supervised his examinations with what I hoped was a masterly squint while Uncle Stash stood by, nodding his approval. After Chiddy pronounced an item "fine, fine," I helped him wrap the piece in a blanket and strap the bundle onto the dolly. He pushed, and I walked alongside with a steadying hand on the cargo. I didn't mind that our squeaky passage through the village drew attention as we made our way past Captain Biggie's, OK Bazaar, and Toolie's one-man bicycle repair business. I felt proud to be a workingman who associated with a person as imposing and worldly as Chiddy. When girls my age turned their heads, I stood a little taller.

"The ladies find you quite attractive, you know," Chiddy said one day as we trundled a chair to the lorry.

Because he said this without sarcasm or teasing, like someone reporting the news, I turned his words over in my mind with care. *Did they? Was I?* "I hadn't really noticed," I lied, casting a glance at a girl I knew from school.

She wore a pale dress and stood in a ribbon of sunlight that silhouetted her legs. I watched her lift a hand in a tentative, below-the-waist wave before disappearing inside the door of Swale's Grocery Store.

Chiddy's laugh was a thunderclap that startled a flock of sparrows into flight. "That one noticed you."

Her name was Mima Swale. In grade school she had borne a passing resemblance to a dandelion. Now her long, lean frame curved in interesting new ways, and the nimbus of curls on her head had lengthened to a free-falling gloss.

"Her name is Mima," I said, uncommonly pleased to shape the syllables with my lips. "From school."

"I see." He nodded thoughtfully, as though I had shared a profound truth. "You must take good, good care not to break her heart."

Break her heart? The notion that Mima's heart could have anything to do with me came as a stunning bulletin. "No worries, Chiddy," I said, tossing another glance toward Swale's Grocery. "No worries."

7

ON DAYS OFF I LOADED my tool belt and went to help Roop repair Rotting House. Although home building pushed the frontier of my abilities, I was eager to practice and expand my trade. Roop and Granny Nobbs were grateful for any effort to patch up their crumbling abode. Until then, I had never gone inside Rotting House. My friendship with Roop was an outdoorsy one that had flourished on his front porch and the banks of the river. As a result, my initial inspection of the premises came as a shock.

Picking my way through the four decent-sized rooms, I discovered a tide of squalor worse than I had expected. The floorboards were spongy with decay. Dark stains mottled the walls. Doors were stuck open or closed. I spied frills of multihued mold, silky white spider nests, and a bedside umbrella Granny opened at night for protection against grainy smut that dropped from the ceiling. The house had a gamey mouse stench that even the odors of Lifebuoy soap and boiling chicken feet couldn't hide.

Poor Roop did his best to keep things tidy and functional. He had swept the floor clean of chicken feathers and used Omo detergent to scrub away the mess created by Granny's walkie business. Laundered clothes hung from a line in back. He had hammered wooden railings into the walls to help Granny move from her bed to the kitchen table and her chair on the porch. He showed me the pot reserved for her private motions and told me he emptied and rinsed it every morning.

What words could I use then? The effort my friend made to care for his aged grandmother left my throat thick with feeling. When I finally spoke, I tried without success to sound normal. "Oh, I see. Well."

The tin roof leaked through rusty, razor-edged gaps that promised tetanus. I owned only one pair of work gloves, so I kept the right-hand one and gave the left glove to Roop. A board placed between two kitchen chairs was all the scaffolding we needed to survey the patched, corrugated mess that served as a lid for Rotting House. Wild creepers had taken hold in some of the mossy, dirt-clogged gullies. Bat guano chalked the dirt beneath the eaves. A scorpion plump with poison popped out of an inch-wide gap and scuttled to safety.

I stepped down and removed my glove, stalling. Roop said nothing, watching me like a patient getting ready for bad news. Clearly, the roof had to come first, but I hadn't the slightest idea how to fix it. To me, the patient was terminal. "We have to replace the roof, Roop. The whole thing," I finally said, guessing a new roof was the simplest solution. "Tear this one off and start over."

He blinked.

"We'll use leftover roofing from the shop. It won't cost a thing." Stash had encouraged me to take surplus materials accumulated in the dark recesses of the workshop. A cleanout was long overdue. More to the point, our growing furniture business needed more space. "You've got to start with a good roof. Otherwise, repairing the rest is a waste of time."

He swallowed hard, unused to big decisions. "Granny can't be exposed to the night air, you know."

"Of course not. We'll do it in one day. Remove the old tin, caulk the beams underneath, and lay on new metal sheeting. How hard can that be?" My bravado impressed even me. "We won't inconvenience Granny at all."

This was a scenario Roop could not refuse. We spent the rest of the afternoon measuring. He held one end of the tape while I reeled out the other and recorded the measurements on a scrap of cardboard.

Granny woke from a nap to sit and watch. She looked as frayed as an old rope, but when she smiled, her eyes were liquid with affection. "You boys are good to me. Without you, I'd have only the chickens."

"And the bats," Roop reminded her, aligning the tape to recheck a dimension we had already measured twice. Laying sheets of corrugated tin on a structure as imperfect as Rotting House hardly required such exactitude. But I was a semiprofessional now, and although I had never swapped out a roof, I did know how to measure.

"Your sister stopped by yesterday," Granny said, waving a broom at an Ovambo that had taken an interest in my ankles.

"My sister? Zola was here?" I looked at Roop.

He looked as surprised as I was. "I didn't see her."

"Her boyfriend bought her a walkie." Granny smiled her checkered grin. I couldn't tell whether she was happy to have made the sale or pleased by the romantic gesture.

"Boyfriend?" My voice rose in pitch, incredulous. I realized I sounded like an idiot. Zola was nineteen years old. Not a few girls in our village were wives and mothers by that age. I looked at Roop. "Did you know Zola has a boyfriend?"

"News to me." His shoulders slumped as if yoked by a great weight. I noted this and stored the image in a corner of my mind to reconsider later.

At the moment, all I could think about was Zola's boyfriend. Who from the dubious pool of young manhood in our village could this suitor be? "Who was she with, Granny?"

"I don't know his name. The chickens go mad whenever he comes."

"He's been here before? With Zola?"

"Once or twice."

Life often surprised me, but seldom in a way that made me feel so ridiculous. Had I expected Zola to stay cooped up at home forever, a surrogate mother caring for our family? The shameful truth: I had.

Roop and I didn't say much after that. We finished measuring and made a plan to transport roofing material from the shop to the yard in front of Rotting House.

Before I left, Granny handed me a bag of walkies. "Don't tell Zola I gave you these free."

I walked slowly, chewing, rattled by the news I had just heard. Zola had a boyfriend, a life I knew nothing about? Her secrecy seemed an impossible betrayal, so unexpected that I began to doubt the whole story. Maybe Granny had gotten it wrong. Maybe she had mistaken another girl for my sister. Or maybe Zola and a guy did show up to buy walkies, but they weren't really together.

The hammer hanging from my carpenter's belt thwacked against my hip. I hardly noticed. My mind leapt forward to the day Zola would leave our house to marry and start her own family. How would Baba, Hannie, and I manage then? Sheepishly, I remembered that I once had assumed *she* worried about *me* leaving home. Life could be very unsettling, I thought as

I bit into a walkie. The reflections so consumed me that I didn't see Mima Swale coming the other way until we stood almost shoulder-to-shoulder.

"Hi, Bonesy," she said, her smile radiant. "I haven't seen you in a while."

"Uh, hi. I've been working. At Roop's. And my uncle's shop." *I sound like a dope.* "Want a walkie?"

She reached in. "Thanks."

"They're from Granny Nobbs."

"Yum. Hers are good."

Zola's secret life fled from my mind as Mima and I stood an arm's length apart, chewing, crunching on walkies. I found myself acutely attentive to the shine of her hair, the arch of her lips, the thudding in my chest. "I've seen you at the grocery store," I said.

"I work there now. With my mother." A shadow crossed her face. I recognized the feeling that hung between us then, the weight of it. Her grief was almost palpable.

The story of her father's recent death had flown through the village. One night Mr. and Mrs. Swale—Kate and Bastian—were driving through the bush when they stopped to reclose the rattling tailgate. Mr. Swale got out and walked around to the back while Mrs. Swale sat and waited. A minute or two passed in silence. Mrs. Swale called to her husband, but he didn't answer. She stepped out to have a look. He was gone. She never saw him again.

Most everyone agreed a cat must have taken him—a lion or leopard that had gone straight for the throat. Apparently there were drag marks in the dust, but no one had found any sign of Bastian Swale, not even a boot.

I hesitated, searching for words. "I'm sorry about what happened."

"Thank you." Her eyes glistened. "It's hard, you know, that he just disappeared. It might have been easier to see him dead."

I wasn't so sure about that, so I looked away and said nothing.

She inhaled, an audible suck of air. "Oh, I'm sorry. Seeing your mother ... it must have been awful."

I nodded, not trusting my voice.

Her voice was a whisper. "Did you get to say goodbye at least?"

"No." I cleared my throat. "When my father carried her into the house, he told me to stay away. Trying to protect me, I guess. When I did see her, she was already dead." I realized I had just admitted I was present when the cobra bit my mother, something I had told no one. I waited, looking at her.

"I'm sorry," she said simply.

"Me too."

We were quiet then, but our silence didn't feel lame or awkward. There was comfort in simply standing next to her. Her calm sympathy fostered a closeness I felt in every channel of my being. I was conscious of breathing the same air as she, of feeling the same breeze that pressed her skirt against her legs. When she lifted her face to say goodbye, I was in the grip of something new.

* * *

Replacing the tin roof on Rotting House turned out to be a bigger project than I had anticipated. Fortunately for me, Uncle Stash intervened early, when Roop and I were rummaging around the shop for supplies.

"Do you have enough roofing felt?" he inquired.

"Roofing felt?"

"To lay between the plywood and the metal."

"Plywood?"

And thus began my lesson in roofing. Stash helped sort and remove the surplus materials from the shop: sheets of corrugated tin, offcut plywood, nails, wood screws, and even an old roll of roofing felt. Where quantities fell short, he quietly ordered and paid for more. Grandpa Nobbs had been Stash's friend since childhood. Granny Nobbs had babysat for my cousin Squeak. Stash even managed a good relationship with the Ovambos. For some unknown reason, the flock simply wandered away, letting him pass without assault, when he limped across the yard.

Once we had assembled all the necessary supplies, Roop and I actually did complete the job in one day. Following Stash's advice, we ripped off the rotten metal in dim, predawn light and by sunrise had exposed the entire termite-chewed mess underneath. Our early start diverted the resident bats coming home to roost. They circled and dived and, finding their quarters demolished, flew off in search of new shelter.

Stash arrived shortly after dawn bearing a large jug of Aunt Letty's homemade soup and a loaf of bread warm from the oven. He showed us how to cut plywood to replace the ruined sections and then lay roofing felt in overlapping strips. At midday we took a break for soup and bread, sitting on the porch with Granny. Roop and I spent the afternoon cutting and laying sheets of corrugated tin, while Stash and Granny laughed and reminisced, and my uncle kept an expert eye on the work in progress. By the end of the day, Rotting House wore a shiny new roof, and I could claim a useful new skill.

I returned the next morning to help Roop haul away the debris we had piled in the yard. The Ovambos clucked and pecked at it, getting in our way. Cleaning up proved almost as much work as the roofing job itself. We sorted metal from wood, picked up rusty nails, and raked the yard clean of splinters and small bits that could injure bare feet. I was dumping a handful of rakings into a barrel when something shiny caught my eye. It fell into the depths before I got a good look, so I almost let it go, imagining a shard of tin. But before I dropped in the next handful, I leaned over to peer inside. It was small and silvery, almost undetectable among the metal scraps: a key.

"Roop. Look what I found." I reached in and retrieved the small treasure, brushing away dirt and crud. Something might have been etched in one side, but the writing was worn and hard to read.

He shrugged. "Probably carried in by a rat. Ask Granny."

She was dozing in her chair on the porch. When Roop gave her the key, she blinked and turned it over a few times, frowning. "I can't think where …" She paused. "Unless …"

"What?"

"My old jewelry box." Her face brightened. "That must be it."

"Jewelry box?" Roop looked at me. I knew we were thinking the same thing: Granny didn't own much jewelry.

"Grandpa gave me a jewelry box the year we were married. When you opened the lid, music played, and a ballerina twirled in a circle. He thought I'd like that." Her eyes misted. "As a little boy, your father liked to wind it up, Rooper. Kids are hard on things, you know. After a few years the box fell apart." A sweet, faraway smile softened her features. "It had a lock and a key."

The mention of Roop's father—another dead parent—tugged at me. Even if the key Granny remembered was long gone, the one I had found gave her the pleasure of a happy memory. I fished out the cord that hung under my T-shirt. "I keep this key with me at all times. I could put yours on a necklace for you too, as a memento."

She touched my hand. "I'd like that, Bonesy."

On my next visit I found her asleep in her chair. Not even the screeches of the chickens woke her. I tiptoed up the stairs and, moving her head just a little, slipped on the necklace with its newly polished keepsake.

* * *

Work with Uncle Stash turned out to be a constant, eye-opening journey of learning and discovery. With practice, I became adept at turning chair legs on the lathe. Then I managed to shape a few only slightly irregular bowls for Zola and Aunt Letty. Stash taught me the art of scribing—making new materials that are a square fit against old materials that aren't, an essential skill for the ongoing repairs at Rotting House. I became conversant in shoptalk and spent hours discussing with Stash the relative merits of wood types, sanding techniques, and various joints. When was the half lap preferable to the rabbet? The doweled butt to the mortise and tenon? My head swelled with new words and their meanings. The language of carpentry became familiar and empowering, and more than once I was reminded of my mother's respect for a rich and vibrant vocabulary. She couldn't have imagined the words I knew now.

Chiddy walked up the path calling, "Hellooooooooo, Bonesy," with increasing frequency. Demand for our furniture was robust and growing. Chiddy delivered to more than one store now, and he liked to tell Stash and me about the customers who purchased our wares. "She was very fine, this missus, very fine," he reported, circling his arms as if to embrace a barrel. "Also very beautiful. And married." He winked at me. "This one needed your strong, strong bed."

He told us about shy, expectant young couples picking out their first cradles, about growing families in want of bunk beds, about grannies with canes testing rockers—"cradles for the aged," he said. He reported that our "limited edition" wooden bowls had caught the eye of an exporter. And one morning, he brought the best news of all.

"I have a very special order," he announced, handing Stash a typewritten sheet. "Six bedroom suites."

"Six? From one buyer?" Stash looked dubious. He held out the paper so I could read along with him.

6 king-size beds framed to support mosquito netting
12 bedside tables, each with one drawer and a shelf
6 wardrobes fitted with hooks and shelves for clothing
6 small desks, one drawer each
6 desk chairs
6 occasional armchairs paired with 6 small coffee tables

Stash stared at the list. "Who has so many bedrooms?"

"Motembo," Chiddy said, leaving us as unenlightened as before. He waved another typed page. "These are the dimensions and specifications. You are requested to use fine, fine woods such as African mahogany, 'with blackwood or ebony accents,'" he said, reading the last few words straight from the page. "Accents are drawer pulls, hooks, and trim, I believe."

"Motembo?" I asked.

"A safari camp. Six new guest tents. Quite far, far away."

Our biggest order ever and from a *safari* camp. I felt a shiver of excitement.

"How soon can you begin?" Chiddy asked.

Stash looked at me. "We'll start today."

From that morning forward, Uncle Stash and I put in long hours, seven days a week. The instructions from the camp referred to furniture we had sold before, one-of-a-kind pieces of the highest quality, made from the most beautiful materials. We were happy to apply that standard again and to charge the premium such work deserved. Cost didn't seem a problem for Jackson Quinn, Motembo's manager. He had signed our contract with a bold slash through the Q and included a down payment of 40 percent. Chiddy told us Jackson Quinn was a certified guide with an excellent reputation in the safari business. He had risen to management in another premier camp. Now he planned to transform Motembo into the finest of them all.

Although I hadn't met Jackson Quinn, he became a valiant figure in my mind. He was enterprising, successful, and particular about quality. He was a man who understood the allure of the African bush and created welcoming outposts for like-minded souls. Best of all, he was a safari guide. I wondered if he knew my longtime heartthrob, Ruby, of Ruby's Amazing Safaris. Ruby had stirred my youthful fantasies for so long that she had grown in my imagination to Amazonian proportions. I doubted even Jackson Quinn could stand up to her.

Mr. Quinn was never far from my mind as I cut, joined, sanded, and finished each piece of furniture destined for Motembo. I expected that our number one customer would personally inspect every knob and hook, and I did not want to disappoint him.

During those weeks, I seldom saw the rest of my family. Baba went through his usual swings, making frequent trips to Captain Biggie's and working hard in the field when he felt well enough. Hannie was consumed by her new school and friends, already bringing home decent teachers' reports. Zola? I didn't want to know how Zola spent her time. Actually, I did. Yet I never asked about her boyfriend because I hoped she would tell me on her own. She cooked and organized for us as always. Our household ran as efficiently as ever. I supposed the boyfriend gave her a sense of a larger life, something that was hers and hers alone. Why should she have to explain?

My new attitude about Zola's romance had a lot to do with Mima Swale. I hadn't told anyone that I had begun stopping at Swale's Grocery after work or that Mima possessed the power to double my heart rate in five seconds flat. Mrs. Swale departed the store promptly at closing to return home and cook dinner for Mima's younger brothers. Fortunately for me, Mima stayed behind to tidy the shelves and sweep. Although my days in Stash's shop were long and intense, I never felt too tired to visit Mima after work—to watch her eyes widen when I tapped on the window, to see the smile that lit her face when she opened the door.

At first, I stayed only a few minutes, nervous, not wanting to get in the way or slow down her chores. I would say hello, ask about her day. She usually told a funny story about a customer or a mishap involving a toppled display or a bird that had flown in the window. Once I brought a small bowl I had made and another time, a sack of fresh sawdust for soaking up spills. More than once, I found myself in speechless thrall to the lilt of her voice, the movement of her lips, or the twist of hair that coiled against her neck. We were unnaturally careful not to touch each other. An accidental brush of our shoulders felt like a seismic event. I looked into her eyes. She looked away. She looked into my eyes. I looked away. The lunacy of young love. She always asked me to come back and see her again, so I did.

8

Stash used some of our windfall from the Motembo project to buy a rugged used van with four-wheel drive, wide rear doors, and a spacious interior. The previous owners had installed a winch and heavy-duty tires for off-road driving. Stash and Aunt Letty owned an ancient station wagon that had served them and the shop for years. But now our booming furniture business required more supplies, more deliveries, and more frequent trips to the bank. Stash said that after I got my license, I could relieve him of most of our errands.

"Driving a vehicle is a big responsibility," he told me. "You could kill someone."

I nodded, trying to hide my excitement. Not many people in our village owned cars or knew how to drive. Baba once had a truck, but he crashed it, and that was that.

"Hitting a donkey at night could be fatal."

"A donkey?"

"They're attracted to the heat of the road. You can't see them until too late. Death by crashing into donkeys is quite common."

"I'll be very careful."

After I studied the rules of the road, Stash drove me to the Motor Vehicle Department in a town some distance away. To my relief, I passed the written test with ease. An eye exam confirmed my excellent vision. While Stash read from a stack of old *National Geographic* magazines, I took a lesson in a shiny new car with an encouraging instructor who afterward pronounced me fit to drive under supervision. At the end of the day, I possessed a learner's permit, a big yellow "L" to place on the dashboard, and permission to "proceed with practice."

On my first outing with Stash, I killed the engine three times before reaching first gear. The van wasn't the well-oiled machine I had driven with the instructor. Then I shifted into second and tore out a patch of road.

"In some places that's against the law," Stash said, gripping his seat belt.

My hands choked the wheel as we shuddered along. But soon I found the rhythm. After I had achieved a few smooth cycles through the shift pattern, driving felt as natural to me as riding my bike.

We careened around a corner. "Early cars didn't have steering wheels," Stash informed me. "You had to steer with a lever."

"Interesting."

"Yes, I think so." He settled back in his seat, relaxing a little as my technique improved. We were nearing a crossroads choked with vehicles, pushcarts, pedestrians, and a cyclist balancing a pig on the handlebars. I downshifted, causing only a minor jolt to my passenger.

"During the polar bear migration in Churchill, Canada, you have to ride in a special Tundra Buggy so the bears can't climb in the windows and eat you. I read it in *National Geographic*."

"Do polar bears want to eat you?"

"Yes, because they're famished." He looked at me. "The inside of a vehicle is the safest place in the bush too, especially at night. You can write that in your journal."

I nodded, wanting to be agreeable. I didn't tell him that so far I had written nothing in my journal. The immaculate, leather-bound volume, still wrapped in brown paper, remained as blank and unblemished as the day Mr. Kitwick gave it to me. What, exactly, I was waiting for, I couldn't say. But I had a feeling I would know when the right time had come.

Although I wasn't superstitious, I had to admit that another graduation gift, the lucky bean seed bracelet from Zola, was serving me very well. "For luck in love and work," she had said. At the time I had brushed off the notion of an easy shortcut to important life goals. But at present I was inclined to look upon her gift with a tad more respect.

For one thing, I was wearing the bracelet the first time I kissed Mima. I had stayed late at the grocery store to help her carry in boxes from the back room. When we were getting ready to lock up and leave, she took off her apron and hung it on a peg, turned out the light, and then hesitated at the door. She must have turned to face me, but all I remember is that our lips came together with predestined ardor and precision. My arms found their way around her. The length of our bodies met, pulsed, rubbed, and said hello. Lucky bean seeds were far from my mind during that first kiss. But I couldn't deny the bracelet was there, on my wrist, while I was touching the girl who so thrillingly wanted to touch me too.

For another thing, work with Uncle Stash was turning out even better than I had hoped. I had never guessed that in addition to learning carpentry and woodworking, I would become a licensed driver—or that my job would connect me even remotely to places like Motembo or people like Chiddy and Jackson Quinn.

After I passed my final driver's test, I used the van to transfer items from the shop to Chiddy's larger truck parked on the outskirts of the village. The furniture Stash and I built for Motembo was solid and handsome, with elegant wood grains and lustrous finishes. "Too fine to wheel down the street," Chiddy declared on his first pickup. "Too classy for street walking, you know," he whispered in my ear, grinning.

Each bedroom suite included eight pieces plus a detachable frame for mosquito netting. Chiddy estimated his truck could hold all six suites if we broke down the beds and frames for reassembly at their destination. Because of limited space in the shop, we agreed that Chiddy would pick up and store the Motembo pieces as we finished them. When the entire order was complete, he would drive the furniture to the camp in one trip, a two-day journey over sketchy roads.

"I believe your furniture will be very well received at Motembo," Chiddy said, puffing as he and I hoisted a recently completed desk into his truck. "The quality is equal to the best I've seen in other lodges, even in the finest lounge and dining areas."

Lounge and dining areas? I knew nothing of safari camps. Details such as this thrilled me. "There are separate tents for the lounge and dining areas?"

"Oh yes, always separate. And quite grand in an outdoorsy, African way. These spaces often have high thatched roofs and sofas with many cushions. There is a bar as long as a canoe. The dining table will seat fourteen or more, with wide, wide arm chairs for maximum comfort." As he said this he patted his own impressive girth. I was becalmed for a moment by the image of fourteen Chiddy-size diners.

"Does Jackson Quinn already have the lounge and dining furniture for Motembo?"

"I couldn't say. The last time I was there, we dined on logs around a campfire."

I wondered how well Chiddy knew Motembo's owner. I didn't need to inquire about this because he added, "Safari camps are quite isolated, you know. Far, far from towns and each other. Sometimes I deliver food and beer and always the latest newspapers. When I arrive, everyone is happy to see me, especially Jackson Quinn."

I suppressed a smile. Of course they were. I could almost hear his cheery greeting as he rolled into Motembo. *Hellooooooooo, Jackson!*

"I spend the night in the staff quarters before returning home, so there is dinner and talking." He gazed into the distance as if remembering a particularly enjoyable evening. "Jackson is an excellent host. Often we have Amarula at his campfire."

"Amarula?"

"I see you have yet to discover the pleasure of Amarula. This is drink made from the fruit of the marula tree. Very strong. Just a little can give you a pleasant feeling. But you must be careful not to drink too much."

I had watched elephants shake marula trees to dislodge ripe fruit. They butted their heads against the tree trunks and pulled down branches as thick as their legs. "Elephants love marula."

He nodded. "People claim elephants get drunk on it. This is a humorous idea, but untrue. Elephants do not say, 'Stop! No eating yet. We must wait for the fruit to ferment.'"

Chiddy's laugh echoed through the cavernous cargo hold of his truck. We had filled about a quarter of the space with furniture. The finished pieces sat at the back, wrapped in felt, securely strapped to the walls. Stash and I still had a lot of work to do.

* * *

Every two weeks or so, Chiddy turned up for the transfer of new items from the shop floor to the van for the ride to his big truck parked outside the village. Driving through our narrow streets with Chiddy by my side swelled me with pride, especially when we passed Swale's Grocery. Often I glimpsed Mima through the open door and sometimes her mother. When they spotted the van passing by, they smiled and waved.

"I see you have won the mother too," Chiddy said, peering through the window. "This is very helpful in a romance."

Although I hadn't made that calculation, I was glad Mrs. Swale seemed to like me. She was a striking woman with long limbs typically clad in pants and sleeved shirts that gave her an aura of unfettered competence. Her hair was gathered in a ponytail that failed to contain the wispy strands floating around her face. She had thanked me for my gift of sawdust, saying she used the compound to absorb and sweep up spills at home as well as in the store. Her brisk, no-nonsense manner concealed the pain she must have felt at the loss of her husband. Bastian Swale had left her with twin boys, Donovan and Drew, in addition to Mima. Caring for the boys while running the grocery business would have been impossible without help from her daughter.

Rather than tying her down, Mima's growing responsibilities increased her freedom and, thrillingly, our chances to see each other. Like me, she had earned a driver's license in order to take over important errands for the family business. Driving the same truck that had seen the last of her father, she delivered groceries to customers, fetched supplies, and made weekly runs to the bank. She was conscientious in these matters, combining two or three errands in one trip for efficiency's sake, not wasting time. We were alike in this way and in our equally serious efforts to meet. We learned to coordinate our business in town, parking side by side on the cool, shadowed side of the bank building. If we felt we could take a few extra minutes, we would stop for ice cream or sit in the van and talk about everything and nothing: our work, bad drivers, happenings in the village.

"Your aunt Letty came into the store," she told me one day. "She's nice."

"Yes."

She leaned closer. "You might want to stop and see her. She's baking pies."

I feigned shock. "What happened to grocer–shopper confidentiality?"

She suppressed a laugh.

"What if I came in to buy, say, condoms?" I managed to pose this question while looking her straight in the eye. "Would that be a confidential matter?"

Her cheeks bloomed with color, but to her credit she did not break my gaze. "That would be a very confidential matter."

Passersby who saw us would never guess the high, intense pleasure that came from these encounters, from simply being together. We were careful not to touch in public, but even then, the slightest tap, the most casual brushing of our limbs, caused carnal upheaval out of all proportion to the apparent cause.

When we were truly alone, at night in the grocery store, Mima returned my kisses with heat and urgency that matched my own. Once she surprised me by parting her lips to admit my tongue, and we both discovered the pleasures of deeper probing. Did all lovers do this? Put their tongues in each other's mouths? I found the practice mildly shocking, even as it felt elemental and true.

Mima's face became my tender playground—her temples, nose, cheeks, and mouth nakedly available to my fingers and lips. Time went unnoticed during these stirring explorations. I got lost in the exquisite topography of her features, the curve of her brow, the symmetrical alignment of cheekbone and chin. One night she turned so that her face was half-dark and half-light, a quarter moon. Closing her eyes, she encouraged my kisses with soft sighs and a dreamy half smile.

But from the neck down, she guarded her body like a no-hunting zone. Whenever my excursion wandered south, to the buttons and zippers that fortressed her clothing, she snapped to full attention. Clamping her hand on my wrist, she redirected the expedition to more neutral territory in the vicinity of her ear or shoulder blade.

On one occasion, she murmured, "Not yet. Let's wait."

I took a deep breath and tried to focus on the delicate contour of her wing bone. Through her T-shirt and whatever she wore underneath, I felt the warmth of her body and a pulse as rapid as my own. "How about in five minutes?"

She pulled away. "I'm serious, Bonesy. I want us to take our time. Everything between us has to be right. Memorable. Like a slow dance."

"A slow dance," I said, considering.

She raised her face to mine, and I kissed her deeply, taking my time. When we came up for air, she gasped, "And a long future."

Stirring thoughts about Mima and our future together took up residence in my mind, where they stepped to the fore, unbidden, at all hours. I walked around feeling weightless, slightly drugged, half drunk. I imagined her fending off other boys who had come before me, saving herself for her future husband, the real deal—a notion that pleased me. She had the confidence of an attractive girl accustomed to setting boundaries. Whenever I ventured into forbidden territory, my inexpert fumblings found a roadblock in the certitude of her limits. But I knew how to wait. Even with my arms around her, when my heart was beating fast and I wanted nothing more than to touch every inch of her, I knew how to wait.

9

Jackson Quinn had not specified a deadline for the delivery of his order. Nonetheless, Stash and I put unrelenting pressure on ourselves to complete the work as quickly as we could. The owner of Motembo, even absent and unintroduced, loomed large in our minds. We were determined to impress him with our diligence as well as our attention to his very particular needs. We were at-your-service custom builders who also valued the prospect of a showcase in a premier safari camp, where guests from all over the world would see, use, and appreciate our work.

The income was important to me and my family, of course. Yet I took the greatest pleasure in daily, hands-on tasks that used and honed my skills. In the shop I felt competent and useful, proud to have a job I did well. Most of all, I welcomed the challenge of creating fine, original, one-of-a-kind objects that would meet the exacting standards of a person such as Jackson Quinn.

But once the magnitude of the Motembo order had come into focus, Stash and I had shared more than a moment of doubt about our ability to fill it. Our preferred practice of creating one piece at a time fostered excellent craftsmanship, but the method would take far too long for this project. The question of increasing efficiency without affecting quality had been asked—and answered with varying degrees of success—many times before. With some reluctance yet seeing no other way, we decided to cut every part needed for like items—say, the wardrobes—and then assemble and finish all six at once.

"Mass production," Stash whispered. "Interchangeable parts. Don't tell anyone."

"Don't worry," I whispered back. "No one will ask."

No one would even notice because we used a variety of wood types and grains. We fashioned different drawer pulls, hooks, and knobs for each set of furniture. The finished suites were compatible in style, measurements, and high-end sensibility. But no two ended up the same. Every piece we built for Motembo turned out as interesting, functional, and unique as any we had ever made.

First, we cut and assembled all six wardrobes, then all the desks, and then the bedside tables. We gave these items priority because their rectangular shapes lined up neatly for storage at the back of Chiddy's truck. The coffee tables came next. Round, they stacked in pairs, top against top. Then we built and finished the chairs: six desk chairs and six larger ones designed to accommodate cushions. Last were the king-size beds and their canopy frames. These we assembled, finished, inspected, and took apart for reassembly in the new guest tents at Motembo.

On the afternoon I slid the last bed rail into Chiddy's fully loaded truck, Chiddy appeared as happy as I was. He planned to leave for Motembo early the next morning.

"I will be there in two days," he said, grinning. "Two days until good company, an excellent dinner, and the lullaby of the snorting hippos."

"And Amarula?"

He tipped back his head and laughed. The diamond stud in his ear twinkled as if plugged into the mood of its host. "If Jackson feels like celebrating, yes. And I guarantee, when he sees this shipment, so beautiful, every piece complete, he will feel like celebrating." He closed the cargo door and twirled the dial on the heavy padlock. When he turned to face me again, the expression on his face had darkened. "Something about this is not quite right, Bonesy. Not quite right." He rubbed his chin as though contemplating a weighty matter. "You are the one who should be celebrating, you and your uncle Stash."

"Uncle Stash said he was celebrating by taking a nap."

"Then you and I must celebrate together. We will go to Captain Biggie's for your first taste of Amarula."

I looked at him. "I'm not eighteen, you know."

"Oh, but you will be very soon, yes? Captain Biggie has a broad, broad mind about these matters." As he said this, Chiddy wrapped his weighty arm around my shoulders and steered us in the direction of the tavern. His innate optimism about everything, including the breaking of rules, endeared him to me as much as his bubbling awareness of his own charm.

"Chiddy, will you visit me in reform school?"

"Reform school? Dear Bonesy. You are too old for reform school. You will go straight to the big house. Of course I will visit you there." He said this with a straight face. "But prison will not be necessary because your celebratory drink will take place under the tutelage of a wise elder—me."

We were halfway to Captain Biggie's when I blurted, "My father drinks too much. Once he starts, he can't quit."

Chiddy stopped abruptly and turned to face me. His voice softened. "I am sorry to hear it. This will not happen to you. Learning to drink is like learning to drive. First, the learner's permit. You drink only under supervision—to know the feel of things, how to handle yourself. In this way, you learn how and when to stop."

"What if I can't stop?"

"Then no license. You must never drink again."

I was thinking this over when we stepped across the threshold of Captain Biggie's. After our walk in the sunshine, my eyes took a moment to adjust. The tavern was long and narrow, like a cave that darkened at the far end. The bar ran along the left wall. Round mats advertising the Beer of Good Cheer dotted the long, polished surface. Behind the bar an old, foxed mirror reflected a string of twinkling lights and the imposing backside of Captain Biggie himself.

He was a big-boned, broad-shouldered man, like a statue missing its pedestal. I had glimpsed the tavern owner a few times in the village, never up close. His face was as wide as a cake plate, but his sparkly little eyes could have fit in the head of a shrew. He wore a white tunic and several long strings of dark wooden beads that clacked against the bar when he leaned in to greet us.

"Hello, Chiddy. I see you brought a friend." The smile on Captain Biggie's face did not indicate the slightest concern about my age. Chiddy settled his great bottom on a barstool that looked insufficient for the load. When Chiddy didn't crash to the floor, I took the stool next to him.

"Yes, this is Bonesy, an excellent carpenter. He's Stash's nephew."

"Ah, the nephew. I've met Zola, the niece." Captain Biggie hesitated before he spoke again, glancing toward the back of the room. Then his big smile returned. "Welcome, Bonesy, friend of Chiddy, nephew of Stash. You are also a friend of mine. What can I get for you?"

"One Amarula," Chiddy said. "We will share."

Zola had been in Captain Biggie's Tavern? That news was just beginning to sink in when I got another surprise. The small glass Captain Biggie set in front of Chiddy held a liquid resembling chocolate milk.

"The cream in Amarula makes the drink delicious and also treacherous," Chiddy explained. "You do not feel the heat of the spirits in your throat. So you must take a very small sip and wait for the pleasant feeling."

I tipped the glass to my lips, thinking of elephants. The liquid tasted fiery and creamy-rich at the same time. I set the glass down on the bar in front of Chiddy and waited for the pleasant feeling.

"Do you like it?"

"I think so." My first taste of alcohol had been the tiniest of sips. "But I think I feel pleasant because Stash and I finished the furniture for Motembo." Then I overcame a fit of shyness to add, "And because you are my wise friend."

He took this in with the seriousness that I had come to trust, with no hint of mockery or condescension. "These are excellent lessons for a drinker with a learner's permit. The drink is not the most important thing." He raised the glass. "Congratulations, Bonesy. To you and Stash and your fine, fine craftsmanship." He took a sip slightly larger than the one he had recommended. "And to friends. Much better than drinking alone."

With that, he drained the glass in one gulp. Fishing a couple of bills from his pocket, he winked at me and placed the money on the bar. "In four days' time I will return with your payment and all the latest news from camp." He heaved his great weight off the stool. "Now, my friend, I must leave you to prepare for my trip. We have enjoyed our drink, and you are sober and happy, yes?"

I felt the same as I always did, so I nodded.

"Good, good. I know you will find your own way home." With a wave at Captain Biggie, he headed out the door.

I was trailing after him when I glanced toward the rear of the tavern. By then my vision had grown accustomed to the dim interior. I blinked. My father was sitting at a rear table with two men I didn't know.

During the second I hesitated—go or stay?—Baba looked up and saw me. A slight rise of his eyebrows indicated surprise. Chiddy had already left, so I decided to stay and explain to my father why I was there. As I approached the table, one of the men got up and went out through the back door. The other man turned to look at me.

"Hi," I managed, clearing my throat. "Uncle Stash and I finished the furniture for the safari camp, all of it." The words came out in a rush. "Chiddy, the driver, brought me here to celebrate."

"I see. Congratulations," Baba said in a neutral voice. He indicated an empty chair. "Have a seat."

The other man held out his hand. "I'm Marks."

My palm felt small in his grip. He had dark, gentle eyes and a chin like an anvil. Beneath the strong planes of his face was a softness that warmed me to him right away. He appeared alert, intelligent, and as fit as a boxer in a trim khaki shirt. I guessed he was only a few years older than me.

"I'm Bonesy," I replied.

"Your dad has told me about you. You're a carpenter, right?"

I nodded. No glassware sat on the table. No food. I was pretty sure I knew what Marks did for a living.

"Carpentry is good, steady work," he said. "He's proud of you, you know."

Like an idiot, I nodded again. My voice had abandoned me. I pictured the elephant slaughter Baba and I had seen, and felt an unpleasant sensation, not yet a fully formed thought. "Your work is steady too," I said, almost in a whisper.

Marks and my father exchanged a look. "He knows I help against poachers," Baba said quietly.

Marks turned to me. "Yes. I'm a wildlife ranger. Protecting the animals and their habitat is a full-time job."

"Are there more dead elephants?" The words felt bulky in my mouth. "Did you find some?"

Again Marks looked at Baba, who nodded and said, "If he's old enough to drink in a tavern, he's old enough to hear it." His tone held a reprimand I didn't miss.

Marks's voice came out flat, a dirge. "A large breeding herd south of the village. Twelve females and their young. The water hole was poisoned." His lips formed a knot. He looked away, as if overcome by what he had seen.

"Then they poisoned the carcasses," Baba continued, keeping his eyes steady on me as if testing my fortitude—my fitness to sit in a tavern among grown men.

I wasn't sure I had heard correctly. "The ivory poachers poisoned the dead elephants?"

He nodded. "To kill vultures so they won't give away the location of the next slaughter." He paused to let that news settle. "You know how quickly vultures can find a carcass—thirty minutes or less. Poachers need longer than that to carve out a single pair of tusks. Mutilating a herd can take all day."

The bloody carnage Baba and I had witnessed swam into my mind, a horrible day's work for some sick soul. I remembered that Baba had spotted vultures over the area the day before we got there. I too had noticed vultures, the ones waiting in the trees near the dead animals.

"We don't have the manpower to track down every kettle," Marks said, anticipating my comment. "But following vultures has been a successful strategy, resulting in more than one arrest." He eyed me. "A kettle is a swarm of vultures in flight."

I knew that, so I nodded.

Marks leaned closer, looking intent. I felt the weight of his words even before he said them. "The poison they use is a cheap pesticide: carbofuran or aldicarb. Readily available, quieter than guns. Of course, all the other animals that come to drink at the water hole or feed on the poisoned carcasses die too, not just the vultures. We've found dead lions, dead leopards, dead hyenas, dead wild dogs, dead birds by the dozen. An atrocious loss of life."

I might have been old enough to hear this news, but I was unprepared to receive it. The pleasant feeling I'd had at the bar with Chiddy vanished. The words, "dead ... dead ... dead ... dead ... dead," struck me like a beating. I was proud Marks had spoken to me seriously, like an adult. But I felt a constriction in my chest and the heat of a rising anger that found nothing to grip. I looked from Marks to my father and back again, waiting for reassurance that never came.

* * *

Stash and I took off the next four days while we waited for Chiddy to return from Motembo. Although what I had learned about the poisoned animals weighed heavily on my mind, I told no one. Even beyond the fact that Baba trusted me not to reveal his involvement with rangers, the criminals who slaughtered elephants seemed too dangerous, too ruthless and wicked to discuss with anyone, as though the mere mention of them would bring bloody retribution. I tucked the news of fresh slaughter into a deep, dark recess of my mind.

Marks became a familiar presence in the village. He had been around all along, of course, but now that we had met and shared something terrible, I felt a kinship that flooded me with pride. I was heartened to know that a man like him had dedicated his life to saving the animals I loved too. Each time I passed him in the street, he had a smile and a friendly word. He told me about individual elephants he had seen in the wild and about the herds he observed and protected. He asked how I was and what I was up to. I suspected he already knew the answers from talking to Baba, but I didn't mind because I relished his attention.

Rangers were often away at work in the bush, of course. But when Marks failed to show up at all one day, my stomach pitched with worry. I knew too well that Africa could give, and Africa could snatch away. The added threat of vicious, stop-at-nothing ivory poachers raised the survival stakes for rangers even higher. I found myself repeatedly scanning the street for a glimpse of him and searching Baba's face for signs of calamity. To ask my father about the ranger seemed a breach of our code, so I worried in silence and tried to think about other things.

Fortunately, during my brief vacation from the shop I found plenty to divert me. First, I volunteered to build a new display area in the grocery store for Mrs. Swale. She was expanding her inventory to include products for home maintenance and gardening. "But we don't want the mops and mousetraps next to the milk," she said, looking pleased by the sound of her words. "What would you think about a separate section in back?"

She asked this of no one in particular while I was in the store with Mima. Although I felt proud that she might have wanted my opinion, I waited for Mima to respond.

"Back here?" Mima asked, indicating an old cupboard currently in use for storage. "I don't see how tall things like mops and brooms would fit."

I eyed the space, taking mental measurements. I cleared my throat. "If you can do without the cupboard, you could remove that altogether. Then you could start over with pegboard and a column of adjustable shelves attached to the wall—about a day's work for a carpenter. Like me."

I kept my face neutral until Mima cracked up, laughing. "A carpenter like you is exactly what we need."

Mrs. Swale wouldn't have looked happier if I had suggested building her a castle. "Would you do it? Of course, I'll pay you. Thank you, Bonesy."

A job that should have taken a day or two lengthened into three because Mrs. Swale brought the twins, Donovan and Drew, to help. Eleven years old, the boys found every tool I brought worthy of inspection and testing. I let them fire nails into plywood and showed them how to saw up scraps of trim. I narrated my own work as I went, thinking of Uncle Stash while repeating at every opportunity, "Measure twice, cut once."

By the second day, I was calling the boys "the Dees" and making them giggle. "Well, look who's here—the delightful, dexterous, discerning Dees. Or could you be the dastardly, duplicitous, dirty Dees?"

"The dirty Dees!" they shouted in unison.

When I finished, Mrs. Swale wanted to pay extra for my attentions to Donovan and Drew. Since I had been happy to help and actually enjoyed the twins, I refused to accept more than the cost of the materials. Mima gave me a melting look and planted a chaste kiss on my cheek.

On my way out the door, Mrs. Swale met me with a basket of groceries. "It's the least I can do, Bonesy. I'm so grateful. Thank you."

The weighty basket held canned goods, packets of rice and beans, and on top, fresh greens and a hand of bananas. Thanks to my income from the workshop, my own household currently wanted for little in the way of groceries. But I accepted the gift gratefully. After I said my goodbyes, I carried the basket straight to Rotting House.

The Ovambos heckled and chased me, pecked on my shoes, and made such a ruckus that Granny sat up in her chair. Roop poked his head through the doorway, laughing as I dodged my way across the yard. *Hyunk-hyunk-hyunk.*

"My life is on the brink, and you laugh?" I said as I hurtled up the stairs. "This is for you and Granny." I handed him the basket. "I hope you feel like a worm."

"Hello, Bonesy." Granny rocked and grinned. She must have just washed her hair because it smelled of Lifebuoy and was fluffed out like a cumulonimbus.

"What's this?" Roop asked, fingering aside the leafy greens for a look underneath.

"From Swale's, for building some shelves." Before he could refuse, I said, "Let's go fishing. If you skunk me, you can hand over your catch."

When it came to fishing, Roop never needed a second invitation. While he put away the groceries and gathered gear for both of us, I sat on the porch with Granny. The Ovambos were giving themselves sand baths in the hot afternoon sun. One by one, they broke out in fits that resembled tribal dancing. Minor dust storms exploded across the yard.

While I watched the chickens, Granny watched me. She fingered the cord on her necklace, looking at me with moony, misty eyes. "You're a good boy, Bonesy. A good boy."

Mima, Mrs. Swale, and now this. I felt heady with popularity. My veins churned with the warmth that comes from being adored for good deeds. I put all thoughts of poachers and dead animals out of my mind and let myself fill with happiness, gratitude, and benevolence toward every living thing. Even the Ovambos took on a handsome air. How vigilant they were in patrolling the yard!

The walk toward the river with Roop by my side and a fishing pole in my hand only heightened my sense of well-being. I loved the outdoors. Today, the bright slant of sunlight, the raucous *zaaak* of a lilac-breasted roller, the shush of grass against my ankles—everything I saw, heard, and felt proclaimed life an excellent business.

We headed for a new fishing spot upstream from our previous encounter with the crocodile. To my great surprise, Zola was there at the edge of the river, sitting on a slab of rock. A fat leadwood tree jittery with vervet monkeys obscured most of her. She looked to be contemplating a flotilla of leaves that twirled in the river's slow current. Her lovely profile caught a shaft of light that accented her cheekbones and the shine of her hair. I slowed my footsteps, taken in by the serenity of the setting and my sister's tranquil beauty. Was this where she came to relax and get away from her domestic duties—from Baba, Hannie, and me?

Roop had spotted her too. I heard his sudden intake of breath. We stopped, sharing a moment of uncertainty. I felt torn between preserving Zola's solitude and calling her attention to the novelty of meeting this way, at the river. Finally, I stepped forward, stirring the vervets as I drew past the tree. Someone was sitting beside her. I blinked in disbelief.

10

I REALLY SHOULD HAVE KNOWN. I had been a fool not to figure out that Zola's secret boyfriend was Skinner. In retrospect, all the clues had been there. His flirtation with every skirt that came along meant nothing next to his lifelong interest in my sister. She was beautiful, womanly, and ripe for plucking by a big, bad boy who could bring excitement to her life—a boy who also happened to be movie-star handsome and a formidable, if villainous, force in the tiny world of our village.

It revolted me to think how Skinner must be savoring his conquest. Zola was more than desirable and capable. She was an almost mystically aloof figure who had left school and the fantasies of a dozen boys to disappear into domesticity under the protection of our father. She was the daughter of a mother who had died due to Skinner's own recklessness, the niece of a man he had tried to rob, the sister of an adversary who loathed and barfed on him. She was a prize he could use to piss off quite a few people.

I stood next to Roop, breathing hard, winded by outrage. Skinner sat with one arm slung casually, possessively, across Zola's slender shoulders. A cigarette dangled from his lower lip. Now I knew why Captain Biggie had met her at the tavern—through Skinner, of course. Who else would have taken her there? Even at a distance, I could see the smug expression on his face and, worse, the lucky bean seed bracelet circling his wrist—at least eight or ten strands, as wide as a cuff.

"Let's go," Roop said, side-valving to direct his voice at me. Both of us had suffered abuse at the hands of Skinner. I suspected Roop hated him as much as I did. "We could take him if we wanted. We could crush that moron. But let's go."

Zola must have heard Roop's voice because she turned and saw us. Her startled expression gave way to a look that resembled a spear in full flight.

She fixed her eyes on me in a highly communicative stare that said, *Be afraid. Be very afraid. He could crush you.*

Roop missed the telepathic vector. Under Zola's liquid gaze, his good sense fled. He moved toward her, ignoring Skinner. His voice came out soft. "Hello, Zola. Is this guy bothering you?"

Skinner swiveled his head, flexing thick, muscular cords in his neck. Ashes dropped down the front of his shirt. "Well, look who's here." He tossed the cigarette into the river. "Nobbskull." Like a cat, he rose to his feet in one fluid motion. His eyes cut back and forth between Roop and me. The lines of his body—the cocked hip, the rounded shoulders—broadcast an infuriating insolence. "Zola's off duty, Bonesy. You'll have to go home and wipe your own bottom."

I dropped the fishing pole and lunged at him. Roop took Zola's hand and pulled her out of the way.

My fist glanced off Skinner's cheek. A dreadful sneer distorted his features. His eyes took on a nasty gleam. Instead of backing away, he thrust out his jaw, pointing at the annoying dimple in his chin. "Bring it on, Bonehead."

Like a dope, I fell for it. My fury coalesced into a single point of molten hatred for that cocky face.

We were the same height now, but I was woefully outclassed in the art of the fistfight. I swiped and punched the air while Skinner danced and bobbed out of reach, smirking, taunting, playing with me. I heard Zola beg me to stop, but I was too far gone, too consumed by rage and frustration, and too close to tears to regain control.

"Give it up, Bonesy. Don't waste your breath on that turd," Roop urged from somewhere behind me.

At least I think that's what he said. My heart was hammering. Blood roared in my ears. The edges of my vision clouded. I punched and swung like a dervish, lost my balance, braced for a blow that never came, regained my footing, and swung again. I was breathing hard, sweating profusely. Skinner looked as fresh as a boyfriend out on a date, which he was. The red slash of his extra-wide lucky bean seed bracelet infuriated me even further, like a cape before a bull. I had never felt such hatred—or felt so utterly useless and miserable. I was beginning to wish Skinner would knock me unconscious and be done with it.

He didn't knock me out, but he finished me off just the same. After dodging another futile jab, he grabbed me by the upper arms, pinning them to my side, and half-walked, half-dragged me to the river's edge. "You need to cool off," he said and threw me in.

I let myself sink in the cold, tea-colored water. A long, silvery fish slanted past. Bludgeoned by shame, impotence, and my sister's devastating betrayal, I felt too crushed to care about the wildlife stirring around me. It didn't matter that Zola knew little or nothing of my bitter history with Skinner. The fact that she would align herself with such a lowlife, a delinquent boy-man who reeked of ill will, shocked me to the core. As I floated, weightless, it came to me like a wet slap—I hardly knew her.

When I surfaced, I felt glad that Skinner had pitched me into the river because no one could see my humiliating tears. Roop had waded into the shallows in case I needed saving, even though he was a terrible swimmer who didn't like to get his face wet. He wagged his fishing pole in my direction, ready to pull me out. In spite of everything, I almost smiled.

I waved Roop off and stayed in the deep channel, treading water, letting my thumping pulse settle. I was in no hurry to revisit the scene of my disgrace while Skinner and Zola stood on the bank, watching me. His arm was around her again. He wore a preening, self-satisfied smirk that made me want to smack him—as if I could. Zola apparently still had the decency to care whether I drowned. But she must have decided I was going to be okay because with an almost indiscernible nod in my direction, she let her wretched boyfriend steer her away from the water's edge. Shoulder-to-shoulder, she and Skinner disappeared from view.

After a minute or two, I swam toward shore, slowed by dejection and the drag of my drenched shorts and T-shirt. Roop had retreated to higher ground and slumped on the rock where Zola and Skinner had sat. I noticed a vulture perched on a branch, patient as an undertaker. I wondered whether its sights were fixed on me.

I made it to the boggy shallows and was squelching through mud when the monkeys erupted in a fit of frantic screeching. A pair of Egyptian geese shot skyward. In my haste to scramble up the riverbank, away from whatever alarmed them, I fell on my belly and skidded back down. Mud slid up my shorts and T-shirt and into my mouth and nostrils. I grabbed a gnarly, half-soaked root and tried to pull myself up, but my hand slipped on a jelly of frog spawn. When I finally found my footing, the mud sucked the shoes off my feet.

Roop was ignoring my sorry struggle. Up on the rock he had stiffened to full alert and appeared fixated on the river behind me. I didn't waste a moment looking back. With a rising sense of threat, I threw myself onto dry land, falling forward, facedown. Without delay I crawled, crab-like, away from whatever Roop saw in the water. When I stopped for a breath, I was caked in dirt and as sodden, slimy, and shoeless as a creature at the dawn of evolution.

"Look," Roop said, pointing.

A mokoro carrying two men I didn't recognize glided into view. From his higher vantage point, Roop had spotted the dugout canoe some distance away. Now the poler standing in the stern ceased poling, and both men turned their heads to stare at us. As they drifted closer, they didn't say hello or lift a hand in greeting. Their steely expressions defied interpretation.

I supposed a mokoro behind me in the water had been less dangerous than a gap-jawed river creature, but the men riding in it didn't look much friendlier. While Roop and I watched, they used low voices to exchange a few words, which I couldn't make out. Between them were a brown tarp and two paddles for use in deeper water. I wondered whether they planned on coming ashore.

With a great thrust of wings, the vulture in the tree took off, circled the river, and flew away. The steersman ignored it, keeping his eyes trained on Roop and me. His face was a mask. Without a word or a gesture, he planted the pole in the shallows and pushed off. In a moment, the mokoro had vanished.

"Cheerful guys," Roop said, his voice as flat and expressionless as the faces of the two men.

I tipped my head sideways to drain water and muck from my ear. "Sorry about fishing; I'm done for today. You go ahead." I hoped he would stay. For Roop, fishing cured almost everything, maybe even the heartbreak of seeing Zola with Skinner.

He shrugged. To my relief, he said nothing about my sister and Skinner, my humiliating defeat, or the disgusting state of my slimed and oozing person. I knew heartache when I saw it, but I felt powerless to comfort him.

When he picked up his fishing pole and turned toward the river, I retrieved my shoes and quietly left.

I made my way home, dripping and filthy, hoping to see no one, especially Mima. She could handle grime, but could she face a boyfriend so soured and beaten and now so closely linked via Zola to a psycho like Skinner? It occurred to me that Mima herself might have had to fend off our village's number one predator. She was far too fresh and pretty to have escaped the attentions of a shameless boy-man on the prowl.

As I neared home, one thought cheered me a little: when he found out Zola was seeing Skinner, Baba was going to throw a fit. My father knew a lazy, worthless lowlife when he saw one. He wasn't blind to Skinner's bullying or his seedy reputation in the village. Stash had told my father about the attempted theft at the workshop. Baba would straighten out Zola. I knew that for sure. Maybe he would give Skinner a good going-over too. I paused to wipe some grit out of my eyes. Physical harm was wishful thinking—Baba wasn't a fighter—but I enjoyed the prospect of my father laying into Skinner with a barrage of choice, red-hot words.

I had almost reached our yard when I spotted Zola and Skinner walking on the path ahead, tight as ticks. I ducked behind a tree. One encounter with those two was more than enough.

While I spied on them, a crushing realization took shape. They were walking away from our house—my house. *She took him there?* The notion that Skinner might have stepped across the threshold of my home, touched things I used every day, maybe even looked at my calendar from Ruby's Amazing Safaris, outraged me almost as much as his attachment to my sister. How could Zola be so unthinking? So heartless and unaware of boundaries? Even though they couldn't have stayed long, my disappointment in her was devastatingly complete.

I rubbed my drying, itchy scalp. A long scratch on my arm was raw and bleeding. My head throbbed. But what I felt most was the sharp, almost unbearable sting of betrayal. Only the notion of support from Baba brought me a measure of comfort. *Just wait until our father hears about this.*

I watched the two of them make their way down the lane. Skinner hooked one finger inside the back of Zola's belt, too lazy to hold up his own arm. When they were gone, I picked my way toward our porch and through the door, keeping a sharp lookout for missing objects Skinner might have pocketed. My nose ran with muddy snot. My wet clothes had begun to chafe. My bare feet felt the punishment of countless small rocks and prickles. A day that had started so well had turned painful and joyless. And the worst was yet to come.

I found Baba sitting in the kitchen, drinking coffee. A newspaper lay open on the table in front of him. With some relief, I gathered from his calm demeanor that Zola and her hideous boyfriend had bypassed the house.

"Hi," he said, eyeing me up and down. "I hear Skinner threw you in the river."

I looked at him. "What? Who told you?"

"Zola." He took a sip from the coffee mug.

"She was here?" I could barely push out the words. "With him?"

He placed the mug carefully on the table, taking his time. Then he nodded. "You just missed them." He paused. "Probably a good thing."

"A good thing?" My words came out leaden with incredulity. "There is nothing good about this. Even the idea of Skinner in our house makes me sick, almost as sick as the thought of him with Zola."

"This is her house too. Their relationship is not your business."

I couldn't believe what I was hearing. "What?"

"Sit down."

I fell into the chair opposite him, stunned.

"Zola is twenty-one years old. She's more than capable of making her own decisions. You and I must respect her, even if we don't agree." He wore a look of weary resignation that incensed me. I wanted to grip his shoulders and shake them.

"Skinner is pond scum, and you know it." I didn't care that I sounded as petulant as a schoolboy.

"Zola's not stupid. Let's give her some space."

"Space to have her life ruined? I don't understand you, Baba."

"Then you must try harder."

* * *

Although my vacation still had a day to go, I got Stash to open the shop so I could return to work early. The workroom became a refuge once again—from Zola, who barely spoke to me, and from Baba, whose sanguine attitude toward the rot that had entered our lives confused and saddened me. Following the altercation at the river, I had made one fruitless attempt to change Zola's mind about Skinner. Now I was keeping my distance from all of them.

"My life is just as important and considered as yours," Zola had said, after I suggested she was wasting hers. "Don't you ever forget it."

Important and considered? Her pathetic effort to become a person of some account by associating with our village's leading delinquent upset me more than I could say. I had woefully misjudged Baba and now Zola too. The apparent ease with which Skinner had exploited my sister's neediness upended my long-held beliefs about her intelligence and strength of character. I had never felt so let-down.

"You could go back to school," I had argued. "You could sell your bead jewelry. Teach beading. Help at Hannie's school. There are many ways to find meaning and worth."

"Yes, and I've found one, Bonesy. So stop preaching and leave me alone."

When Stash heard about the discord in my household, he joined me in the shop. "Work can be therapeutic," he said kindly. "The shop needs a day for maintenance and repairs. You can start by sorting the scrap wood into piles. Then sweep the floor."

While I got busy, Stash inspected the tools, and we fell into our familiar, comforting roles as apprentice and teacher. "Woodworking is mostly about cutting," he reminded me, frowning at the jagged edge of a jigsaw. "When it comes to cutting, friction is the enemy. Dull, dirty tools create friction—drag, vibration, heat. All of those affect the quality of the cut."

We spent the rest of the morning vanquishing our enemy, friction. Stash showed me how to use a solvent to clean built-up pitch and resin from the cutting blades and taught me techniques for sharpening chisels. When we had restored the cutting equipment to peak condition, I lubricated the moving parts on the power tools. I felt calmer, more removed from Zola and her miserable boyfriend with every passing hour. I polished the screwdrivers, wrenches, hammers, and clamps until they shone, then hung each one on its peg in descending order of size. I was rubbing the workbench with mineral oil when Aunt Letty arrived with coffee and a plate of sandwiches.

"Hello, Bonesy."

"Hi. How did you know I was about to drop from hunger?"

"Aren't you always, dear?" She set the tray on a stool and looked around with her hands on her ample hips. "This shop is cleaner than my kitchen."

"We're out of mineral oil," I said, turning the bottle upside down.

"I'll put it on my list for Swale's." She made no effort to suppress her smile. "Kate and Mima showed me the new display area. They're smitten with it—and you."

My face warmed. "Have they stocked the shelves?"

She nodded. "With everything for cleaning and the garden. Very convenient."

At the end of the day, I headed straight for the grocery store, as eager to see Mima and the new display as I was uneager to go home. As usual, Mima was there alone, straightening up before closing. When I stepped through the door, she took my hand and led me to the back, pointing at an arrow-shaped sign that read "House and Garden." A fresh carpet and some plants helped define the new area. Orderly rows of brightly labeled jars, cans, and boxes filled the shelves. The pegboard supported a tidy, parallel lineup of brushes, brooms, and mops.

"See? Everything fits perfectly." Using the little spade of her fingers, she moved an item a fraction of an inch. The smile on her face was sweet and uncomplicated. Pleasure in the meticulous geometry of the display was another thing we shared. I kissed her then and there, standing next to the Omo, the Happy Suds, the plant food, and the snail bait.

Later, on my way home, I realized how much better I felt after a day in the shop with Stash and an evening with Mima. Work and Mima had become the cornerstones of my life. I tried not to ruin my improved mood by thinking too much about my sister and Skinner. What did Skinner know about work? Or love, for that matter? All the lucky bean seeds in Africa couldn't redeem Zola's appalling boyfriend. She would come to rue her choice—of that I was sure. But I was beginning to accept the unpleasant truth that she needed to discover her mistake on her own, without help from me.

The next morning, my excitement about Chiddy's return eclipsed all thoughts of Zola and Skinner. I couldn't wait to hear every detail of Chiddy's trip. Had the furniture arrived in good condition? Did the suites look beautiful in the tents? Was Jackson Quinn pleased?

Uncle Stash tried to present a calm front, but I knew he shared my anticipation. On that day, he would receive the biggest check he had ever seen, the final payment from Jackson Quinn. I suspected he hoped for a new order too, for furniture to complete Motembo's dining area or lounge. In light of the day's quivery expectations, he did not ask me to work on anything important. "Experiment a little, Bonesy. Build whatever you like."

While he paged through a catalog of power tools, I searched piles of scrap lumber for inspiration. Several decent cuts of knot-free plywood suggested a long box or two. I struck upon the idea of building tool caddies for Donovan and Drew. The twins' interest in carpentry recalled my own enthusiasm at their age. Whether the fascination would develop into a lasting pursuit remained an open question. But I liked encouraging the boys, and of course, there was the added benefit of pleasing their sister.

The power of interesting work to challenge and absorb gripped me again that day. A tool caddy is an uncomplicated project: three long boards, two peaked end panels, and a dowel handle to secure inside bores at the ends. But cutting, routing, joining, and sanding something even so simple requires precision and care. I lost all sense of time. Hours passed. Stash left the shop and returned. I had just applied a final coat of tung oil to the finished pieces when the voice chimed through my concentration: "Helloooooooo, Bonesy."

With an almost magisterial sense of timing, Chiddy filled the doorway.

In my excitement, I came close to upending the can of oil. "Hi, Chiddy." I made myself seal the can and properly stow the brush before turning to him. "Welcome back."

He held a manila envelope against his chest and wore a slightly lower-wattage grin than usual. I wondered if the long drive had tired him. Or was he feeling the aftereffects of too much Amarula?

"Hello, Mr. Stash," he said, dipping his head toward my uncle.

"Greetings. Have a seat," Stash said, pushing a stool across the floor.

"How was your trip?" I asked.

"Quite eventful." He sank down with a sigh. "The rains washed away the track in many places. Very difficult driving for a big, big truck." He shook his head as if remembering a mournful occasion. "Too much mud. Very good for getting stuck."

"I am sorry to hear it," I said, recalling his words to me. "Did you deliver the furniture?"

"Oh yes. The furniture is at Motembo."

"Well?"

"Well what?"

"Come on, Chiddy. Does Jackson Quinn like it?"

He produced a sad expression that looked feigned but nonetheless gave me a moment of anguish. "When Jackson saw the bedroom suites"—he paused for maximum effect—"he was silent for many minutes. He touched the finishes, opened and closed the drawers, sat in the chairs. Then he wanted to see the furniture arranged in the six tents, so I and some others moved it all in."

"And then?"

"He walked from tent to tent—this took some time because the guest quarters are quite generously spaced—and inspected each one."

Behind me, Stash exhaled audibly.

"What did he say then, Chiddy?"

"I will repeat exactly what he said." Again he paused for maximum effect. "Effing brilliant."

Stash looked uncertain and then broke into a smile. "Effing brilliant? That's effing great, isn't it Bonesy? Don't repeat that."

I grinned. "Brilliant is good enough for me."

"But there is a small problem." Chiddy's face turned grave. "Jackson says the job is not complete. The beds and their net frames are still in pieces. He wants one of you to go there and assemble them."

"One of us?" Stash looked at me and then back at Chiddy. "But we wrote down the directions. Assembling the beds isn't difficult."

"Not difficult, no. Yet Jackson insists. He said he ordered beds, not rails and headboards." Chiddy reached into the manila envelope and withdrew a check. "Here is half the balance he owes you. He will pay the rest when the beds are complete."

Stash examined the check, considering. Then he looked at me. "Would you like to go?"

"Me?" I said stupidly.

"Who else? I'll stay here and run the shop."

My heart was doing flips. "Yes. I'd like to go."

Chiddy handed me a sheaf of papers. "While you're there, Jackson wants you to build a bar."

11

Due to the washouts Chiddy had encountered on his recent trip to Motembo, he plotted a different itinerary for me. "This new way is too rugged for my big, big truck," he said, waving a hand over the map he had drawn. "But for you, in your excellent van, it will be a scenic journey."

His sketch of the route was so crude it could have decorated the wall of a cave. Actual roads, rendered in thick black strokes, formed less than a quarter of the trip. The rest of the way followed a dotted line between landmarks he had drawn with imaginative flourishes that he explained in detail.

"This is the oxbow where you will see a large pod of hippos," he said, pointing at a series of squiggles meant to represent ears poking out of water. "Follow the ridge south past the marula grove to a large rain tree growing on an island in the middle of the river."

I squinted at the umbrella he had sketched atop a column in the center of a circle. I moved my lips: *rain tree, island.*

"Here you turn east and continue to three large, flat-topped boulders." He looked at me. "Three Flat Rocks is home to a pride of lions. Do not exit your vehicle in this place." To emphasize the point, he picked up a pencil and drew a large paw with long black claws.

From there, the dotted line I was supposed to follow led past a pair of pointy termite mounds, a dense thornberry thicket (curly scribble), and a colossal baobab tree "visible for miles." Beyond the baobab was a kilometer or so of chalky hardpan—"flats, hills, and a few tilting dune slopes you must drive around." These led to a manmade track cut into thick mopane woodland.

"This track leads through the woods and over a plank bridge to Motembo," Chiddy said, sounding triumphant, as though talking me through the route was as good as getting me there. "You will not, not miss it."

Instead of a map, I would have preferred Chiddy himself along on the ride with me. He knew the terrain and would have been a good travel companion. But his one-man delivery operation could not shut down for the several days it would take to drive to Motembo, assemble the beds, build the bar, and return. So I assured him and Stash that I could make the trip by myself. I hoped this was true. The thrill of an expedition to an actual safari camp canceled any misgivings I might have felt about crossing wild, vaguely charted territory in a questionable vehicle, alone.

During the days it took to prepare for the trip, I felt too dazed with excitement to show a flicker of worry. I studied the sketch of the bar Jackson Quinn had in mind for Motembo and did my best to anticipate the tools, hardware, lumber, and finishing materials I would need to build it. Most of the required wood was already on hand there, according to notes from Mr. Quinn—boards from a giant mahogany tree that had fallen over near camp.

In addition to carpentry supplies, I packed a duffel bag with extra clothes and made room in the back of the van for a bedroll, a basket of food from Aunt Letty, two canteens and a jug of water, extra gasoline, and my shotgun. Chiddy gave me lessons in jacking up the vehicle to clear obstacles along the way or to change a punctured tire. We tested the winch. "For getting out of mud, Bonesy. Please avoid mud if you can." At the last minute, I unzipped the duffel and added the journal Mr. Kitwick had given me. I hadn't yet touched a pen to its creamy pages, but I suspected my life might be taking a noteworthy turn.

Now, just three days after Chiddy's return, I found myself gripping the wheel of Stash's van, swaying and bouncing in my seat on the pitted road to Motembo. I had been driving only a couple of hours when I glanced for the hundredth time at the map on the seat beside me. A long, dark slash indicated actual pavement for the next several kilometers. "Straight, straight as the nose on your face," Chiddy had said.

I passed thinning garlands of shacks on either side of the road. An agitated dog ran out and nipped at my tires. The mongrel's barks were almost inaudible over the thrum of the engine and the rattle of the van's desiccated rubber seals. When the intervals between homesteads grew wider, the dog gave up and slunk away. The traffic—mostly bicycles, carts, and an occasional goat or chicken—lightened and then disappeared. In time, the empty road made a line across the plain true as a runway, as far as I could see. I relaxed a little, sat back, and let my thoughts drift to Mima.

My excitement about the trip had sparked something in her too. When I told her where I was going, her face lit with enthusiasm. "A safari camp! How wonderful!" She told me her mother and father had gone on safari for their honeymoon. Her favorite photo of them was taken in the pink glow of an African sunset, with giraffes silhouetted in the background. At bedtime, her brothers still liked to hear the story of the Cape buffalo that had appeared out of nowhere and charged. "Our parents escaped by climbing onto the roof of their truck. The buffalo hung around for hours, snorting and pawing the dirt."

I pictured Mrs. Swale, unperturbed, enjoying the view.

"My father said that from then on, he always made sure the champagne bottle stayed within reach of the roof."

She told me this one evening as we lounged on the silky new carpet that decorated the home and garden section at the back of the store. We had turned off all but one light near the front door. Even though we were alone, we talked in whispers that seemed to fit the dim shadows. Our faces were inches apart.

She touched a finger to my lips. "While you're gone, may I take the twins to visit your uncle in the shop? They're inseparable from their new tool caddies."

"Of course. Stash would like that."

I inhaled her familiar scent, something sweet mingled with the damp perfume of our overheated bodies. Our carnal explorations still followed a cautious, near-silent ritual, step by step, to a stopping point determined by her rapidly evolving sexual policy. On this night, as we talked and kissed and touched, I felt the familiar wallop of my slamming heart. My long-suffering loins sent out the usual memos. I was nearing the moment when I would have to release her hot body, get up, and leave. But instead of drawing away, she pulled me closer. "Don't go, Bonesy. Stay."

I drew back. *Now?* The moment I had longed for, dreamed about, and imagined on a daily basis caught me by surprise. She was breathing audibly, tilting her hips into mine, lifting my shirt.

"Are you sure?"

She nodded, solemn, panting softly. I touched my forehead to hers, steadying myself, giving us both another minute. Soon we were fumbling with buttons and cloth. She shimmied out of her dress. I slipped off my shirt and pants. Her skin was luminous in the gauzy light, the arcs and slopes and dark, secret narrows so lovely I had to catch my breath. I braced myself above her and felt our heat cook the humid air between us. She was holding my arms in matching grips, tight enough to staunch blood.

"You are beautiful, Mima Swale," I murmured close to her ear.

Now I blinked and downshifted to climb a rise in the road, grinning into thin air. My eyes followed a bateleur eagle kiting overhead, but I didn't really see it. I was remembering the next night, the last before I left, when Mima and I made love again. Afterward, we had talked about our future together with the certitude of matched souls. My future seemed impossible without her. I couldn't imagine it, and I didn't want to. I had never awoken to a day more radiant with promise than this day, today, when Motembo waited for me at one end of my journey while Mima Swale waited for me at the other.

*   *   *

The paved road soon dwindled to gravel and then became a dusty track, as Chiddy had said it would. I left my wandering thoughts and steered the van onto rough, pitted turf. The vehicle pitched and rocked so violently that I worried the aging metal might shake apart. The going was very slow. I made frequent stops to clear tinder-dry grass caught in the undercarriage and top off the coolant in the van's steaming radiator. The sun produced a dazzle on the hood. Funnels of dust rose in the hot air, twirling across the plain and through the open windows. Sweat streaked down my cheeks. I had hung a canteen around my neck for easy access to water. Chiddy had warned about mud, and in the dry heat of that searing afternoon, I almost longed to find some.

Even as I sweated and clutched the wheel with white-knuckled intensity, my spirits soared with the joy of being outdoors, a dot on the vast open plain. As much as I liked my work in Stash's shop, I was hungry for the wilderness I had explored since my earliest memories. Chiddy's route was taking me through a vast wildlife reserve nearly untouched by human activity. I spied a pair of giraffes browsing in the distance. They reminded me of Mima's parents and the photo she loved. A small herd of zebras grazed near the giraffes, taking advantage of the taller animals' superior sight lines. When a giraffe bolted from danger, the zebras knew to run away too—and in what direction.

I stood in the shade of a winterthorn tree and ate a sandwich in the company of a hornbill that cocked its head right and left, watching me. The bird had followed the van for hours, feasting on insects spun up in the dust behind the tires. Across the plain, a copse of torchwoods swayed and shook. I heard the crack of a breaking branch and knew an elephant was snacking on the tree's oily fruit. It occurred to me that Marks could be in the vicinity too, working to protect that very elephant and all of its pachyderm relatives.

Color was draining from the sky when I parked for the night next to a gully with a trickle of water running through it. I used a stick to fish grass and seeds from the van's smoking exhaust pipe and checked under the chassis one more time. The ticks and pings of cooling metal gradually gave way to the evening sounds of the bush—the bark of a baboon, the churring of a scops owl, a nightjar's haunting five-note call.

Within minutes, darkness fell, and the temperature dropped to a dense chill. I pulled on a jacket and unrolled my bedding in the back of the van. The flip of the switch from day to night sent a shiver through me that had nothing to do with the cold. Africa's sharp-eyed nocturnal hunters—lions, leopards, jackals, hyenas, and countless smaller predators—would soon rise from their heat-induced slumber, peckish, stomachs growling, and begin looking for fresh meat. I had never spent a night alone in the bush.

I closed the doors and windows and crawled under my blanket. The hour was early for bed, but I hoped to rise before dawn and make a good start. I was lying with my head near the rear doors, facing forward, positioned to see through portions of the windows. The night sky glittered with stars. I watched a comet streak across the darkness. I wished Mima could see it too. Then I thought about my destination and felt a little fluttery, too excited to sleep. If all went well, the next day I would arrive at Motembo. Mo-tem-bo. The very name struck a deep, thrilling chord.

My wakefulness didn't last long. When I awoke in the middle of the night, druggy with slumber, I almost rolled over and let myself succumb again. But something I couldn't name made me sit up and look outside.

The stars had disappeared. Through the windows the sky had turned a dark, impenetrable black. I scrambled to my knees and peered at ... what? A chill shivered through me. I crawled forward and leaned over the seat backs for a better look. I didn't feel afraid, exactly. But my heart was beating fast.

Something shifted to admit thin moonshine. The light fell on a gleaming arc of tusk. Mountainous shapes moved against a starry background that had been there all along. Elephants stood in front, in back, and on both sides of the van. I was surrounded.

Compared to the behemoths outside, the van was a puny thing. A few stomps of elephantine feet could flatten it—and me. To my great relief, I did not sense agitation in the animals or even the slightest unease among those gathered almost within reach. Their ears were gently flapping, and their trunks were relaxed. I moved slowly, not wanting to cause alarm, as I reached forward and cranked the window a fraction. The gurgly, sloshy sounds of elephant digestion wafted in along with the rich, woody scent of fresh elephant dung.

As my vision adjusted to the shifting scene, I made out individual animals, their mighty trunks and great columns of legs. I had never been so close to elephants, certainly not in the center of a herd. With awe, I watched the movements of their bodies, sensed their familial bonds, listened to their rumbling language and the grinding of molars as big as babies' heads. Most amazing was the near silence of the elephants' giant, delicate footsteps, quieter than the footfall of men.

Then, with a start, I found myself gazing into the liquid eyes of a calf that seemed to be looking back at me. Its face was window-high, hairy, wrinkled, adorable, even in the dim light. As I stared at the wizened little features, the calf swung its barely manageable trunk up in the air and heaved it forward. The mitten-like tip landed hard on the glass, inches from my nose.

I gasped, both charmed and terrified. Nose-to-nose with a wild elephant was a singular and risky position, especially when the elephant was a calf. What if the mother sensed fright in her offspring? She could decide to obliterate the offending party and do so with dispatch. I tried not to move, not to even blink. The calf wrangled its loopy trunk into the stratosphere again and smacked a spot higher on the pane. I guessed it was sniffing out the opening at the top, aiming for a good whiff of me.

While I held my breath, a trunk the width of a smokestack swooped down and swept the curious infant away. The calf trundled off to disappear among pillars of legs. An inaudible message must have vibrated through the herd because the elephants began moving slowly, noiselessly, away and into the night.

* * *

The next morning, I awoke to the chorus of birdsong heralding a new day—predawn trills, chirps, and warbles as effective as any alarm clock. I tumbled out of the van in pink light. The air was still cool and morning-fresh. If I hadn't witnessed the elephants passing quietly in the night, I would have been shocked by what I found outside: trampled earth, crushed foliage, huge fresh tracks, and steaming piles of scat a single stride away from the thin metal walls of the van.

I stood in the spot where the calf had stood, reliving the thrill of our brief encounter. It came to me how vulnerable that small elephant and its relatives were, with fabulous bounties on their ivory tusks, their huge feet, and even the hair that tipped their tails. What were the chances those critically endangered animals would escape the scourge of poaching and grow to old age?

While dawn enflamed the horizon, I peeled and ate a hard-cooked egg, sliced an orange, and silently thanked Aunt Letty for the delicious cinnamon cake. But when I climbed behind the wheel of the van and started the engine, disturbing thoughts of elephant slaughter remained vivid in my mind.

My mood improved when the day opened to bright, temperate sunshine. I rolled down the windows and consulted the map, turning my thoughts to the landmarks that led from my current location to Motembo. The route Chiddy had sketched no longer relied on roads of any kind. I tried to ignore the unease I felt about traversing a dubiously scaled realm marked only by dotted lines between cartoonish drawings. At present, I was looking for a river that curved like an oxbow and held a pod of hippos.

I drove along the gully toward a scrim of dark foliage that looked to be riverine woodland. Staying on the open plain, I followed a thicket of brambles and trees that ran in a straight line for about a kilometer. Then the greenery made a wide curve, suggesting a change in the course of the river. I parked in the shade and picked my way down through crackling underbrush, aware that an elephant would make less noise. When I came within sight of the water, a dozen pairs of hippo eyes were already trained on me, each eye paired with a twiddling ear. The parts seemed to float on the surface, independent of the great, submerged bodies treading water below.

Encouraged by evidence that Chiddy's crudely drawn map could actually lead me in the right direction, I turned my back on the wary pod and returned to the van. Proceeding south, I drove around the oxbow on relatively open turf outside the fringe of trees. I passed the stand of marulas my friend had drawn with special care, a salute to our celebratory drink of Amarula. Next, I was supposed to find a rain tree growing on an island in the river some distance away. But how would I locate an island from up on the ridge where I couldn't see the water?

Even as I asked myself this question, I spotted a possible answer: a well-trod opening in the foliage, wide as a truck: the path worn by hippos going to and from their nocturnal grazing pastures. I brought the van to a halt in the shade of a flat-topped acacia tree—already the heat held a suffocating grip—and followed the track on foot down a gentle slope to a wide swath of floodplain. The shrunken river had created a dry and shady thoroughfare, solid as a road.

I walked along this corridor for a few minutes, wondering whether I should hike to the rain tree and exit the riverbed there to mark its location or go back to the van now and drive to the tree on the hard-packed floodplain. Chiddy's drawing was inconclusive on this point. The dotted line clearly followed the river, but was I meant to drive in the riverbed or up on the open plain?

I paused for a moment in the emerald-green shade, watching a glossy ibis peck in the shallows. A pair of ducks plied the open water. Floods from an earlier deluge had eroded the riverbank to a mild slope that promised easy egress once I found the designated tree. The beach was firm and smooth, free of grass that could catch and ignite. Compared to the desiccating oven of the plain, this was a gentle, moist, welcoming paradise—surely the route Chiddy intended me to take.

A few minutes later, the damp fragrance of moss perfumed the air as I steered the van along the river's margin. I felt cool and refreshed, pleased I had chosen this calm, sun-dappled course. Date palms leaned in on both sides. Flowering caper bushes lined the riverbank. Occasionally, the tires splashed through runnels of water that braided away from the main channel. Here I would not have to worry about an overheated engine or the peril of snagged combustibles.

As I passed a spreading leadwood tree, the riverbed turned dark with moisture. I noticed hoof marks in the soft earth and the trails of animals that had ventured in to drink. I downshifted, slowing to search for the driest way forward. Chiddy's warning to avoid mud was never far from my mind. I shifted again and eased up on the clutch.

The tires bit and rolled ahead. A flock of blacksmith plovers scattered, calling *tink-tink-tink*. The chassis swayed and lurched. I was aiming for a wide swath of dry beach just ahead, beyond a few more meters of damp. I took a breath and stepped on the gas.

The van lunged like a pouncing animal and abruptly stopped, jerking me forward in my seat. I turned the wheel and spun the tires but succeeded only in churning up black spew on all sides, digging in further, killing the engine. The van bellied into sucking mud, marooned.

After the brief silence that followed, local residents made themselves known. The leadwood tree came alive with vervet monkeys leaping from branch to branch. A black-winged stilt worked its long red legs across the beach. A fat caterpillar dropped onto the windshield along with a clot of wet leaves welded together by decay. Nature seemed more than ready to close in and bury me.

I removed my shoes and socks and opened the door, relieved to find I wasn't pinned inside. I stepped out. Pungent muck oozed between my toes, over my feet, and up my ankles. The van had sunk to the axles. I high-stepped through squelching mud to the winch mounted on the front. My lesson on getting unstuck was about to prove invaluable, as Chiddy must have known it would. I pulled on a pair of leather gloves. I was unspooling the winch cable when a faint snap of twigs made me look up. A man had emerged from the woods downriver. He was walking toward me.

At first, I felt too surprised to do more than stare. The man was twig-thin, with jaundiced eyes and corroded teeth. A silvery machete rested in his hand. Behind him, two younger men carried old, small-gauge rifles. They were not smiling.

Hunters who carried rifles and looked poor and hungry were as familiar to me as my own family. The men's predatory air didn't worry me as much as this sudden visitation in the middle of nowhere. Did they plan to rob me? Steal everything in the van? They were talking in low voices, speaking words I could not make out. The older one with the bad teeth suddenly grinned and gestured. I realized he was offering to help get me unstuck. So they could steal the van too? My schooling in the malfeasance of humans had eroded any charitable expectations I might have held. It came to me that a pack of wild dogs would alarm me less.

Before I could make a move, the men had reached me. One of them grabbed the winch cable from my hands, reeled it out, and strapped and hooked a date palm with the efficiency of a person who had performed similar ambushes many times. The old guy pointed at the driver's side door, wanting me to get in. Did I have a choice? I climbed in, connected the winch control, and turned the key in the ignition. One light touch on the accelerator, and the van groaned and heaved. Two men pushed from the sides. Then, with a mighty gush, the tires rolled, the undercarriage came up for air, and the vehicle lurched to shore.

I felt like a fish reeled to dry land, panicked about what would happen next. The man in front took his time unhooking the cable and disconnecting the hook. At the speed of a side-necked turtle, he folded the strap into a neat coil and set it on the ground. The line was respooling when he ambled toward me—and then past me. To my surprise, the two others were already striding away, back down the riverbed. I stared at them for a moment, unsure of their intentions. When all three were quite far away, I leaned out and yelled at their receding backsides. "Thank you!"

The old man raised a hand above his shoulder, but no one turned around. Only then, in hindsight, did I discern the kindness in the old man's face and the admirable spirit of cooperation among the three men. With a stab of shame, I realized they were not unlike Baba and me. They were subsistence hunters, probably looking to feed themselves and their families—decent people ready to help a kid stuck in the mud. With a sigh, I eased the vehicle forward. I wondered whether I would ever see them again.

Some time later, I rounded a curve and came within view of Chiddy's next signpost. The rain tree growing on the island signaled a turn to the east. Opposite the island, the gently sloping riverbank wore the flattened, exhausted look of a route well traveled by animals. I rotated the wheel and followed the trail out of the ravine, squinting as I emerged into the stare of the sun.

The lion hangout known as Three Flat Rocks showed itself vividly in the distance, a trio of dark granite slabs. Beyond the rocks, I made out what looked like the oddly branched tip of a very tall tree. The baobab? My excitement about the expedition—the prospect of visiting a safari camp and meeting real guides—burbled up once again. According to Chiddy, after passing the baobab, I would cross a stretch of hardpan and enter the woodland that sheltered Motembo. I was almost there.

But I made myself drive slowly, rumbling forward in low gear toward the great, boxy boulders. In the cauldron of midday, the lions that resided around Three Flat Rocks were probably asleep, invisible in the golden grass. Although heat freighted the air inside the van, I raised the windows almost all the way to the top.

Leaning toward the windshield, I studied every lump and bump in the flat, sunlit terrain. I hardly dared to blink. Chiddy had indicated a pride, probably five or six females, their young, and maybe a male. Females and cubs usually slept close together, almost in a pile. The male would be separate but nearby.

I was about even with the middle boulder when a honey-colored tail tipped with black popped up like a flag. I pressed on the brake. Another tail flipped up diagonally off my right front tire. I turned the wheel and eased away, squinting at the straw-colored turf. I drove so slowly that a blade of grass that had drifted onto the hood did not stir. Even as I sucked in hot air and felt the sweat streak down my face, I resisted the urge to go faster. Tracing a wide, slow arc around the lions took many minutes. I didn't open the windows or breathe quite normally again until I had cleared the third boulder and could see Three Flat Rocks shrinking into the distance behind me.

With the windows down and fresh air filling my lungs, I drove as fast as I dared past the termite mounds and the thornberry bramble. Approaching the baobab, I eased up on the accelerator to stare at the biggest tree I had ever seen. The ancient trunk rose like a fortress. Multiple silver-gray columns had fused together to form a growth wide enough to hide an elephant. A tangle of surface roots snaked out in all directions. At the top were a dozen fat, forking branches, each one the circumference of a normal tree.

I parked in the shade of the giant limbs and got out. My cramped legs tingled as I stretched and bent my knees, eyeing the largest living thing I had ever seen. The tree's fat, extruded roots formed ridges and canyons that made walking precarious. Placing each foot with care, I moved in for a closer look.

Animals had stripped away patches of bark, but the damage didn't seem to have harmed the big galoot at all. I stepped past a series of columnar outgrowths as fat as water tanks. A curb-like root led to another circular wing skinned of bark. The exposed surface felt as smooth as sanded pine. A gathering of twittering Cape sparrows drew my attention upward. To my surprise they sat on a fig tree growing out sideways from the baobab about nine feet above my head. The interloper must have sprung from an airborne seed that had lodged in a crevasse and taken hold.

I had walked almost all the way around when I came upon the biggest surprise of all: a split in the trunk as wide as a door. Stepping cautiously, I peered through the opening. My eyes took a moment to adjust. The tree was empty, hollow, as if a colossal router had scraped out the insides. Multiple trunks had melded together over decades—centuries maybe. The result was a cool, humid interior that resembled a small round room with clean walls and a high ceiling. Somewhere far above my head, a shaft of light cast shadows on a colony of bats clinging to the upper reaches. The air inside smelled, not unpleasantly, of damp wood. It reminded me a little of Rotting House before Roop and I replaced the roof.

Although I had read about baobabs, I had never seen one. This goliath more than lived up to the legends: baobabs used as animal pens, post offices, even jails. I imagined sheltering inside the tree, building a gate of branches and a bed of leaves. Although I was tempted to step through the opening and investigate further, I made myself turn back. Midday sun and heat were pressing down. To reach Motembo in daylight, I needed to stay on track.

My clothes looked and smelled like I had slept in them because I had. I stood next to the van and peeled off every stitch. Using water from a jug and a sliver of soap, I showered under the gaze of the hornbill that had followed me all day. The bird clucked and cocked its head as if sizing up the naked specimen under the tree.

The safari guide I had once stared at through a window at school remained vivid in my mind. He had looked clean and groomed, wearing shorts with a matching shirt and very fine boots. After suffering through school without the proper uniform, I understood the importance of appropriate dress. Jackson Quinn would not expect me to be as well turned out as a safari guide. But like Mr. Kitwick, he very likely would notice if I arrived looking as though I had made no effort at all.

I dried myself with my T-shirt and put on clean shorts and a shirt that repeated washings had turned almost the same color. I didn't own boots, but my newish sneakers looked presentable enough. I stuffed the dirty clothes in a bag and straightened the interior of the van. After a quick lunch of biltong, groundnuts, and a banana, I set out on the final leg of my journey.

12

MY HEART WAS BEATING IN sync with the tires as they thumped across the plank bridge. I had reached Motembo in good time. Sunlight dappled the mopane woodland and played on the rough-hewn signpost that marked the entrance. I swallowed hard, straightened up in my seat, and gripped the wheel tight.

The first person I saw was a long, skinny, round-headed man built along the lines of a lollipop. He was sweeping leaves from the floor of an open pavilion under a soaring, dramatically thatched roof higher than any I had ever seen. When he looked up, a grin split his face so readily that I knew he was expecting me.

He leaned the broom against a chair and stepped out. "You must be Bones. Welcome to Motembo."

Bones? I liked it. Just like that, I had a new name.

"I'm Teaspoon." He held out a hand. Instead of shaking the usual way, he gripped my wrist, so I gripped his. It felt solid, like a double knot.

"Like knife and fork?" I asked, hoping the question wasn't rude.

He laughed, a surprisingly deep basso for such a slender guy. "Yes, like knife and fork. We all do a little of everything here, but I mostly set and wait tables, maintain the pavilion, and help in the kitchen." He put on a serious face. "My name, though, comes from my sterling character."

"I see," I said, smiling as he grinned again.

"Would you like a bottle of water?"

Although I wasn't thirsty, I accepted simply because I wanted to say yes rather than no to this agreeable man. He showed me where to park the van and, against my protestations, lifted out my duffel and carried it while I followed. We walked down a narrow path leading away from the pavilion. He pointed out a small structure on a slab of cement. "The kitchen." He then pointed to another. "The laundry."

A little farther on, we passed several large canvas tents tall enough to enter standing upright. "This is where Jackson and his wife, Kiki, stay," he said, pointing. "This one is for Luke and Jaleen. Newsom sleeps over there, and over there, Nate, the chef. We're quite separate from the guest quarters, for everyone's privacy."

I realized that at least one or two of the people he had named must be actual safari guides. I nodded and surveyed the scene, trying not to look like an awestruck dope. When we arrived at the last tent, he swept aside the canvas door. "This is where I stay. I will be pleased to share with you."

Inside were twin camp beds with fluffy quilts, bedside tables bearing shiny kerosene lanterns, shelves of neatly folded clothing, and a washstand and mirror. The window flaps had been rolled up to admit patchy sunshine and a slight breeze. The bedroom was nicer than my own room at home.

"Thank you for sharing. I'll only be here a few days."

"No worries." He set my duffel on one of the beds. "The loo and the shower are that way." He pointed through the window to a fork in the path. "Jackson and Kiki and most everyone else will be back in time for dinner, around six thirty. When the camp is empty, we dine early. Would you like to rest after your long journey?"

I was not sure what I had expected at Motembo, but to be treated so deferentially, like a guest, wasn't it.

"I'm really not tired, Teaspoon. Could you show me where the bar is going to be? After that, maybe I can start putting together the beds."

He nodded. "Of course. You are here to work. Please follow me."

We retraced our steps past the staff tents, the laundry, and the kitchen. At the pavilion he indicated an empty space on one end where the bar would go. A stack of lumber sat to the side. The bar was planned to face a seating area that was already handsomely furnished with deep rattan chairs, earth-toned cushions, and tables made from djembe drums. An imposing wooden tribal sculpture stood in one corner. At the far end were a long dining table and a dozen or so leather chairs. The furnishings looked solid, understated, elegant. It pleased me to know that the bedroom suites Stash and I had built lived up to this high standard. But I regretted that I would have to inform my uncle we should not expect orders for lounge furniture or a dining set.

"I'll take you to one of the guest tents," Teaspoon said. "The furniture you made for them is a great success."

After we stopped at the van to retrieve my tool belt, I followed Teaspoon down a well-raked path leading away from the tents we had visited earlier. On each side of the walkway, selective pruning and clearing had reined in the woodland without ruining the sense of barely tamed wilderness. An unlit lamp marked the turnoff to a narrower path that ended at the first guest tent.

"Tent" was inadequate to describe this dwelling. The large, green canvas-walled structure sat on a raised wooden platform accessible via four steps, sturdy handrails, and a front deck furnished with rattan chairs, a hammock, and a sisal floor mat. The deck faced the open plain and a water hole situated for prime animal viewing. We entered through a screen door with a tricky latch. "To keep out the baboons," Teaspoon explained.

He went in first to raise the window covers. As light flooded in, I caught my breath. Even with the bed rails lying loose, this was the most beautiful room I had ever seen. The polished mahogany floor broadcast warmth and light, softly mirroring the chairs, desk, tables, and wardrobe Stash and I had built. Thanks to specifications from Jackson Quinn, the furniture was perfectly scaled. The rich wood hues partnered well with generous kuba cloth cushions and canvas walls. "Bedroom suite" didn't convey how integral the furniture was to this welcoming space. Each piece looked as though it had grown where it stood, from a seed that had taken root in the hardwood floor. I felt a surge of pride mixed with regret that Uncle Stash wasn't here to see the room too.

A partition behind the bed concealed a granite vanity with two porcelain sinks outfitted in gleaming chrome hardware. In one corner stood a loo, and in the other, a showerhead as big as a hubcap. Teaspoon unzipped a side door that opened to a second shower on a slab of granite overlooking the water hole.

"You can see why we are forbidden to go near the water hole when guests are present." He lowered his voice. "Especially when one of them is a shapely lady."

He looked quite serious, so I nodded, straight-faced. Clearly, maintaining privacy in a camp so open to the wilderness required a certain amount of forethought.

"In ten days' time, we will welcome our first visitors. Until then, we will be very busy."

"I'll help however I can." I looked around. "Do you know where the mattresses are?"

"Chiddy will deliver them when the beds are finished. I believe you know Chiddy?"

"I do." I recalled Chiddy's account of jolly evenings around the campfire. I hoped I would still be here when he arrived.

"Good. Now I will leave you. Please latch the screen door behind me and always when you go in or out." At the door he turned. "I will be working at the pavilion. Come there before dark. I wouldn't want the lions to get you on your first day."

After he left, I quickly latched the door, thinking more about lions than about baboons. A kudu with magnificent spiral horns had come to drink at the water hole. I had seen kudus in the wild, but never so close, with so little effort. The sight held me rapt. For a moment, I imagined myself a guest in that splendid tent, gazing at the untrammeled Africa I had flown a great distance to see. I wondered if actual guests understood the significance of well-tended comfort so close to nature, in the heart of a fragile ecosystem. People like Jackson Quinn surely did. I knew this because every calendar from Ruby's Amazing Safaris proclaimed "the symbiosis between tourists on safari and the wilderness they visit, photograph, and support through their spending." According to Ruby, the safari business was a mainstay of wildlife conservation.

The kudu looked up, apparently alert to some faint vibration on the far side of the water. I watched as the animal listened, motionless, frozen with primordial anxiety. In a moment, another imperceptible shift in the atmosphere signaled the all clear. The kudu resumed drinking, and I turned to my work.

Assembling the long rails of the king-size bed by myself proved awkward but not impossible. The components Stash and I had built fit together smoothly enough, and by jockeying everything into place, I managed to complete the bed frame in only a little longer than it should have taken. I was sliding in a support for the mosquito net when footsteps sounded on the deck outside. The person who tapped on the screen door could only be Jackson Quinn.

"Hello, Bones," he said in a hearty voice. "I see you haven't wasted any time." He was broad chested and not too tall, with light green eyes and a

THE STORY OF BONES

full head of curly blond hair recently flattened by a hat. His fair skin, pale on the forehead, pink below the hat line, was as wrinkled as a road map.

"Uh, hello." I hurried to unlatch the door. "Mr. Quinn?"

"Jackson. We go by first names here." He shook my hand the way Teaspoon had, by gripping my wrist. "You drove here alone?"

I nodded, a little tongue-tied in the presence of the man I had revered from afar. I noticed he wore the uniform of a guide—shorts and a coordinating shirt with two pockets and rolled-up sleeves. He had no doubt spent the day in those clothes, yet he appeared neat and pulled together. I was glad I had taken the trouble to change before coming into camp.

"Good for you." He regarded me for a moment. "Not an easy trip."

"I got stuck in the mud. Some men helped winch me out."

"They did? Old guy and a couple of younger ones?"

I nodded.

"That would be Sam and his sons. 'Good Sam,' we call him. He lives in the village and washes dishes here on the condition he stays out of sight. Sam is a benign soul, but he can look scary to visitors."

At that, I nodded again.

"When no guests are present, we let Sam and his boys hunt small game in the area—strictly for the pot, you understand. They built a blind overlooking the river. When a vehicle gets stuck, they're always the first to know." He gripped the upright I had just installed, testing its stability. "You're an excellent carpenter. You and your uncle."

"Thanks."

"Teaspoon got you settled?"

"Yes, he gave me a nice welcome."

"Sorry I wasn't here to greet you." He hesitated, regarding me thoughtfully. "Have you been to a safari camp before?"

I shook my head.

"We'll show you around." He turned to go and then looked back. "Thanks for coming."

* * *

By dusk, I had finished assembling the support for the mosquito net. The bed and its roof-high frame were as big as some of the houses in my village. At home, I could rent this bed as a dwelling. I gathered my tools, covered the windows, latched the door, and hurried back to the pavilion minutes before darkness descended.

Teaspoon was lighting kerosene lamps grouped around the seating area. He had set seven places at the dining table and lit a row of candles down the middle. Darkness had fallen as fast as a curtain dropped over a window. Against the warm pools of light, the surrounding blackness took on a profound, almost tangible density. I hoped I wouldn't have to walk back to Teaspoon's tent by myself.

Jackson and two women were the first to arrive. "Bones, meet my wife, Kiki," he said, touching the shoulder of a slender, small-boned woman. A smattering of freckles dotted her nose. "And this is Jaleen. She puts up with Luke and manages our housekeeping."

Kiki and Jaleen each shook my hand the conventional way. I was struck by Kiki's iron grip, unexpected in a person so slight. Both women welcomed me warmly, Jaleen with a girlish giggle, Kiki in a crystalline English accent that suggested generations of unruffled prosperity.

"The furniture you built is brilliant, Bones. Absolutely brilliant," said Kiki. "We are very pleased."

I suppressed a smile. *Not effing brilliant?* "Thank you. My uncle Stash helped."

Her eyes shifted. I turned to see two men walking in. Each wore a guide's uniform similar to Jackson's. But unlike Jackson and the others, these two were unsmiling and grim. When Kiki introduced us, the younger man, Luke, nodded in my direction. The other, Newsom, shook my hand absently, his face taut.

Luke sank into a chair. He rested his elbows on his knees and rubbed his face with both hands, not looking up.

"Something wrong?" Jackson asked.

Newsom stood to the side, upright and dignified, hands folded in front. He had a bristle of white hair. I couldn't guess his age, but in looks and bearing, he struck me as a wise elder, a man who had seen and done just about everything. In a soft voice he said, "BB is dead."

Audible intakes of breath preceded a shocked silence. Jaleen lifted a hand to her mouth. Kiki leaned into Jackson's side. Teaspoon stood slack-jawed, shoulders slumped.

"We found what was left of him on the flats near Jackal Pan," Luke said, locating his voice. He tilted up his face to address Jackson. "He was killed at least a day ago with an automatic rifle. We tracked boot prints to the river, where the prints ended."

"Bloody hell." Jackson ran a hand through his hair. "Have you told his family?"

"Yes. And we got word to Marks. I tried to radio you, but we were out of range."

"Marks?" I couldn't help blurting the name. "The ranger?"

Jackson looked at me. "You know him?"

I nodded. "He lives in my village."

"Then you might know he leads the antipoaching effort in a big region. BB—full name Bongani Baas—was Marks's friend and one of the best rangers we had."

I hadn't known this about Marks—that he led many people. My admiration for him, already bright and shiny, took on even more wattage. I remembered the anguish on his face when he described the poisoned water hole and the animals that had died there, his emotional investment in causes that mattered. I couldn't imagine the grief he must feel at the murder of a ranger who was also his friend.

"Why don't we sit down," Kiki said, nodding toward the dining table. She directed me to a chair. "I'm sorry, Bones. This is very hard news. We've known BB a long time."

No one spoke as we settled around the table. Jackson took the seat next to me. A heavy silence hung in the air. When Jackson finally spoke, he turned to me. "BB, Kiki, and I started here as guides when the old camp first opened. Bongani became a master tracker—one of the finest and most capable men I've ever known."

The others nodded and murmured. Jaleen sniffed, dabbing her nose with a tissue.

"He had a special way with elephants," Luke said. "The guests he guided almost always got a close-up look at a herd. They could sit quietly in an open vehicle while the elephants lingered close enough to touch, even when newborn calves were present." He shrugged. "The same elephants that trusted BB could be skittish around other guides. We never figured out exactly how he did it."

They took turns speaking, filling in for each other. I supposed it was a way for them to process the news and pay homage to a remarkable man. I was beginning to understand how tightly knit they all were, so isolated out in the bush. My own throat tightened. I swallowed and blinked.

Kiki spoke next. "When ivory poachers moved in to terrify and slaughter the elephants, BB gave up a top job as a guide to become a ranger and risk his life every day. He was fearless in his pursuit of poachers. He would track them far into hostile, lawless territories."

"Marks will tell you BB was a good soul," Newsom said in a quiet voice, looking at me. The older man was calm and serious. I could feel his years. At the mention of Marks, I sat up straighter. I felt proud that a man who had befriended me was so closely associated with their hero, Bongani Baas.

"Once," Newsom continued, "BB and another ranger followed vultures to an elephant carcass. The poachers were still there, two men working on a tusk with a handsaw. They weren't the organized criminals who kill with AK-47s and maim with electric tools. These men were locals—farmers, with crops to protect and families to feed.

"One of the men, trembling and very afraid, aimed a rifle at BB. Using a calm voice and the language of a kinsman, BB told him to put down the weapon. He said even though he had caught them breaking the law, he knew they weren't bad men. He persuaded them to leave the ivory behind. He said if they did, instead of remembering their faces, tracking them to the end of the earth, and throwing them in jail as he surely could, he would forget he ever saw them."

No one at the table made a sound while Newsom talked. It was the longest speech I would ever hear from him. Somewhere in the inky distance, a hyena whooped and cackled.

Jackson picked up the story. "Marks heard about this when BB and the other ranger showed up carrying a fresh pair of tusks. Although more senior authorities pressured BB to reveal the identity of those two men, he never did. The problem of locals protecting their crops from destructive animals or hunting for bush meat to feed their families isn't going away anytime soon." He shook his head. "We try not to be too aggressive against them. It is very difficult to convince subsistence farmers that wildlife is an asset that needs protection."

"What happened to the tusks?" I asked, almost in a whisper.

"They went into a government stockpile of confiscated ivory. Periodically, the authorities incinerate the tusks in a public place. A tragic waste from start to finish."

Newsom spoke up again. "Some version of BB's forgiveness got around. The villagers started helping him track the routes of ivory traders working for bosses far away—the ones who fund resistance armies and drug cartels. Many people gave him leads. In time, BB led the disruption of more than one heavily armed poaching ring."

"So of course, he became a target," Luke said. His face looked gray, prematurely aged, though he wasn't much older than me. I guessed Bongani Baas had been important in Luke's life.

Teaspoon passed bowls of steaming stew and a platter of corn bread warm from the oven. Hunger gnawed at my gut. I was glad that even in their grief, the Motembo team appreciated good food. No one said much while we ate. The tinkles and plinks of cutlery filled the pavilion. When we finished, Kiki poured coffee. Teaspoon cut and served wedges of apple tart with warm custard poured on top. The meal was delicious, better than anything Zola had ever cooked. I made this assessment of my treacherous, misguided, Skinner-loving sister and her culinary abilities without the slightest twinge of guilt.

Jackson got up and announced that he and Kiki would depart in the morning to visit BB's family. They said good night and left. Luke and Jaleen excused themselves too. I watched Newsom light a cigarette and stare into the darkness. Teaspoon and I left him to his thoughts as we cleared the table, working silently, weighted by the sad news.

When the dining area was in order, we put out the lights and made our way to our tent. Like the others who had stepped from the pavilion into blackness, Teaspoon carried a rifle and a flashlight. "You must hold these in your hands whenever you walk on our paths at night," he told me, shaking both items for emphasis. "Animals often visit after dark. It is best to make some noise so you don't surprise them."

We hurried through the chill with him in the lead, chatting about nothing much, just to create sound. He moved the light rapidly back and forth across the path in front of us, occasionally darting the beam up into the trees. When we reached the tent, he unzipped the door flap and made a quick inspection inside. I was beginning to understand that the lessons I had learned about vigilance in the bush applied equally here, even in a camp as civilized and well-appointed as Motembo.

Teaspoon changed into sweats, folded his clothes, fell into bed, and began softly snoring almost instantly. He slept on his back in the dead-potentate position: legs straight, feet together, hands folded. Sealed away in slumber, he looked as neat and tidy as everything else in his carefully maintained quarters.

I assumed the dead-potentate position too but felt too wide-awake to go to sleep. My mind reeled with images from the preceding twenty-four hours. Already the elephant herd that had surrounded my van in the middle of the night seemed an ancient memory. I silently thanked Good Sam and his sons for rescuing me from the river. I relived my visit to the hollow baobab tree and every detail of my arrival in camp. The story of BB and his connection to Marks claimed another half an hour. I tried to shift my thoughts to less stimulating reaches of my brain. But I got stuck on the thrilling fact that I had just dined with actual safari guides who had treated me almost as an equal.

Staring up into darkness with excitement churning through me, I doubted I would sleep at all. On top of everything, wild creatures were making a racket outside the tent. I tried to put animal names to the sounds I heard: the honks, grunts, hoots, and coughs. I was straining to identify a faint rustle at the threshold of the audible when a mighty, full-throated roar jerked me up to sitting position. I held my breath and stared into the darkness.

Teaspoon skipped a snort and then continued snoring as before. The night chorus outside took a pause too, lion-alert and waiting, but only for a moment. In seconds, the blabbering, muttering, whispering bush came alive once again.

Sleep seemed further away than ever. I lit my bedside lamp, taking care to keep the flame low. I was pretty sure that if Teaspoon could sleep through a tooth-rattling roar, he wouldn't be bothered by me. Slowly, I unzipped my duffel bag. I had never written in the journal Mr. Kitwick gave me, yet the soft leather volume felt familiar and comforting in my hands. In the circle of yellow lamplight, I turned back the cover. I rubbed my palm across my shirt and took up a pen. For the first time since high school graduation, I felt I had something truly worthy to record.

On the first page I printed in neat block letters, "BONGANI BAAS." I considered adding an account of BB's heroism and tragic death at the hands of wildlife poachers. But then I remembered the journal was for me and me alone. To me, the name Bongani Baas said everything.

13

In the days that followed, I found many things to record in my journal. I wrote down every snippet of bushcraft I overheard from Teaspoon and the guides, starting with the importance of making noise on the pathways at night. I made lists of the birds I saw for the first time and plants that were new to me. Equally notable were the realities of life in an actual safari camp. My fantasies about Ruby and her amazing safaris had never included spacious quarters with fluffy duvets or excellent meals prepared by a chef. They certainly had not included afternoon tea.

Teatime came as a surprise on my first full day in camp. I had worked steadily since breakfast on the assembly of beds, taking only a brief break for a sandwich with Teaspoon and Jaleen. By midafternoon I had finished the last bed. I returned to the pavilion to find Teaspoon arranging a tray of cups and plates.

"I was about to come and find you," he said. "Would you like a scone?"

"Uh, sure."

He placed a triangular pastry on a plate and handed it to me. "Do you like your tea white or with lemon?"

I looked at him. "Tea?"

"We're rehearsing. Nate is trying out new recipes and a new oven. When guests are present, tea and biscuits or cake are served every day at three thirty."

"They come in from exploring the bush for *tea*?"

"No," he said patiently, as if explaining to a child. "They rise from their beds for tea. Our schedule follows the patterns of the animals. We are active early and late. During the hot midday hours we rest. Teatime gathers everyone for the late-afternoon game drive that lasts into evening. Dinner isn't served until eight or eight thirty."

During the day's swelter I had never stopped working, of course. No one had told me that a rest and a shower after lunch were perfectly acceptable, even for staff.

Jaleen, who was pouring herself a cup of tea, overheard. "Don't get the idea that we sack out for three or four hours like the guests. There is plenty of work to keep everyone busy until teatime."

I didn't doubt this. Jackson had mentioned that Good Sam helped in the kitchen, and I had seen a girl with cleaning supplies following Jaleen. But for a camp that hosted a rotating roster of twelve guests in six tents for weeks at a time, the staff seemed pretty lean.

"The beds are finished," I told Jaleen, swallowing a delicious bite of scone. "When do you expect Chiddy and the mattresses?"

"Late tomorrow. Jackson asked him to start out today, with a stop at your shop to pay the balance owed. He should be well on the way by now."

It pleased me that Jackson had approved the final payment to Stash even before he had inspected the finished beds. His trust in me squared my shoulders, made me stand a little taller. I noted the pile of lumber waiting to become a bar, both pleased and nervous about the chance to prove myself again.

With no guests at Motembo, teatime was a sketchy business. Luke rushed in, took a few swallows from a cup, grabbed a scone, and turned to leave. I was studying the plans for the bar when he looked back. "I'm going out to search for leopards," he said. "Want to come?"

I was so surprised that all I could think to say was "Now?"

"Yes, now. Bring a hat and your canteen. I'm parked behind the kitchen. Meet you there."

I ran to Teaspoon's tent, pulsing with excitement. The only hat I owned was a black baseball cap I had long ago unearthed from a pile at the Sisters of Charity. I grabbed it and my canteen and hurried out.

"What is SOX?" Luke asked, looking at the hat.

I shrugged, having no idea.

"Best not to wear black in the bush. The tsetse flies will think you're a Cape buffalo, their favorite thing to annoy."

Another nugget to record in my journal, I thought, taking off the cap.

Luke rummaged in a rucksack and pulled out a tan, balled-up wad of canvas that turned out to be a hat. "Here. You can have this."

I looked at him. "You mean keep it?"

"Not exactly a prize. But yes, you may keep it."

Wrinkles and frays and a small, jagged tear in the crown suggested a lifetime of adventure in the bush. I pulled the hat down over my ears. It was too large by only a little. I had never owned anything so wonderful.

Luke drove out of camp fast. The Land Cruiser jostled and bounced, not in a precarious way but with the authority of a machine with great heft and weight. The vehicle crashed through the underbrush, forded axle-deep streams, and sped over rocky terrain that would have destroyed Stash's van. Luke worked the stick shift with unconscious ease, smoothly navigating steep, sandy rises and sudden ditches where the earth fell away without warning. We did not retrace the route I had taken into camp. Instead, we headed for a shady glen wooded with acacias and old-growth leadwood trees.

"Like all leopards, ours are very shy," he said over the thrum of the engine. "We've seen three this season, a female and two males. The female is pregnant, due to deliver. We're keeping an eye on her."

I nodded and turned my gaze up into the trees.

From time to time, Luke stopped to step out and clear a fallen branch or study the ground for tracks or scat. Occasionally, I anticipated his purpose and jumped out first, dragging aside a limb while he stayed behind the wheel. A few times I pointed out spoor I had noticed from my seat. Once, a large baboon swaggered across our path, causing Luke to stomp abruptly on the brake.

"Alpha male," I murmured, watching the animal's confident, butt-swinging knuckle walk.

Luke nodded. "He's fearless. He rules a large troop. You see why we latch our doors."

We had been on the move for about thirty minutes when Luke downshifted again, holding the engine at a low hum while we rolled slowly forward. He was staring intently into dense brush. My pulse quickened. I had seen a leopard only once, on a hunting trip with Baba. We had gotten a fleeting glimpse as the cat slunk into long grass and disappeared. "The Prince of Stealth," Baba had called it.

Something a distance away caught my eye, a tree trunk streaked with … what? I squinted and raised my eyes to a horizontal limb about four meters above the ground. "There," I said, pointing.

Luke killed the engine and raised his binoculars. "That's her. Nice spotting."

The leopard rested on her belly, watching us. "She's guarding a kill," I whispered. A sticklike leg with a dark shin stripe hung from the tree. The appendage was attached to a shredded mess of flesh that had bled down onto the trunk. "A duiker, I think."

He peered through the lenses a moment longer. "You know your antelope."

"From hunting with my father." I quickly added, "For the pot."

While we watched, the leopard rose from her perch and bounded down the trunk. She was a beautiful animal, sleek and fluid. Without a pause she nosed into a dense thicket, where the white tip of her tail remained visible for a minute or two.

"She looks like she's already given birth. The cubs are probably in that brush," Luke said in a low voice. "She'll suckle them in hiding for about three months."

"I hope they last that long."

"Yes. It's a dangerous time. Newborns weigh only four hundred grams, about fourteen ounces. They're defenseless against predators. We'll keep our guests away until we see the cubs climbing trees. We don't want to broadcast their hiding spot."

As if summoned by Luke's words, a brown spotted hyena appeared from the shadows and nosed the base of the bloodied trunk. Drool swung from its mouth, a scavenger's somatic response to the scent of a kill. Other hyenas would gather soon and stick around for days, waiting for bones to fall. A shiver shuddered through me as I watched the hyena circle and sniff so close to the newborns' hiding place.

Luke and I left quickly then, not wanting to draw more attention. We took a longer route back to camp, finding interesting, guide-like chores at every turn. Several of the tracks we followed disappeared into nothing, but Luke never diverted the Cruiser. He got out to clear brush, rebuild washouts with a shovel, or push sticks and stones under the tires to roll us out of sand. Once we got out to clear a spiderweb as big as a badminton net. Its builder, the size of an almond, hung motionless in the middle, alert for the slightest tremble in the outer threads.

I helped Luke as much as I could, watching him, learning fast. I wasn't a novice in the African bush, yet I realized how far I was from a trained professional. Luke's comments hinted at a vast store of knowledge, but even more instructive was his demeanor as we rolled along. His eyes never rested. They swept with laser focus right and left, up and down. Even over the thrum of the engine, he detected sounds I missed: the screech of an owl, the sneeze of an impala. He anticipated flowering trees, dead animals, even bodies of water before we came to them, apparently by sniffing the ever-changing currents of air. All his senses seemed sharper than mine, honed through practice and necessity.

"See that?" he said as we came to a full stop in the middle of nowhere.

A length of wire hung from a branch. At the end of the wire, a slipknot formed a loop the size of a truck tire.

"A near-perfect killing machine—simple, cheap, portable, easy to set up, difficult to see, and nearly impossible to escape. Tension in the loop slides the knot along the wire, closing the loop tighter and tighter."

I hadn't seen the wire, but I knew about snares. They were one of poachers' favorite weapons.

Luke took a wire cutter from the storage box between our seats. "Poachers set these indiscriminately, wherever they please. Often they forget or abandon the location, leaving a snare to trap some unlucky creature by the leg or neck, where it dies a slow, terrible death." He snipped the wire in several places and threw the pieces in the back seat. "An animal that manages to escape suffers wounds that can fester and cause an even longer, more terrible death. A sorry business all around."

After that, I kept my eyes open for snares. I both wanted to be the sharp lookout that spotted one and hoped never to see the evil device again. We had driven another ten minutes or so when I pointed toward a copse of trees at the same instant Luke turned the wheel in that direction. The snare wasn't difficult to see—or smell. The loop had closed around the neck of a wild dog sprawled near the track, garroted to death, buzzing with flies.

Luke freed the carcass and clipped the wire. Disgust contorted his features as he climbed back into the driver's seat. He started the engine without a word. I felt a knot between my shoulder blades. The senseless, manmade death of an innocent animal felt worse than any of nature's bitter realities.

He drove slowly on the way back to Motembo, holding the engine at a low hum. By raising our voices only a little, we were able to talk. "We're always on the lookout for snares and gin traps," he said, finding his voice.

"Gin traps?"

"Filthy, often rusted metal jaws with jagged teeth that clamp shut on a leg—or a tire."

"They set them in the tire tracks?"

"Sometimes. More often they cut gaps in the brush to encourage animals to move in a certain direction, toward the traps. We drivers can be fooled too."

"You must be good at changing tires."

He nodded, grim. "We are."

We rolled into camp as the sun fattened and fell. I helped clean the Land Cruiser by crawling underneath to clear away grasses snagged on the undercarriage. Luke rinsed the insulated camp box stowed in back. Together we washed the windscreen before covering the vehicle with a tarp. As we left the parking area, he handed me the cut lengths of snare wire to deliver to the maintenance shop. Nothing even remotely reusable was thrown away at Motembo.

After dinner that night, I was measuring lengths of wood for the bar when Luke came up beside me. "You did well today, Bones. Thanks for your help."

Praise had never pleased me as much. Out of gratitude, respect, and something akin to hero worship, I quickly stood and removed the canvas hat I had put on again when I left the table. "I liked helping you."

Instead of turning to go, he just stood there. Perhaps he was remembering his own past helping Bongani Baas, followed by the sudden, unbearable weight of the ranger's death. His face sagged and grayed in what looked like renewed grief.

My voice almost deserted me. But I had the presence to add, "I'm sorry about your friend Bongani Baas."

He extended his hand in a new way, with the fingers pointed up about eye level. Although I had never shaken hands like that, my response was automatic, as if by instinct alone. My palm met his and together we made a fist in the air that felt more solid and reassuring than anything we could have said.

***

When Chiddy arrived after teatime the following afternoon, I had almost finished framing out the bar. I was kneeling behind the long, rough mahogany structure, fitting in shelves, when I heard the hum of a motor, the squeal of heavy brakes, and Chiddy's unmistakable voice. "Hellooooooo, Teaspoon."

The greeting reminded me that Chiddy still thought I was "Bonesy." I hurried out to say hello and set him straight. "Hi, Chiddy." I was wearing my safari hat, as I had been all day. I gripped his wrist, demonstrating one of my new handshakes, and wondered if he thought I looked different, more manly. "I'm called Bones now."

"Well, of course. Very fitting." He shook my wrist, smiling and nodding. "Bones, I bring greetings from your uncle and the twins, Donovan and Drew. The boys have been busy, busy learning to be carpenters."

"Stash is teaching them?"

"It looks to be so. Of course, they are very young," he added, probably in case I might be worried about losing my job. "Just playing at it now."

"I'm glad Stash has company while I'm gone," I said, meaning it. "Did you see Mima?"

"Your lovely girlfriend was not at the workshop. But I believe I saw her through the door of the grocery store. There were many customers inside."

Only four days had passed since I left the village. Although Mima occupied a central role in my ongoing fantasies, my home, Swale's Grocery, and Stash's workshop seemed very far away.

Teaspoon helped Chiddy and me carry the mattresses from the truck to the guest tents. It was hot, sweaty work that left us drenched and puffing, especially Chiddy, whose girth remained as impressive as ever. On the way back to the pavilion, I pointed out a thread of green boomslang hanging from the thatch.

Teaspoon nodded. "We know it lives up there. We never tell guests, of course. Boomslangs are reclusive, and they help control pests, so we coexist peaceably." He looked at me. "This snake makes an appearance quite often, high above our heads. You are the first visitor to spot it."

I nodded, solemn. "I promise not to tell."

We stopped to observe the coffin-shaped head dangling in the air.

I wondered if the snake had detected our voices or the vibrations of our movements and come out to take a look. While we watched, it suddenly vanished, as if yanked by the tail.

The evening in camp was almost festive, much happier than the two previous nights. Even before I arrived at Motembo, I had known the importance of resilience in people who live close to the realities of the African bush. In a safari camp, both the realities and the need for resilience seemed amplified many times. Everything there struck me as larger, more consequential than the rest of life and at the same time simpler, more focused and intense. I felt a constant undercurrent of excitement. I was deeply attracted to the sense of purpose and camaraderie that knit together everyone who worked at Motembo, no matter who they were or where they came from.

Jackson and Kiki returned from their condolence visit with supplies, including a large bottle of Amarula. After dinner, just as Chiddy had described a lifetime ago, all hands settled around the campfire. Everyone except Teaspoon and Newsom, who didn't drink alcohol, held a glass of Amarula. The fire snapped and spit. Sparks climbed into the sky. A scorpion popped out of a smoldering log and scurried past my foot. Beyond our circle of light, another outer realm had come alive with the cackling, chuffing, hooting voices of nocturnal creatures on the prowl.

I took a small sip of the deceptively smooth and creamy homegrown brew I had sampled at Captain Biggie's. Through plumes of smoke, I studied the bright faces of the people I had come to know. Everyone at Motembo, and Chiddy too, had been accepting and kind. Now they were in high spirits, relaxed, tongues loosened by camaraderie and the sweet, fermented fruit of the marula tree.

Jaleen revealed impressive storytelling skills when she recalled the time a leopard dragged a dead impala into her laundry. Her voice commanded a low, creepy register, and she paced her words for maximum effect. The others must have heard the tale many times before, yet no one made a sound as she described stepping across the threshold and almost tripping over a magnificent cat ripping flesh from a carcass.

"The leopard peeled back its bloody mouth and hissed," she said, drawing out the s's. "I can still see its haunches bunching and flexing as it braced for a lunge." Her eyes were wide, glistening orbs. "I knew not to run, so I backed away as slowly as I could. S-l-o-w-l-y. Back, back, back. I didn't stop or turn around until I was all the way to the pavilion."

"Brava," Luke said. "Never run from a cat."

I was pretty sure that bit of wisdom was meant for me.

"We're always on guard for animals that wander into the tents," he continued, glancing my way.

I felt a wave of affection for him—and all of them, as it dawned on me that the stories and banter were directed mostly at me, a fresh audience. I was enjoying myself very much, and my enjoyment seemed to please them. Grinning, I took a sip from my glass. Chiddy had been right about the pleasant feeling.

Jackson told about a long-departed guide who had thrown scraps and bones from a barbecue into a ditch behind Jackson's tent. Before long, a pack of snarling, cackling hyenas had shown up for the feast.

"Did they keep you awake?" I asked. Maybe I wasn't the only one disturbed at night by animal sounds.

"Until dawn. But I must say, the hyenas did a thorough job of cleaning up."

Chiddy dipped his head toward Jackson. "See how good-natured he is? Our Jackson is an excellent man—for a *soutpiel*."

Hoots of laughter got my attention. "Soot pill?"

Jackson explained, "Afrikaans for 'salt penis.' One foot in Africa, one in the UK." He puffed air. "I'm supposed to be insulted."

"It is a terrible insult," Kiki said in a mild voice, pouring a little more liqueur into Chiddy's glass. "He really should slap you."

"I would never insult my dear friend Jackson. He is a fine, fine man—for a *soutpiel*."

More hoots told me that insults were part of the fun.

"We haven't asked about your drive, Chiddy," Kiki said. "Was the mud a problem this time?"

"No, no, not mud. This time a Cape buffalo gave me a fright. I came upon an old male that was feeling quite unrelaxed." He took a sip from his glass while we waited to hear more. "I had parked and gotten out to kick a tire."

"That means 'take a leak,'" Luke interjected, looking in my direction. "Women say, 'pick a flower.'"

I nodded, feeling a little dizzy.

"And I was kicking the tire when I saw the buffalo about as far from me as that tree." Chiddy gestured with his head. "The monster hoofed the ground as if to say, 'See me grind this dirt into more dirt? This is what I'm going to do to you.'"

"What did you do?" Kiki asked.

"I ran for the truck, quick as a bee."

The others looked amused, but I needed a moment to put together the image of Chiddy and "quick as a bee." It came to me that I might be drunk. Had someone poured me a refill? I had been careful to sip the Amarula slowly, but when I peered into my glass, I found it empty.

Teaspoon must have noticed me eyeballing the tumbler like a telescope. I don't know what else he noticed, but he got up and said, "Let's go, Bones. It's getting late."

I would have liked to stay by the fire and listen to more stories, but I did not want to walk back to Teaspoon's tent alone in the dark. So I got to my feet, feeling quite unstable. The earth I relied on to be solid and stationary rocked beneath my boots. Walking proved tricky. With my back as straight as a plum line (or so I thought), I faked sobriety by taking abnormally careful, measured steps. I was pretty sure all eyes were on me as I tried to forge a dignified exit. Of course, I fooled no one. For what seemed a very long distance, I swayed and slewed behind Teaspoon's wavering back. I must have made it all the way to the tent and my bed because that was where I ended up.

14

I opened my eyes to searing light. Sunshine burned through the window. My headache was a warthog in a snare, kicking and tusking against my temples. The inside of my mouth felt like the hide of an old goat and tasted worse. It took me a minute to sort out who had made me eat the remains of dead vultures. Just thinking the word "Amarula" made bile rise in my throat.

Teaspoon was long gone. At least that's how it looked when I managed to sit up and peer through the narrow slits of my eyelids. My vision was in ruins. The other bed appeared neat. Teaspoon's sweat clothes were folded on the shelf. Something crackled. I looked down to discover a note pinned to my shirt, the one I had worn yesterday.

Good day, Bones. I am sorry if you do not feel well. You have learned a lesson about Amarula, yes? I left you a present. Chiddy.

A pair of dark glasses sat on the table next to my bed. I couldn't believe I had slept through Chiddy's departure—and way past the hour Teaspoon and I usually got up. I put on the glasses and crept out of the tent. To my relief, I encountered no one on the way to the shower except a tiny elephant shrew that dashed across the path and into a hole. I wanted to crawl in with it. Besides feeling embarrassed beyond measure, I suspected I couldn't manage a simple "Good morning" without causing more havoc inside my skull.

The cold water hit my skin like a spray of gravel. I emerged from the shower battered but awake, head pounding. Jaleen had left my other set of clothes, laundered and folded, in a basket outside Teaspoon's tent. I put them on. In the tiny mirror above the washstand, my face looked shrunken, the hue of algae in a swamp. Luke's hat and Chiddy's glasses gave me the appearance of a person wanting to hide, which I was.

In the pavilion I found another note, this time from Teaspoon. Would anyone actually speak to me today? A large camp box like the one I had seen in Luke's vehicle anchored the paper against the breeze. *Bones: Here is your brunch. Coffee's in the thermos. I hope you feel better. T.*

I had slept through breakfast *and* lunch? The news came as a shock. Yet it was true; the sun had passed its summit. Afternoon heat bore down. I blinked with the dawning realization that I had slept through half the day. I must have been blotto out of my mind. Did everyone in camp know? Even Jackson Quinn?

A severe tribunal set up court in my mind. I tried but could not remember how the previous night had ended. My last recollection was a story about Chiddy and a bee. The thought that I might have acted sloppy and out of control in the company of people I admired so much mortified me. It made me even sicker to think I might have lost their trust and respect. I sank on a chair and cradled my throbbing head in my hands.

A shaft of sunlight angled in to spotlight the unfinished bar. Through the dark glasses I squinted at my work. Even in their rough state, the long boards pegged together without a nail in sight formed a handsome focal point that transformed one end of the pavilion. I inhaled the familiar scent of fresh-cut wood, absently fingering the lucky bean seed bracelet that never left my wrist. *For luck in love and work.*

Even as my head pounded and my stomach churned, I registered a tick of hope. Maybe diligent effort could save me. I had always found respite in the calming rhythms of sanding, staining, sealing, and lacquering. Finishing the bar well wouldn't erase the humiliating mistake of drinking too much. But if I produced a beautiful result in spite of my sorry condition, maybe I could redeem myself in the eyes of Jackson Quinn and the others. I felt it was my only chance.

With a renewed sense of purpose, I opened the camp box. *Food first.* Teaspoon had packed thick slices of ham and cheese, quartered tomatoes, an apple, and a buttered baguette. I made myself chew and swallow everything. A bottle of water and two cups of strong, sugared coffee helped sluice it all down. My thirst was a force unto itself, unstoppable. I flashed on the image of my father pumping water after a night at the tavern. *So this is how it feels.*

Overfull and quietly belching, I made my way to the van. The finishing materials from Stash's shop sat in the back: sander, stain, sealer, woodgrain filler, and several cans of high-quality lacquer. I silently thanked the hot, desiccating breeze that played on my bare arms and legs, favorable conditions for drying the coatings between each application. The circulating air would also minimize the fumes' potential to abuse my already trashed and throbbing head. I intended to sand, lacquer, sand again, and buff every square inch of mahogany as many times as it took to make the bar shine like a jewel.

During several trips back and forth between the van and the pavilion, I encountered no one. A lizard scooted across my path. A golden-tailed woodpecker tapped on a nearby tree. The human residents of Motembo were nowhere to be seen. Solitude suited my current, fragile state, yet what did it mean? Where was everybody?

I took a deep, steadying breath and tried to focus on the job at hand. After I finished assembling all the necessary supplies, I took stock of my workspace. Motembo was an orderly place, with prescribed ways of preparing guest quarters, setting tables, and serving food. In general I was a neat and orderly person. But my current display of tidiness out-tidied all the usual standards. Overcompensation for my woozy, unstable state felt entirely appropriate, a matter of control. An observer might have concluded that strict laws of geometry ruled a carpenter's alignment of pots, brushes, and tools. Was an inspector due?

With my materials lined up in careful rows, I plugged the sander into the generator behind the bar and turned it on. Although I was grateful for the gift of electricity, the noise from the machine vibrated inside my skull like a swarm of hornets. A few small birds shot into the air. I tilted my head for a look at the thatched ceiling but did not see the resident boomslang. Like every human being in camp, the animals were deserting me too. I felt alone, sick, too pathetic for words.

I had been at work for some time, maintaining an impeccable workspace and making decent progress, when I noticed two boots standing next to me. They belonged to Jackson Quinn.

"Don't stop, Bones. We can talk while you work."

I swallowed. My tongue felt fat and useless, stuck to the roof of my mouth. I remained on my knees and tried to focus on the brush in my hand. My palm was damp against the wooden handle. Chiddy's dark glasses sat on the floor. I wasn't ready to part with Luke's sheltering hat.

"I'm glad to see you working. Everyone in camp feels a bit woolly-headed today." He paused, waiting for me to say something. When I didn't, he added, "Kiki said to tell you she's sorry for overserving you. Amarula can sneak up on a person."

An apology, to me? I wasn't sure I heard right. I didn't know how to reply, so I shrugged, glancing at him. The underarms of my freshly laundered shirt felt wet with sickly sweat.

He turned his gaze upward. "Teaspoon said you spotted the boomslang."

"Yes."

"You know you're the first visitor to see it."

I nodded. "I promised not to tell anyone."

This brought a smile to his lips. "Luke was impressed by your spotting abilities too. He told me you were knowledgeable in the bush—and helpful."

The conversation was not what I had expected. "Thank you. I liked driving with him to find the leopard." I hesitated, unsure of my role. "I hope the cubs are okay."

"They are as far as we know. We won't get a reliable count until the litter comes out from hiding. Or, if we're lucky, we might see the mother moving the cubs to a new location."

"She was beautiful. The first leopard I've seen up close."

He fell silent for a moment. I kept my head down, working.

"Do you like it here, Bones? At Motembo?"

An odd question, I thought. Was he asking in a general way, trying to be nice? Or was he leading up to a reminder about correct behavior in camp?

"Well, yes," I answered, wary, looking up.

"I'd like to suggest something for you to think about."

Giving up alcohol? Buying an alarm clock? I waited.

"Would you consider becoming a guide? A safari guide like Luke and Newsom?"

My face froze in a vacant expression that must have made him think twice about what he had suggested. "Me?" I finally said. Amarula had cudgeled my brain.

"Yes, you."

The string of arguments that followed sounded preplanned, as though he had given them a lot of thought. As I gradually came to my senses, I registered an intense, flattering, almost unprecedented interest in me and my future. In one remarkable speech that I will never forget, Jackson gave me accolades, guidance, and an offer I could not refuse.

"You already have your secondary school certificate and a driver's license. You're an experienced hunter. With a little training, you could both pass your four-by-four vehicle test and obtain the required firearms license. You're smart and a hard worker too. A few months of dedicated self-study would ready you for the Level One Guide Certification Exam. Six more months of on-job training, which you could complete here at Motembo, would qualify you for a Level Two Certificate, the same as Luke's. Newsom wants to cut back a little, spend more time with his grandchildren. Soon we'll have a full-time opening for you."

"Here?"

"Of course, your carpentry skills would be very welcome in camp too."

I put down the brush and rose to my feet. My brain felt sluggish, but my heart was beating fast. I took a breath and hoped I would be able to put together an intelligent sentence. "I would like to be a safari guide."

The declaration felt bold on my lips, revelatory. It was an utterly true admission I had never before put into words, even though I had lived in awe of safari guides for as long as I could remember. Ruby of Ruby's Amazing Safaris dwelled in a world so far from my own life and circumstances that the idea of emulating her or any guide had never occurred to me—that is, not until Jackson laid out a reasonable path I knew I could follow. Now, all at once, my future seemed obvious, preordained, enlarged far beyond the well-trodden paths of my village and the four familiar walls of my uncle's workshop.

"But I will have to ask my uncle. He might not want me to leave the shop."

Jackson nodded. "Yes, of course you must ask him. In the meantime, I'll give you a Level One syllabus and the study materials it covers. They'll help you understand the learning required and the commitment you must make." He turned to go. Over his shoulder he added, "I hope you feel better."

* * *

I drove home from Motembo with my mind so far from the journey itself that afterward I hardly remembered the route I had taken. Instead of Chiddy's map, the Level One syllabus, workbooks, manuals, and logbooks sat on the seat beside me, drawing my eyes away from the windscreen with precarious regularity. I had already memorized the syllabus by reading the pages over and over in the light of a lantern on my last night in camp.

I had always assumed guides were well informed, but I had never guessed the range of subjects they needed to know—for starters, geology, ecology, climatology, astronomy, biomes, botany, taxonomy, conservation management, local culture and history, lodge and game drive management, vehicle rescue and maintenance, and first aid. These were just a warm-up to the core curriculum: learning the life cycle, habits, and characteristics of hundreds of species of animals and plants, as well as how to locate, spot, and identify each one. With every line I read, my respect for safari guides grew. Not even my school principal, Mr. Kitwick, knew so many things.

Jackson had assured me that I could return the study materials if I decided not to go forward. But he must have known that turning my back on such an opportunity would be unthinkable, no matter what my uncle said. Among the materials Jackson had given me, I discovered a receipt that revealed he had already paid to register me as a self-studying guide candidate. That brought a smile to my face. In Jackson's mind, there had been no doubt.

Now, driving home, wearing Chiddy's dark glasses and Luke's canvas hat, I tapped a cheerful rhythm on the steering wheel. Sunlight silvered the hood of the van. The open bush, scene of my future career, felt benign and welcoming. From time to time, I tested myself by casting a keen and practiced eye on a plant or animal. Already I knew the names of the trees I saw and most of the birds. A pair of antelopes with white circles on their hindquarters darted away from the sound of the engine: waterbucks.

My hangover had finally vanished. I was uncommonly grateful to feel normal. During casual conversations following my regrettable night at the campfire, I had learned that both Luke and Kiki had also slept late the next morning.

"I was in ribbons," Kiki confided.

"Hounded by the black dog," Luke said.

I suspected the condition wasn't entirely new to either of them. For me, one visit to the punishing aftermath of inebriation was more than enough. I doubted I would overindulge again.

The bar in the pavilion had turned out as well as I had hoped. My workmanship had drawn praise from everyone, including Nate, the cook, who christened the shining masterpiece by smashing a glass of sparkling wine against it. Jagged shards and a shower of *grande cuvée brut* were no match for five glossy coats of clear, hand-buffed lacquer. I felt confident that the lustrous finish I had labored over for days would stand up to anything—spilled drinks, crashing objects, even marauding baboons.

In less than a year, if I worked hard and learned fast, carpentry would become an interesting sideline to my real profession. I couldn't wait to tell Mima the news and describe the rosy-hued future I envisioned for the two of us, living and working together at Motembo. Of course, she could work in camp too, at almost any job she wanted. During our farewell conversation, Jackson had assured me of that. I told him Mima was even more industrious than I was and smart too. We would do her parents one better and not just honeymoon on safari, but start our life together in the welcoming embrace of a premier, world-class camp, a camp that wanted us to stay.

I turned over in my mind how others would react. Hannie, my sweet little sister who loved Ruby's calendars as much as I did, would no doubt light up at the prospect of having a guide for a brother. How Baba and Zola were going to take the news, I couldn't predict. Those two had disappointed me so thoroughly that I almost didn't care how they might react. I intended to cut myself loose from their opinions, or at least not try to change them. My world was expanding far beyond their influence. In return, I would try to look the other way when they did exactly as they pleased, without regard for common sense or my objections. "Give her some space," Baba had advised. He was about to see just how much space I could give.

My biggest, most sobering worry concerned Uncle Stash. What would he say when I told him I wanted to be a safari guide? Even if my beloved uncle stood up and cheered, would I be wrong to leave him alone in the shop? Abandon him just as he was getting older, frail, his gimpy leg more troublesome than ever? Stash and his friendly workroom had provided a haven for me through difficult times, a place where I had found purpose and a sense of belonging. Under his patient instruction I had learned skills to serve me for a lifetime. And of course, through Stash I had met Chiddy, gone to visit Motembo, and watched my world open wide.

For two days I drove with these questions spinning through my head. Underpinning all of them was the assumption that I would pass the tests necessary to become a guide. I did not minimize the time and effort success was going to require, the hours of study and review. I saw before me a tricky rope bridge that stretched from my present life to a remarkable future. I wanted nothing more than to make it all the way across.

15

Afternoon shadows were lengthening when I rolled into the village. The crumbled roads and shabby, leaning buildings looked the same as always, but I felt I had been away a very long time. I wondered how Roop and Granny were. Finding time to visit them and help fix up Rotting House, or even go fishing, would be more difficult between working in the shop and studying for the guide exam. The chickens, at least, would not miss me.

I was too excited to dwell on the pitfalls ahead or on any qualms I felt about leaving Stash. Putting them aside, I headed straight for Swale's Grocery. At that hour, Mrs. Swale was likely to be in the store with Mima. I welcomed the chance to tell both of them about Jackson Quinn's proposal and the bright, new path that had so unexpectedly opened for me—and Mima too.

It would help that Mrs. Swale had gone on a safari with her late husband. She had seen firsthand the work of professional guides and witnessed their importance in a thriving industry. I hoped to spark happy memories for her, as well as build support for Mima's eventual departure. Now that the twins were old enough to help in the store, I felt sure that Kate Swale would not stand in the way of a markedly enriched future for her daughter.

As I neared the grocery, I removed Chiddy's glasses and Luke's hat and ruffled up my flattened hair. Earlier I had stopped by a stream to wash and change into fresh clothes. I felt fluttery at the prospect of seeing Mima again. In an hour or so, Mrs. Swale was likely to go home, leaving Mima and me to reconnect in the most intimate ways.

I parked in the space behind a shiny new delivery truck. Mrs. Swale had finally parted with the old vehicle that held sad memories of her husband's disappearance. A dog chewing on a bone sat in the dust next to the truck. It wasn't until I had stepped out of the van that I noticed the door to the store was closed, unusual for Swale's on a sunny afternoon. A sign in Mima's printing hung from the doorknob: *Closed today. Please come back tomorrow.*

Closed? I was taking in this startling fact when I heard a noise inside—voices. I tried the knob. The door was unlocked, so I went in. What I saw made me catch my breath.

The floor was strewn with debris—ripped bags spewing rice and beans, mangled cereal boxes, broken bottles, dented cans, pools of sticky liquid, and over everything a dusting of fine, white powder that must have been flour. Mrs. Swale stood in the middle of the mess, looking stricken and drawn. She held open a large trash bag. Mima was on her hands and knees, collecting pieces of glass. For a moment they didn't notice me.

"What the …?" I picked my way through the wreckage. "What happened? Are you okay?"

Mima looked up in surprise, her face a pale moon. "We found this when we opened today." She got up and kissed me lightly on the cheek. "I'm happy you're back."

Too stunned to fully appreciate the kiss, I looked around, dumbfounded. "Was anything stolen?"

"Not a cent. The cash drawer wasn't touched. Everything else is such a mess we can't tell what's missing."

"What's missing almost doesn't matter. So much is ruined. Hello, Bonesy." Mrs. Swale's voice came out thin and weary.

I crouched next to the bag she was holding and began to pick up glass.

"The new section in back is even worse," Mima said, kneeling beside me. "The shelves you built were torn off the wall. I'm so sorry, Bonesy."

No sorrier than I was. This wasn't the homecoming I had expected. Selfishly, I felt crushed that my big announcement would have to wait. I would even have to put up with "Bonesy" a little while longer. "I'll rebuild the shelves, of course. I'll do whatever I can."

Mima placed her hand on mine. In other circumstances her touch would have sparked something notable. But now, instead of the usual hot rush, what I felt was, well, just her hand on top of mine—lovely and soft to be sure, but for now, in light of the current situation, platonic. It startled me to think I had become so responsible.

I squared my shoulders and looked around. "How did they get inside?"

"Through the back. The screen door was locked, but the screen itself had been ripped from the frame."

In the pause that followed, I noticed the sound of a broom sweeping glass. I gestured toward the rear of the store. "Are Donovan and Drew here?"

"No," Mrs. Swale answered. "I wanted to spare the boys the worst of it. They're at your uncle's. He's been so kind."

"Then who …" I didn't finish because a person holding a broom stepped into view. I wouldn't have been more surprised if a goat had trotted forth. It was Skinner.

"Well, hello, Bonesy," he said, feigning friendliness. A serpent-like smile split his face. I think it was the first time he had used my name instead of "dung beetle" or worse. "Isn't this an appalling mess?" His words were civil, but they held a dagger edge.

I was too appalled to speak.

Mima looked at me questioningly before filling the void. "Skinner stopped in this morning for cigarettes. When he saw what had happened, he offered to help."

I watched her smile at him and felt a tightening in my chest. She was just being friendly, but even so …

"Glad to be of service," he said with exaggerated politeness, dipping his head.

I wanted to smash in his face. Why was he here, flirting with Mima, when he was supposed to be my sister's boyfriend? I didn't believe for one second that he was just trying to help.

He leaned the broom against the wall. "But now I have to go. I have a date." He flashed an evil smirk my way before composing his features and turning to Mrs. Swale. "Ma'am, you might want to report this to the rangers. It could have been monkeys or even baboons. A troop has been causing trouble near the village."

"I thought of animals too. Such random, senseless damage." She shook her head. "Thank you, Skinner, for all you've done."

"Anytime, anytime at all." He fixed a loaded stare on me that brought to mind an ape marking territory. I half-expected him to piss against the door. "Goodbye, Mima, Bonesy. See you around."

I scowled at him, taut with antipathy. Mima saw my expression and gave me another puzzled look. I had never told her how much I loathed

Skinner. I had seen no need to bring that sour note into our relationship. Now I regretted that I hadn't confided in her because clearly, she and her mother were blind to Skinner's true nature.

"Did you check his pockets?" I asked when he had gone out the door. I immediately realized it was a stupid question since no money was missing. What would he steal, a bar of soap?

"Why don't you like him?"

"It's a long story. Skinner's not a sterling character." I thought of Teaspoon and missed him. "If you need to know more, I'll fill you in while we work."

For the next several hours, we bagged debris, swept, and scrubbed almost every square meter of the store. Mima reshelved the salvageable items and created sale tables for lightly damaged goods. The wreckage in the house and garden section alone took a long time to clean up. The fallen shelves, ripped from the wall, looked as though someone had tried to climb on them. Torn and broken packaging littered the floor. A sweet-smelling glop coated much of the debris. It looked to be a toxic stew of furniture polish, Omo, plant food, Happy Suds, lamp oil, and some other wet and gritty substances I couldn't identify. Skinner, unsurprisingly, had cleared an area smaller than a doormat.

At Mima's insistence, I explained why trusting Skinner was not a good idea. I told her and her mother about how he had dropped out of school and how he harassed, bullied, stole, mistreated animals, and worse. I explained that he ran around with a gang of thugs and generally led a violent, disreputable life. I described him as cunning, unstable, and malevolent. I omitted the part about his infuriating the cobra that subsequently killed Mama. Even then, years later, the memory of my mother's death was too raw.

The women nodded and cooed, taking my side right away. Their support warmed my heart, especially when I told them about Skinner and Zola and how my own father wouldn't stand in their way.

"How awful. I'm surprised your father doesn't put a stop to it," Mima said, sounding indignant.

"Your father may be smarter than you think." Mrs. Swale looked at me kindly. "Sometimes a parent has to stand back. Trying to keep Zola and Skinner apart could make them all the more determined."

I was not convinced. But at least now Mima and her mother knew the worst about Skinner. I felt so pleased to have them thinking poorly of him that I was almost disappointed when I discovered baboon tracks in the gunk on the floor—enough tracks to explain the random, senseless damage. Skinner had been right about that.

* * *

I awoke to find Hannie jumping on the foot of my bed. "You're home! Wake up. Zola's making pancakes."

Mima and I had worked until nearly dawn. Mrs. Swale had stayed for a while, slowing with fatigue, until Mima urged her to fetch the twins and go home. We got the store in good enough shape to open in the morning with a reduced but adequate inventory. Then, too worn out for more than a tender hug, we had said goodbye and gone our separate ways. I had crept into the house in my stocking feet and fallen into bed, but not before noticing with some relief that Zola was asleep in her room, alone.

"Hello, Hannie Pannie." I pulled my little sister into my arms. "Did you miss me?"

"Yes," she said, solemn. "I missed you very much."

"Did you do your homework every night?"

She nodded.

"Good. We can do our homework together now. I'm going to study to be a guide."

"A guide?"

I nodded. "A safari guide. Like Ruby."

Her eyes went wide.

"And my new name is Bones. Not Bonesy, Bones."

I didn't have to tell Baba and Zola because Hannie got to them first. "Bonesy's going to be a safari guide, like Ruby," she announced, rushing into the kitchen. "And his new name is Bones." Her excitement was exactly as I had imagined. Baba and Zola were harder to read.

"Welcome back," Baba said, setting down his coffee mug. "What's this about being a guide?"

Zola was at the stove, turning pancakes. She cast an interested look over her shoulder.

I repeated Jackson Quinn's proposal, including his opinion that I already met several qualifications. "With a few months of study and six more months of on-job training, I could be certified. Jackson offered me a full-time job when Newsom retires."

"Newsom?"

"A guide who's ready to spend more time with his grandchildren." I paused, thinking of Stash. "I would like to accept."

Baba and Zola exchanged a look I couldn't interpret.

"What does Stash have to say?"

"I haven't told him yet." This wasn't going the way I wanted. I sounded thoughtless, as though Uncle Stash hadn't been on my mind since the moment Jackson made his offer. "Actually, Uncle Stash is my biggest worry. I don't like the idea of leaving him alone in the shop."

"Maybe he won't be so alone," Baba said between sips of coffee. "The Swale twins have been there almost every day."

That was welcome news, the same as Chiddy had reported. Eleven-year-olds could lose interest, though. And soon Mrs. Swale would need help in the store.

"Did you know Swale's Grocery was ransacked the night before last? By baboons, we think."

Baba's startled expression told me he hadn't heard. I felt a tick of satisfaction.

"I was there cleaning up with Mima until early this morning." I looked at Zola. "Didn't Skinner tell you?"

She turned. "Skinner?"

"He came by for cigarettes and saw the store in shambles, before your *date*." I tried to make the word "date" sound as off-putting as I could, like "decapitation" or "descent into hell."

"He didn't say anything about that," she said. A frown creased the space between her eyes. "Was anything stolen?"

"By baboons?" Sarcasm oiled my voice. "Uh, the baboons didn't seem to want money. Everything else was upended … or eaten." I looked pointedly at Baba. "Someone should tell the rangers."

He nodded, keeping his face neutral.

I couldn't help pressing my advantage. "By the way …" I glanced at Zola, choosing my words carefully to protect Baba's somewhat undercover relationship with Marks. "The guides at Motembo are friends with a ranger from our village. His name is Marks."

"Interesting," Baba answered.

I gave him a steady look. I was certain he knew the true extent of Marks's involvement in antipoaching efforts—that Marks was not just a local player but the head of a big antipoaching operation, a man admired by rangers as far away as Motembo. By mentioning his name, I gave notice that I too was in the loop. Maybe I knew even more about these matters than my father did.

"It's a small world, Bonesy."

"Bones. I'm called Bones now."

***

I hurried to Stash's workshop, fueled by pancakes and an urgent desire to escape the uninspiring atmosphere at home. Baba and Zola seemed interested in my news yet too preoccupied by issues of their own to express much enthusiasm. To my mind, the culprit was Skinner, of course—Skinner's relationship with Zola and the strain it put on all of us. Once again, I resolved to separate myself from my sister's foolish attachment. My main concern now was making things right with Stash.

The first thing I noticed when I walked into the shop was how tidy it was. The floor had been swept clean, and the tools hung on pegs. The second thing I noticed was a pair of footstools sitting under the workbench. The twins were nowhere to be seen, but Stash hurried forward to greet me.

"Hello, Bonesy." He wrapped me in a hug. "I hoped you'd be back soon."

The warmth of his welcome filled me with affection. I hugged his fragile bones, regretting the news I would have to share.

"I want to hear all about your trip. Tell me everything."

We settled on the two taller stools while I described Motembo and filled him in on the furniture we had built for Jackson Quinn. I assured him that everything had arrived in excellent condition and looked beautiful in the tents. When I described the bar I had constructed in the pavilion, he engaged me in workmanlike questioning of the joinery and finishes. Finally, I felt proud to hand him Jackson's payment, almost double the amount we had requested. "He said it was a bonus for all the brilliant work we did." I couldn't say "brilliant" with a straight face. "That's a quote," I explained with a grin.

He stared at the check. "This is very generous."

"Yes. Jackson is generous." I paused and took a breath. "I have something else to tell you."

"More good news?"

"I hope you'll think so."

During the next several minutes, I described the unexpected opportunity that had come my way, the new career that would provide a different life and a new name to go with it. Even as I saw him watching me, taking it all in, possibly worrying about his own future, I could not conceal my elation. I slid off the stool and tried not to look overeager as I paced back and forth, talking and gesturing. I outlined Jackson's thinking, the encouragement he had given me, and all the steps required to become a guide.

Uncle Stash was a good listener. His eyes never left me as I told him about the leopard I had seen with Luke, about the stories I had heard at the campfire, and even about the sad death of the legendary guide and tracker, Bongani Baas.

Finally, I took a breath and sat down, turning to face him. "The only thing I don't like about this is that in a few months I'll have to leave you and the shop." I realized I had stated my departure as a fact, not a request for permission. "I mean, if leaving is okay with you."

While I was talking, his face had remained flat and expressionless. Now his features softened. A smile puffed his cheeks and crinkled the leathery skin around his eyes. "Leaving is more than okay. You're practically airborne with excitement. I'm happy for you and proud too. You must follow this big chance."

"After all you've taught me, making me your apprentice and everything, I don't want you to think I'm unhappy here or ungrateful."

"Of course I don't. You must remember that time is not a fixative. It's a solvent." He paused to let that sink in. "You taught me something too—that I enjoy teaching." He pointed to the footstools under the workbench. "Donovan and Drew are my new after-school students. They built those stools. We're starting on drawers soon. By the time you're a guide, they'll be making decent furniture."

Relief washed over me, along with an enriched sense of my uncle's goodness. "I'll help with the boys, if you like. For the next few weeks I can work my normal hours and study at night."

"The twins will be glad to see you. They still call themselves 'the Dirty

Dees.'" His amused smile and the warmth in his voice proclaimed an understandable affection for the twins. The attachment had come at an opportune time since I was about to ease my way out of my responsibilities in the shop. I decided I wasn't going to worry yet about the day Mrs. Swale would need the boys in the grocery store.

Looking wistful, my uncle put a hand on my shoulder. "I'm going to miss you, Bonesy ... er, Bones."

My eyes welled. "I'll miss you too."

16

And so began a disorienting period during which I lived and worked in the village of my birth but my hopes and dreams resided at Motembo. I wasn't a *soutpiel* exactly, but my situation appeared similar to Jackson's: one foot at home, one foot in a welcoming African outpost. As for my *piel*, it and the rest of me were quite happy to remain in the vicinity of Mima Swale.

For a few days, though, I seldom found time to see Mima, let alone be intimate with her or even tell her my plans. With Stash's approval, I enlisted the Dirty Dees to assist in rebuilding the home and garden section in the grocery store. My uncle had already taught the boys excellent work habits and the basics of tool safety. Donovan had become proficient at measuring, marking, and cutting lumber. Drew appropriated the nail gun and handled the tool with due respect.

Once we had finished the carpentry, the boys made a game of restocking the shelves. Like Mima, they paid meticulous attention to order and symmetry, although their efforts more closely resembled boys building forts with blocks than storekeepers arranging goods on shelves. Without direction, Donovan picked up a broom and swept the construction area more or less clean.

On the days Mima and I worked together in the store, floods of customers claimed her attention. Her sale on damaged products attracted a significant number of shoppers, who added regular merchandise to their baskets of bargains. As the shelves emptied, the cash register filled up.

"I'm going to the bank, Bonesy," she whispered one afternoon when I was preparing to leave. "Want to go too?"

I leapt at the chance to be alone with her, to tell her the news I had been itching to share. We left right away, with her at the wheel of the new truck. She stopped in front of Stash's workshop to let me run inside. Excitement motored through me as I explained our errand to my uncle, retrieved the fat check from Jackson Quinn, got Stash's endorsement, and hurried back out.

Yet once I was sitting in the passenger seat again, I found myself in no hurry to talk. I gazed sidelong at Mima's fine profile, watching her hair stream in the breeze. While she talked about the unexpected success of the damaged goods sale, I imagined us speeding through the bush in an open four-by-four. The life we would share at Motembo—the never-ending variety and adventure along with well-paid, meaningful work—seemed almost too good to be true.

I recalled a conversation I'd had with Luke about the advantages of employing committed pairs. "Everyone in the safari business prefers to hire couples," he had said. "'Twofers,' we call them. Twofers have no problem sharing a tent. They form a working team from the start and, importantly, exert a cooling effect on khaki fever."

"Khaki fever?"

"A common ailment among guests. They see a handsome guide in khaki shorts and a manly khaki shirt …" He paused. "A guide doesn't even have to be that handsome or wear khaki, if you want to know the truth. Women, and sometimes men, get the hots for him. Serious, aggressive hots. It happens once or twice a season. Female guides can spark it too."

My jaw had dropped. I pressed my lips together and made an interested sound.

"As you might imagine, khaki fever puts the guide, man or woman, in a difficult spot. Everyone in camp can detect a flirtation a kilometer away, no matter how discreet the parties think they are. A liaison, real or imagined, between guide and guest wreaks havoc in every corner of the property. The other guests feel slighted or jealous. The husband or wife may be furious, embarrassed, morose, or all three. Resentment sours the rest of the staff because they have to work twice as hard to maintain a cordial and positive atmosphere.

"So of course, we don't encourage flirtations with guests. We make sure the newcomers know right away that Jackson and Kiki are a couple and Jaleen and I are a couple. It helps a little. Newsom, whose wife lives in a village about five kilometers away, has to fend for himself."

"Newsom?" He was at least seventy years old.

"Even Newsom."

"Are you listening, Bonesy?" Mima glanced my way.

"Uh, yes," I said, hoping I hadn't missed anything important. We had almost reached town.

"I brought the title to the new truck for the safe-deposit box," she continued. "Mother made me a signer along with her, so we both have access."

I nodded as though I regularly visited safe-deposit boxes. In truth, I had never seen one. For a moment, silence hung between us.

I cleared my throat. "Mima, I want you to know why I haven't been coming to the store after work."

I regretted this opening as soon as I said it. Her face went slack, pale as an antelope's belly. She looked as though she expected something bad, news of another girlfriend or a horrible contagious disease.

"It's all good, Mima. Really. I haven't been avoiding you. I've been studying."

"Studying? For what?"

"To be a safari guide. If I work hard, I can be ready for the written exam in a few months."

She took a moment to absorb the news. "And then?" Distracted, she eased up on the gas pedal. A boy on a bicycle cruised past. Someone honked a horn.

"Maybe we should pull over."

She steered the truck off the road and onto a patch of hardpan. When we came to a stop, she shut off the engine and turned to face me. Her expression said nothing. My heart thudded as I took her hand in mine. Over the next several minutes I explained it all, from my bone-deep connection to Motembo and the people there to Jackson Quinn's encouragement and offer of a good job when I completed guide training. I mentioned the advantage of having couples on staff, leaving out the part about khaki fever. As I talked, I watched the color slowly return to her cheeks.

"I want you to come with me, Mima—after training, when I'm certified. I'd like us to start our life together at Motembo."

Now her face was alight with something I couldn't decipher. The hint of a smile played on her lips, but she still hadn't said a word.

"Would you like that?" I pressed. "To live and work in a very nice safari camp? With me?"

"This is a lot to take in, Bonesy."

"Oh, I forgot to tell you. My name is Bones now. Just Bones."

"Well, Just Bones, I'll tell you one thing. You never stop surprising me."

* * *

At the bank we made our cash deposits and then followed a clerk to the safe-deposit vault. I had never seen a door as thick as the one guarding the chamber inside, a room lined with rows of small metal doors. Mima signed a slip, and when the clerk looked questioningly at me, Mima nodded. The clerk hesitated and shrugged, apparently bending the rules. I too could enter.

When we got inside, Mima fished in her bag for a key and handed it to the clerk. He produced another and used both of them to unlock and swing open a numbered door. Mima extracted a long metal box. The clerk invited her to step inside a booth for privacy, but she declined, taking only a second to slide the title under the lid.

Witnessing such extreme security measures got me thinking about the items stored inside the walls all around me. Jewels, probably. And vehicle titles, like the one Mima had brought. But couldn't a person put in anything that fit? Especially in the privacy of the little booth? I felt a shiver. This was a chamber of deep, dark secrets.

Mima slid the box back in its cubbyhole. The clerk relocked the door. Something about the proceedings gave me a pang of recognition, but I couldn't figure out what. I had never been inside a vault or owned anything so precious that it required two keys and a signature to protect. Maybe the locks had captured my attention. They weren't too different from the one I had installed on Stash's cash drawer. The slender hinges interested me too.

I imagined a tour in which I pointed out obscure details to a following of fascinated hardware tourists, not unlike a safari guide noting a tiny frog or the notches in an elephant's ear: Bones's Amazing Safe-Deposit Safari. The notion put a smile on my face. But it wasn't the only reason I felt lighthearted as we left the bank. I saw Mima's guarded interest in my news about Motembo as our first step down a thrilling new path. Her caution seemed appropriate and prudent in view of the radically altered future I had proposed. Though her response hadn't been the outpouring of enthusiasm

I had hoped for, I wasn't the least bit discouraged. On the contrary, I felt almost giddy with happiness and relief.

In the following weeks, my campaign to convince her turned almost playful, a sweet courtship. Whenever I talked about guiding or the camp, she listened carefully, laughed in the right places, and asked probing questions about Motembo and its staff. I saw her a few times a week. My visits usually were short and, when we found ourselves alone, intense. Lovemaking took on a heated, breathless urgency. When we were apart, I couldn't wait to be near her, yet we both accepted that for now, studying and work took precedence over everything else.

Early on, I sought out Marks both for guidance and as a conduit to Jackson Quinn. I was a little nervous about seeing him for the first time since I had discovered his elevated status in the world of guides and rangers. But I wanted to dispel any doubt I might have left in Jackson's mind about my determination to become a guide.

I found Marks at Captain Biggie's. He was sitting at the same table in back where I had seen him with Baba. On this occasion he sat alone, peering at a map. As I passed the bar, I nodded at Captain Biggie, who surprised me by remembering my name.

"Hello, Bonesy." The long strings of wooden beads around his neck clattered against the bar.

"Uh, hello. It's Bones now."

"Well then, Bones, what can I get you?"

Being recognized at my local bar was a new and heady experience. For a moment, I imagined myself bellying up and ordering a beer. But I said, "Coke."

"Welcome back," said a friendly voice. I turned to find Marks standing beside me. He pointed toward the table with the map. "Let's sit and catch up."

As it turned out, Marks didn't need much catching up. He already knew I was preparing to be a guide. He knew my uncle supported my decision. And he knew I was studying for the exam.

"Who told you? Baba?"

"Word travels fast, doesn't it? I hope you don't mind. I already let Jackson know you're on track. He and I are in touch almost daily."

"I don't mind. I want him to know." I sipped my Coke, thinking about the tight-knit world of guides and rangers. "I'm sorry about your friend Bongani Baas."

A shadow crossed his face. "Thank you."

"Did you find out who killed him?"

"We don't know the identity of the person who fired the AK. But we know the network—paramilitaries who've recruited, pushed out, or murdered almost all the subsistence poachers in the region." He glanced over my shoulder. "I come to this table once or twice a week. If anyone has information to share, they know where to find me."

I felt the skin tighten on my scalp. I turned and peered into the dark recesses of the tavern, looking for informants and assassins. "Is it okay I'm here?" My voice was reduced, almost inaudible.

"Of course. Come whenever you wish. I'll quiz you before the test." He wagged a finger at me. "I can be a tough examiner."

I swallowed. "You're on."

* * *

The workbooks and manuals Jackson had given me held a daunting volume of information. I often studied late into the night. For relaxation, I read a memoir by a guide, who wrote tips such as "When you don't know the answer to a question, look it up. Clients do not expect you to know everything." I found this advice so reassuring that I recorded it in my journal.

Soon after I began my studies, I took a Saturday morning off to visit Roop and Granny Nobbs. The Ovambos went berserk as usual. I wove my way across the yard with an alarming number of chickens squawking and pecking at my shins. Roop appeared on the porch. When he saw me, he laughed, same as always.

"Hi, Bonesy. I heard you were back."

"Sorry I didn't get here sooner." I swatted away a savage hen and vaulted up the steps. "How's everything at Rotting House?"

"Less rotten. The new roof has made a big difference. Granny's fine too." He gestured toward the chickens stirring up dust in the yard. "I'm expanding the business."

A rooster that had chased me up the steps spun around to attack Granny's empty rocker. I moved away, keeping a wary eye.

"A vendor in town wants a regular delivery. He sells poultry and supplies a restaurant. After hearing about Granny's walkies, he came to find us. He said, 'Chicken feet usually lead to chickens.'"

"A reasonable assumption."

"Yep. And I'm learning to drive."

"Oh man. No road will be safe."

He ignored me. "The Swales sold us their used truck. Did Mima tell you? They were very generous in their pricing."

"She didn't say." I felt pleased that Mima and Mrs. Swale had been kind to my friend.

"Who didn't say what?" Granny asked, appearing at the door. When she saw me, the familiar gap-toothed smile transformed her face. "It's Bonesy!"

"Hi, Granny." I kissed her lightly on the lines scored into her cheek. "I hear you have a new truck."

She toed away the rooster and settled in her rocker. "Parked in back. Now Rooper can make deliveries far and wide." She was wearing a cotton dress with a droopy collar, and her cord necklace swung into view.

I stared at the small silvery key. "Uh, Granny. That key …"

"Never leaves my neck." She fingered the cord. "How you found this little thing in the rubble … I still can't believe it."

Something tugged at me, a memory. "May I have a closer look?"

"Sure." She shrugged. "It hasn't changed much."

As she sat forward, I turned the worn metal in my fingers, squinting at the faint imprint on the surface. "This might not be for your jewelry box."

"What?"

"I think it's a safe-deposit box key. Mima Swale has one like it."

Roop leaned in for a look. "Safe-deposit box?"

"For valuables. You can store jewelry and important papers in a locked box in the bank. Mima put her truck title there."

Roop stared at me. Then he turned to Granny. "Did you and Grandpa have one? A safe-deposit box?"

"If we did, I didn't know about it." She slumped back in her rocker, blank-faced.

I felt a pang of regret. Had I ruined the keepsake that gave her so much pleasure? Or uncovered a hurtful secret? I looked at Roop. "I'm probably all wrong. You could ask at the bank."

Before I left Rotting House, I mentioned that I was studying to become a guide. I kept the news casual, almost offhand, dreading my friends' reaction almost as much as I dreaded leaving them behind. Granny nodded and smiled, not really understanding.

A cloud passed over Roop's face. Then he grinned and slapped me on the back. "That's great, Bonesy." He tried to sound enthused, but his voice came out strangled.

I didn't have the heart to tell them I also had a new name.

* * *

I didn't see Roop again for weeks. My days started early and ended late, crammed from end to end with work, studies, and as much time with Mima as I could fit in. Stash had received a big order from an exporter for handcrafted baby cradles and a commission for a custom walnut-slab dining table. Mr. Kitwick wanted bookshelves for the school. The twins came to the shop most afternoons to hone their drawer-making skills and stuff themselves with Aunt Letty's fresh-baked cookies. The shop pulsed with noise and activity.

I stayed up later and later each night, cramming as much information as I could into my overtaxed brain. I had moved through the training syllabus to the heart of my studies: flora and fauna and how to identify individual species in the wild. On weekends I hiked far into the bush or sat by the river with Baba's binoculars and a backpack weighted with reference books, trying to name every plant and animal I saw. I collected unfamiliar seeds and leaves between the pages of my journal to study in detail at home. I filled a rucksack with small rocks: granite, limestone, quartzite.

When the guide exam was only a week away, I went to see Marks. "I'm ready for you to quiz me," I said, hoping this was true.

He sat alone at his usual table with some paperwork spread out in front of him. He wore his olive-green ranger uniform, the sleeves rolled to the elbows, and double-knotted boots coated in dust. A canteen and binoculars hung below the field jacket slung over the back of his chair. Although I had seen him there before, in the dusky light of Captain Biggie's, the tavern still struck me as an alien habitat for a man so attuned to the open air. He looked ready to bolt at a moment's notice.

I placed my study manuals on the table in case he wanted to consult them. He laid a hand on top of the pile. Later I would realize that he had questioned me without opening a single book.

"The umbrella thorn belongs to what genus?"

"Acacia."

"What survival tactic does this tree use?"

"It releases a chemical into the soil that prevents the germination of other seeds. This eliminates competition for space and water."

He nodded. "Even trees can be territorial. What's another name for the gray tree frog?"

"Foam nest frog, because the female uses her hind legs to whip up a protective froth that surrounds her eggs. The result is a foam nest the size of a melon that hangs from the tree."

"Good. Male weaver birds go to what lengths to attract a female?"

"They weave complicated nests with fresh materials and advertise them with preening displays."

"Not so different from us, eh?" He winked.

We went on like this for over an hour. A few questions stumped me, such as the Latin name of the weeping boer-bean, *Schotia brachypetala*, and the function of the syrinx, a fleshy membrane below a bird's windpipe that vibrates to create birdsong. I must have looked crestfallen when I didn't know the answers because Marks smiled and said, "Don't worry. Those were to remind you there's always more to learn."

Then he moved back into more familiar territory. "What ungulate walks by moving both right legs and both left legs at the same time?"

"Giraffe."

"Tell me two other interesting things about giraffes."

"They're most vulnerable to predators while drinking, splay-legged, at water's edge. Bending down also subjects their brains to excessive blood pressure, partially counteracted by a network of capillaries that control blood flow. Not surprisingly, giraffes don't drink very often. As a result, their urine is thick, like honey." I took a breath. "Giraffes are the only ruminant with a gestation period of more than a year. Life span is about twenty-five years. Each individual eats roughly thirty-four kilos of deciduous foliage a day." I could have said more, but I sat back, quite pleased with myself.

Marks gave me a severe look. "If you talk like that on a game drive, you'll be thrown to the lions."

"What? Why?"

"Because you sounded like a lecturer, something you never want to do.

Point out one or two things of interest at a time. Answer questions clearly and briefly. Some people want to know more, others less. Watch to see what they're looking at, and talk about that particular thing. Being alert to your guests' level of engagement is an important part of guiding."

I was mulling over that bit of wisdom when a man I recognized from the village rushed up to the table, his face a ball of sweat and worry. His worn clothes and muddy boots told me he worked outdoors, perhaps as a farmer. He snatched a look at me and then turned to Marks. "Another slaughter."

"Where?" Marks was already on his feet.

"North about five kilometers. At least eight elephants dead."

Marks shrugged into his jacket and gathered up the papers on the table. "How recent?"

"The carcasses were warm less than an hour ago. Lions are there."

"I have to go, Bones. Good luck on the exam."

He was speaking to me, but his attention had already gone elsewhere. As he headed for the door, he talked in an urgent voice on his long-range radio. I watched him and the other man hurry out and wished they had asked me to go too.

A few days later, I learned from Baba that the elephants hadn't been shot. They had eaten pumpkins and watermelons poisoned with an agricultural pesticide.

"Poachers are trying quieter methods of killing," he said, his face rigid. "Poisoned arrows, poisoned bait. This time they chose aldicarb, a pesticide farmers use to protect their crops against thrips, aphids, and spider mites.

"A concentrated version called Temik is a readily available rat poison. Less than a tablespoon full can kill an elephant." He shook his head. "It's also called 'Two-Step' because an animal that swallows it takes two steps and dies."

It sickened me to picture elephants falling to their knees and keeling over in the throes of death by poisoning. Now Baba sat silent. He had gone outside himself for a moment or two, looking past me, perhaps imagining the horrible scene. I watched him, waiting.

"It was a breeding herd, including two pregnant females. After the poachers were done killing and sawing away the ivory, they left a message carved into the flesh of the matriarch." He let out a long, weary breath, as if the whole bitter truth was simply too much. "'Follow us and you're next.'"

17

Everything went faster then, as though life itself had sped up. One day spilled into the next at a dizzying rate. I drove myself to an official site in town to sit for the Level One Guide Certification Examination. Unlike the morning of my school exam, I made it to the site in good health and clean clothes, without working up a feverish sweat or vomiting on any passersby. The questions on the test were similar in focus and detail to the ones Marks had put to me. As I penciled in my answers, I silently thanked him for preparing me so well.

Three weeks later, I learned from Jackson Quinn that the results had been posted. I had passed with a nearly perfect score. Jackson congratulated me but didn't seem particularly surprised. His confidence was like wind at my back. I felt my new career racing forward at a high, heady velocity. I wanted nothing more than to live up to Jackson's expectations.

My on-job training at Motembo was to begin in ten days, coinciding with the arrival in camp of twelve foreign guests. Jackson said Teaspoon would arrange a trip for supplies and pick me up on the way back. In the meantime, I was to purchase good boots and a rugged pair of waterproof binoculars. My guide uniform and a new rifle would be waiting in camp.

Jackson couldn't have imagined the thrill I took from the words "guide uniform." How eagerly I welcomed the obligation to put on clean, regulation clothing and a good pair of boots every day. For the first time in my life, I would wear clothes that were correct, official, and worthy of respect.

I lightened up on the studying but did not abandon my manuals and books. Leading foreign visitors on safari, even as a trainee, seemed a daunting assignment. I read and reread the chapter titled "Creating a Meaningful Guided Nature Experience." An even more sobering one, "Caring for the Safety of Tourists," became dog-eared with review. The guide code of conduct, a lengthy list of principles, rules, and protocols, made my hair prickle—could I ever be such a paragon?—even as the words filled me with pride. I was entering a profession with high standards and clearly stated expectations. Tourists with little or no experience in the bush were going to rely on me to lead, enlighten, and protect them. I was fully tuned in to the responsibilities ahead.

Already, guide training had sharpened my view of the world and everything in it. On a fishing expedition with Roop, I found myself acutely aware of each plant and rock, of every insect that whined past or landed on my arm. *Dragonflies lay eggs in fresh water. More than seven hundred dragonfly species exist in Africa.* I wasn't merely aware. I was continually searching my store of knowledge to identify and label, dredge up facts, and figure out when to speak and when to shut up.

I tried watching Roop to discover what interested him on the way to the river, but he mostly looked down, staring at the path in front of us. At water's edge, he zeroed in on the ripples and currents like the angler he was, reading the shady depths to locate a catch. Even as he hunted for fish, my friend seemed unusually preoccupied. Something was on his mind, so I gave up guide practice and encouraged conversation.

"Nice day," I tried. Lame, but it worked.

"Could have been." He tossed in a line. "Zola and Skinner came to buy walkies."

"Again?" Hearing my sister's name paired with Skinner's never failed to sting.

"Twice more. Granny likes Zola. Skinner, she can do without."

I shook my head. "What does Zola see in that loser?"

"I suppose he's hot," Roop said, glum.

I suppressed a laugh that rose unbidden. My friend looked too heartsick to be seen as funny. "Well, if you put aside Skinner's deplorable character, morals, conduct, ethics, and personality, I suppose you could say he's a fine specimen."

That drew a smile. Or maybe it was the barbel tugging on Roop's line. He pulled in the fish, silvery, whiskered, flopping. "Too small." He unhooked it and threw it back. "I got my driver's license."

"Oh. Congratulations. Are you delivering chickens now?"

"Yep. And I took Granny's key to the bank." He paused, concentrating on a ripple in the water.

"Well?"

"You were right. Grandpa had a safe-deposit box."

I didn't know how to feel then. This could go sweet or sour. "Did you open it?"

"Nope. Only Grandpa could, with his signature. The lady at the bank, Mrs. Dubin, was nice, though. She said if Grandpa left a will, the person named could get access."

"Did he leave a will?"

"Granny says he did. He wrote it himself, in front of her, leaving everything he owned to her. At the time, she thought this was sweet but unimportant because he didn't own much. Now we've searched everywhere. We can't find the paper." Roop spent a moment reeling in another fish. This one was a keeper.

"What do you suppose he did with it?"

"Mrs. Dubin said he probably locked it in the box for safekeeping, a common mistake. He might even have rented the box for that very purpose." Roop rolled his eyes. "It's going to take a lawyer and probate court to give Granny access. If she gets it, she'll probably find nothing more than the will that says she's allowed to open the safe-deposit box and find the will." He looked at me blankly for a second before we both erupted in laughter.

"Your grandpa got that backward."

Roop nodded, wiping away a tear that wobbled from his eye. "He was a backward guy, you know? Not much schooling. After my parents died, he worried about their old age—his and Granny's. He did what he could to take care of her."

We fished a while longer without talking much, muted by thoughts of lost parents, old age, and my coming departure. I watched the current stir the river into whorls and thought our fishing spot must have changed little since our grandfathers were boys. The usual insects flitted above the surface. Shorebirds worked their stick legs along the moist bank. *Blacksmith plover. Slaty egret.* A few times Roop and I had met elephants coming to this spot to drink, but we hadn't seen any in a while.

The thought of absent elephants cast an even greater pall over the sunny afternoon. In Grandpa Nobbs's day, before habitats shrank and wildlife poaching surged, thousands of elephants must have roamed this plain and drunk in the river—tens of thousands. Now the pace of killing for ivory was unsustainable. Even as Marks and others risked their lives to save elephants, the species was headed to extinction.

I hadn't seen Marks since the day I watched him rush from Captain Biggie's to the scene of fresh slaughter. I could imagine his reaction to the threat carved in the side of the elephant carcass. Although I still feared for his safety, I understood the fury such a mutilation would ignite. If the poachers believed they could scare Marks with words, they were gravely mistaken.

* * *

I did what I could to ease my departure from Stash's workshop. I handed in my key to the cash drawer and cut back my hours, pulling away little by little from involvement with the Dirty Dees. The twins had become proficient enough to assist Stash in building and finishing the dozen or more cradles on order. They took turns sawing flat boards to size while Stash cut heart-shaped dovetails and worked the corner joinery. The repetitive slab construction suited the boys' skills, and with every cradle their confidence grew.

Stash, too, got to stretch his skills while working with Donovan and Drew. I watched him deliver a crisp lesson in determining the radius for rockers that wouldn't tip. Then he claimed his students' nearly undivided attention while demonstrating the use of the palm sander. The boys leaned in, shifting and scratching only a little while keeping their sights fixed on the tool. My uncle's clear, patient explanation reminded me once again what a fine teacher he was.

A final project for me was to build and finish the bookcases Mr. Kitwick had ordered. On the day I delivered the shelves to the school, my former principal welcomed me with a broad smile and a knuckle-crushing handshake.

"I understand you're called Bones now," he said, pumping my forearm.

"Um, yes."

"Have you heard the expression 'make your bones'?"

I flexed my smashed fingers, thinking of fractures. "No. What does it mean?"

"To earn a respected position in a field of work. The phrase is a corruption of 'establish your bona fides.'"

"I didn't know."

"Well, now you do. It's fitting. You've already made your bones as a carpenter. I expect you'll make your bones as a safari guide too."

I liked it. *Make my bones.* "I'll write that in the journal you gave me."

"Using it, are you? Good."

Since he had answered his own question, I decided to change the subject. "Mr. Kitwick, my uncle Stash is teaching carpentry to the Swale twins. He's an excellent teacher, for little school-age kids."

He held my look, and I knew he was thinking what I hoped he would think. "He taught you too, didn't he." It wasn't a question. "Interesting."

I had planted the seed. Whether or not Stash wanted more kids to teach, I couldn't say, but if Mr. Kitwick approached him, my uncle could decide for himself. I carried the bookshelves into the school and said goodbye. Mr. Kitwick stood in the doorway, watching me go. He was still there, standing like a sentinel in his shiny gray suit, when I drove the van around the corner and out of sight.

* * *

The rest of my guide training could keep me from home—and Mima—for six whole months. I hadn't asked Jackson Quinn about time off. With two days' travel each way, a decent visit would require almost a week's absence. To make such a request even before I had started seemed foolish and ungrateful. I decided to assume nothing except a long separation from everyone in my village, including Mima.

The short time until I departed only sweetened my days with her. We picnicked by the river, went on long walks, and worked together in the grocery store. She took an encouraging interest in my training manuals and guidebooks and rode with me when I drove to town for new boots and binoculars. On the way there, she quizzed me, squinting at an open page as sunlight streamed through the window.

"An elephant's tusks are actually …"

"Modified upper incisor teeth."

"When do tusks stop growing?"

"They grow continuously during an elephant's lifetime."

"Too easy." She flipped some pages. "Name the five golden rules of tracking."

I steered the van around a dip in the road. "Place the first track you see between the sun and yourself. The best time to follow tracks is when the sun is low in the sky."

"That's one."

"As you track, look ahead about five meters to see the bigger picture. Sometimes you can take a shortcut from one point to another."

She nodded.

"Three, use your understanding of the animal's behavior. Is it heading for water or a favorite grazing spot? This can help you pick up a lost trail. Four, mark the last track you see by circling it with a stick or your finger. Then, if you search ahead without results, you can come back and easily find your starting point. And five, use a cloverleaf pattern to look for a lost trail. Circle right, circle left, and circle straight ahead, gradually enlarging the loop."

"You knew that without studying, didn't you?" It was more of a statement than a question. She closed the book. "You'll be an excellent guide." She looked straight ahead, unreadable.

My throat tightened. "You haven't said you'll come … when I've finished training, I mean."

"Six months is a long time, Bonesy." Like Roop and Granny, she still called me Bonesy.

She must have seen my face fall because her voice went soft. "Of course, I want to be with you. Motembo sounds like a dream, for both of us. But you know I can't leave until Mother and I figure out how she's going to manage without me. In time, we'll form a plan. We don't have to decide everything right now."

This wasn't the answer I wanted. But it came as some consolation that Mima had once put the brakes on our lovemaking too. *Not yet, Bonesy. Let's wait. Everything between us has to be right. Memorable. A slow dance.* That first slow dance had turned out just fine. Better than fine.

"So for now, we'll just dance?"

"Dance?"

"A slow, memorable dance?"

Her lips hinted at a smile. "Slow and memorable works for me."

During my last days at home, I spent long hours in the grocery store just to be near her. Together we restocked and straightened shelves, took inventory, and flattened cartons. Once again, I noted how well she and I functioned as a team. The observation stirred up thrilling images of us working side by side at Motembo, but I kept that nugget to myself.

While Mima and her mother were busy helping customers, I found plenty to do on my own. I made repairs, polished windows, and unloaded deliveries. It wasn't lost on me that Mrs. Swale would have difficulty running the business alone.

That troubling notion weighed on me during my last afternoon in the store. I was restocking shelves I had rebuilt in the home and garden section, a task that did little to distract me from worrisome reflections. Lost in thought, I unpacked a case of Omo and lined up the containers in their usual place. When I knifed open a second box and folded back the corrugated flaps, I needed a moment to register what I saw—a moment that felt like slipping into icy water.

The box held twelve cartons of Temik, the concentrated form of aldicarb known as "Two-Step." It was enough poison to kill all the elephants from here to forever. I sat back on my heels. *Swale's sells Two-Step?* I hadn't noticed the pesticide in the store, but I had never actually looked for it. I supposed rat poison belonged in a shop that sold home and garden supplies. Even so, I shuddered to think of the potential for slaughter so tidily packaged and ready for display on shelves I had built myself. Temik, in the wrong hands …

My mind was racing when Mima walked toward me wearing a broad smile. She must have seen the look on my face because her lips flattened into a line. "What's the matter?"

"I didn't know you sell Temik." My voice came out sharpish.

"Well, of course. Without poison, rats would overrun the village." She sounded practical, matter-of-fact. She looked relieved that this was all that was bothering me.

"Was Temik on the shelves before the break-in?"

The question seemed to startle her. "We stocked extra for the new section. So yes, I suppose it was. Why?"

"I didn't see cartons like this in the debris on the floor, or on the sale table afterward. But I bet you had to reorder right away, didn't you? After we cleaned up?"

"Mother does the ordering." Her words trailed out slowly. She let her eyes rest on the open box. "I can check our records."

My thoughts rushed forward like bats from a cave. I didn't spare her the onslaught. "Poachers kill elephants with Temik. They've wiped out entire breeding herds not far from here. The killers massacre in silence, mutilate beyond description, and take ivory worth fortunes." I stopped for a breath and lowered my voice. "Do you think people like that bother with shopping? Do they walk into Swale's and stand in line to pay for their poison?"

Her mouth hung open. The questions didn't require an answer. We both stared at the open box sitting between us. She took a step back, as though the cartons inside might explode.

I ran a hand through my hair. "I think whoever broke in here came to steal Temik. The mess was meant to look like random vandalism or the work of a wild animal."

She regarded me with narrowed eyes. "What about the baboon tracks?" Her voice came out thin and reedy.

"Temik kills more than elephants."

"You mean …?"

"The footprints were from a baboon. But I'm guessing a baboon didn't put them there."

18

Marks was not in the tavern, but I found Baba talking across the bar to Captain Biggie. A tankard of beer sat between them. I hoped the beer was my father's first. When he saw me, he looked clear-eyed and rock-solid, so I settled on the stool next to him. Captain Biggie put a Coke in front of me and moved away.

"What brings you here?" Baba pushed the beer to the far side of the bar.

"The break-in at Swale's. It wasn't baboons. I think the person who did it was a poacher, or someone helping poachers. He stole the entire inventory of Temik."

"And then wrecked the store to cover up what he took." His tone was flat. He looked away. This hadn't come as a surprise.

"You knew?" I felt the blood drain from my head.

He threw a glance toward the rear of the tavern. "Let's go to a table."

Without a word I got up and followed, roiling with disbelief, outrage, and questions. *You knew a thief—a poacher—and not a baboon wrecked Swale's?* I wanted to ask. *And you kept this to yourself?*

Baba settled in a dim corner facing the front, training a stare on everyone who came and went. I took the chair opposite. I wanted him to look me straight in the eye.

"You leave tomorrow," he began, stating the obvious. "Before you go, there are a few things you should know."

I was ready to pop. "Like what? That you can't trust me and I can't trust you? That I'll be the last to know everything that matters? What about Mima and Mrs. Swale? Don't they count either?"

He exhaled audibly. "For one thing, Zola is engaged to be married."

The needle of shock I felt almost prevented me from speaking. I sucked in a breath. "Engaged? To *Skinner*?" I spit out the name. For a terrible moment I believed my father had kept the theft of Temik a secret to protect Zola's boyfriend.

"No. To Marks."

"What?"

"She's marrying Marks."

The dumbstruck look on my face must have told him that an immediate response would not be forthcoming.

"I introduced them several years ago. Zola was unhappy then, not ready to love anyone—or to be loved, for that matter. Marks was smitten right away, of course. And he was very patient." The hint of a smile played on his face. "They met only occasionally at first and always out of the public eye. Zola was adamant about avoiding the kids who had taunted her. Remember how she kept to herself after Mama died? She wasn't even sure she wanted a suitor."

I blinked. I knew she had been happy to leave school. It embarrassed me to realize I had never noticed her isolation—that she had shied away from everyone.

"Marks was clearly in love with her. Steadfast. Little by little, she came around. She gained the confidence to be vulnerable, Marks said. They became almost inseparable. Anyone could see they were meant for each other."

Inseparable? Meant for each other? I put those interesting assertions aside. I had never seen my big sister and Marks within ten meters of each other.

While Baba waited, letting the news take hold, I worked up enough spit to loosen my tongue. "But Zola and Skinner …"

He studied his hands splayed on the table. "For many months we've suspected Skinner of aiding ivory poachers. We believe he delivers supplies to poachers' boats on the river. He might also inform the network when Marks is in town and therefore not out patrolling. We think Skinner stole the Temik from Swale's and returned the next day to cover up or at least legitimize his footprints. He must have laid the baboon track with a severed foot."

I flashed on the revolting image of Skinner dismembering a baboon and pocketing a foot—the exact, disgusting scenario I had suspected myself.

"Lately he's been seen talking on a radio as far away as a two-day drive."

A two-day drive? That put him within reach of Motembo, *my* territory, where I hoped to be rid of him once and for all. A deep stab of resentment knifed through me. Would Skinner *ever* stop interfering?

We fell silent as Captain Biggie approached our table with the drinks we had left on the bar. "I thought you might want these," the tavern owner said, setting down Baba's beer and my Coke. We said thanks but didn't encourage conversation. With a nod and a smile the Captain turned and left.

Baba glanced behind me. "Even with range and a radio, Skinner is a very small fish." He lowered his voice to a barely audible murmur. "Zola engineered their relationship to help Marks. She's trying to find out more about the poaching rings Marks wants to stop—who the bigger players are and where to locate them."

The revelations were detonating in my brain like a string of fireworks. I fell back as if blasted into my chair. "Marks is okay if she and Skinner …" I couldn't finish, but he understood my meaning.

"Zola, it turns out, could have a fine career in espionage. She has managed to create a honey trap while keeping the honey at arm's length, so to speak. Skinner apparently finds the chase intoxicating—so much so, he's fallen for her. Professed undying love, I understand. For now, at least, he accepts her limits."

If either of us felt awkward discussing Zola's sex life, we didn't show it. I was not surprised to learn that my beautiful, intelligent sister had claimed the love of two men. And now my near-idol, Marks, was going to be my brother-in-law. As the truth of that sank in, I felt an overwhelming sense of good fortune and gratitude. All traces of my previous disappointment in Zola vanished. I admired her more than I could say. But I was afraid for her too.

"She's risking a lot," I said. "You know that."

He nodded.

"Has Skinner told her anything useful?"

"He's taken her to the river a few times, to the place where we think he meets the boats. We don't have the manpower to watch around the clock. We need him to tell her in advance when the boats are coming. Marks plans to follow the deliveries upstream. He believes the supply line will lead us closer to the command center of the poaching operation, the ones in charge."

"Roop and I saw Zola and Skinner there, at the river. After they left, a mokoro with two men in it came by. The men stared at Roop and me, then kept going."

"When was that?"

"One afternoon before I went to Motembo."

Baba picked up the tankard of beer and set it down again without drinking. "She thinks she can learn more before Skinner insists on taking their 'romance' to the next level."

I shuddered, making room in my head for "the next level." "Insist" was a mild word for what Skinner could do when he wanted something.

"I'm sorry we couldn't tell you sooner." Baba ran his fingers through his hair, the way I often did. I noticed more gray than I had seen before. "That's not exactly true. Your disgust at Zola's attachment to Skinner was one of the best covers she had. You couldn't hide it from him, and we didn't want you to."

"By being furious, I helped protect her." I couldn't avoid a small, complicit smile that must have told my father I forgave everything. Nothing could please me more than a covert operation against Skinner, especially when I was part of the deception. "I'll stay furious as long as it takes. What more can I do?"

"Keep all of this to yourself, obviously. Go to Motembo tomorrow and become the best guide you can be."

"But I'm worried about Zola. Skinner is—"

"I know," he cut in. "I worry too. But this is her choice, her way to find meaning and support her man. Marks is looking out for her. There's no one better."

* * *

Mima and I spent the last evening before my departure at Swale's. After closing, Mrs. Swale wished me well, kissing me on both cheeks. I noticed unusual pallor in her skin and dark circles under her eyes, evidence of the strain she must have felt putting things right after the break-in. She seemed happy enough about my new career and prospects. Like Mima, though, she displayed a guarded optimism about the rest of it—about Mima eventually joining me in the safari business.

On that score, I was trying not to lose patience with both of them.

They acted as though Mima and Mima alone could help in the store. *Hire someone new, for cripes' sake!* Yet in view of my own misgivings about leaving Uncle Stash's workshop, I knew I would be wrong to underestimate the familial tug. I felt the chances were good that in Mima's absence, Donovan or Drew or both would step up to help—maybe divide their time between the workshop and the store. Although they were still very young, the boys had already demonstrated excellent work habits and an eagerness to learn. Even better, they were Swales.

After Mrs. Swale bid me goodbye and left for the day, Mima set out a picnic on the new carpet in the rear of the store. Candles on saucers cast a soft light over sliced chicken, potato salad, and a crusty loaf. She opened a bottle of shandy and poured the fizzy drink into two jam jars. "To our future." She tapped her glass against mine. "Wherever it takes us."

We talked about everything and nothing, feeling the weight of the long separation ahead. She said she hoped the rangers would catch the poachers who had stolen the Temik. I said I was sure they would. Skinner's name never came up. Keeping the revelations about Zola, Marks, and Skinner from her felt disloyal and wrong. But although I wanted to tell her everything, I felt equally powerful ties to the others who relied on me to remain silent. I said nothing.

After we cleared away the food, we held each other in the flickering light. Our farewell embrace became a tender, unhurried savoring of touch and taste. Each new intimacy, slow and deliberate, ignited sensations we wanted to prolong. While the candle guttered and died, our lovemaking gathered heat and intensity. I felt her currents matching my own, as if our bodies had been wired with common circuitry that sparked and flared and flamed out in sync. Thick-tongued from an urgent round of kissing, we murmured our love and our hopes for a shared life. In the small hours of the morning, we spooned together and fell asleep. She was still sleeping at dawn when I got up and quietly left the store.

I had expected an emotional farewell with Mima. I hadn't predicted the turbulence I would feel later that morning when I said goodbye to Zola. The more I thought about my sister's liaison with Skinner, the more precarious her situation seemed. She was walking a very thin line between autonomy and submission—a line Skinner would do his best to drag her across. I didn't trust him one bit, of course. I didn't trust that he really loved her or even knew what love was. Most of all, I worried about how he would react when he found out the truth.

Zola and I sat alone at the kitchen table. Hannie had thrown her arms around me in a farewell embrace before running off to school. Baba had gone out on an unknown errand, promising to return before I left. Teaspoon would arrive to pick me up within the hour. My packed duffel sat by the door.

"Your necklace is working too well," I said, tweaking the collar of crimson lucky bean seeds that circled Zola's neck. "Too much luck in love can be hazardous to your health." At close range I was struck anew by her beauty—her fine skin, her thick lashes, the elegance of her cheekbones. For a time, her supposed liaison with Skinner had, in my eyes, eclipsed her striking looks. She had, I believed, become so reckless and reprehensible, such a bloody traitor, that all I could see in her was my own disappointment.

Now her lovely eyes danced with pleasure at my renewed affection. "Sometimes I am afraid," she admitted. "But the hazards are worth it when you're saving elephants—an entire beloved species. Marks must have taught you that."

I nodded and shrugged, agreeing yet reluctant to include my sister in the ranks of humans endangered by murderous wildlife poachers.

She took a breath that powered her next confession. "Actually, deceiving you about Skinner has been the most difficult part."

"Harder than acting like his girlfriend? Come on."

"He's just a guy trying to feel important. His life hasn't been that easy."

"Don't ever make excuses for Skinner." Irritation hardened my words. "He's a dangerous, reckless, violent person. You must be very careful."

She touched my cheek. "I am careful. This has gone on for some time, you know. I'm almost alarmed by how smoothly I fool him."

"He wants to believe you." I hesitated, not wishing to stoke her fears yet worried she hadn't thought things through. I took a breath. "How is it going to end?"

She answered so readily that I knew she had considered the finale carefully. "Romances die all the time. When I've learned all I can from him, I'll drift away—lose interest, break it off. Then I'll wait a decent interval before turning up with Marks."

You really think Skinner will fall for that? Her confidence struck me as naive and dangerous. I was about to say so when I looked stepping through the door and, behind him, Marks. Th with themselves, like boys who'd pulled a fast one.

"Marks wanted to say goodbye." My father's gaz supposed he could see you too, while he's here."

My hero, mentor, and future brother-in-law headed straight for me. I sprang up and reached out to shake his hand or wrist or whatever, but he wrapped me in a hearty hug instead. "Greetings, my man."

My man. I felt a rush of feeling that swept aside my misgivings about Zola's breakup with Skinner, at least for the moment. The words pushed out fast. "You're marrying Zola!" As if he didn't already know. "I'm so relieved."

"That makes two of us—four, actually." His glance flitted to Baba and my sister. "We couldn't let you leave without full disclosure, for many reasons, including the fact that Zola hated deceiving you." He was looking at her now, the angular planes of his face softened with affection.

She went to him and touched her lips to his cheek. She looked radiant, happier than I had ever seen her. *Meant for each other,* Baba had said. I couldn't believe I hadn't figured this out for myself.

"I feel like an idiot. My own sister. How did you—how *do* you—keep everyone from seeing you together?"

They shared a quick, intimate laugh before Zola answered. "Aunt Letty and Uncle Stash have been very welcoming. I go in their front door. Marks comes in through the shop. We've gained kilos from Letty's cooking."

I shook my head as I swallowed another not entirely unpleasant dose of chagrin. Of course, Letty and Stash would help Zola, just as they had helped me for so many years. More subterfuge right under my nose. "I never saw you in the shop."

"That's because I only went when you weren't around. You would have figured out in a minute that I wasn't looking for a new dining table."

"I have a long-wave radio like the one Marks uses," Zola explained. "When he's within range, I can call him with information I get from Skinner. We use it to plan our dates too."

A small smile played on Marks's face. "I was in the workshop on the morning of your school exam—the day Skinner walked in and took the money from the cash box. I had left the door open for Zola."

"You were there? When I barfed?"

hid myself in the back, but yes. I could see and hear everything. When Skinner took it broadside and dropped the cash, I almost laughed out loud. I was sorry you were sick, though," he quickly added.

"Stash agreed not to make a big deal of it," Zola continued. "Better for the larger cause if Skinner felt himself in the clear—emboldened even."

So Stash, too, had known Skinner was under suspicion. That, and not forgetfulness, explained why he had taken the blame for the open door and said he didn't want to report the attempted theft. I sank down in my chair. Next, they were going to tell me Hannie was a double agent.

Marks drew Zola closer. "Skinner has been on our radar for years. Now, thanks to your brave and intelligent sister, he could lead us to the beating heart of the ivory trade."

I understood the plan, but the words sat like a heavy weight on my chest. *The beating heart of the ivory trade.* Elegant language for the leaders of a ruthless, militarized, multimillion-dollar criminal network. Very bad actors who used wildlife poaching to finance insurgent wars, drug and weapons trafficking, and human slavery. Those were the people my sister Zola was trying to find.

19

ON-JOB TRAINING AT MOTEMBO WAS truly on-the-job. The afternoon after Teaspoon and I drove into camp, I stood in a row with the rest of the staff to welcome twelve new guests. Like the other guides, I wore khaki pants and a matching shirt with two breast pockets and the regulation pointed collar. Jackson said I was allowed to wear my lucky bean seed bracelet, so I had that on too. My boots had looked so new that I had scuffed them in the dirt to more closely resemble Luke's well-worn footwear. As I smiled at the new arrivals, I was struck by the social power of uniforms. To the guests, I shared equal status with Luke and the others. I had never felt such pride in my clothes.

The guests included a British family of four and eight adults from Japan—the first Asians I had ever seen. As the twelve descended from the van that delivered them, Jaleen stepped forward with a tray of lemon scented hand towels. Teaspoon offered fresh fruit drinks. Jackson said a few words of welcome and introduced the staff, naming me—thrillingly—as a guide along with Luke, Newsom, and Kiki. Nodding toward Kiki, he added, "my wife." At that, Luke and I exchanged barely suppressed smiles.

The Brits were George and Margaret Haviland and their teenage daughters, Lacey and Slim. Both girls were closer to twelve than twenty, yet they no doubt raised the khaki fever flag in Jackson's ever-wary mind. They were flaxen haired and lithe, seemingly unaware of their power to disturb every male in sight as they stretched and yawned and redid the elastic bands that held their ponytails. I never found out where Lacey had gotten her name. But Slim was tall and built like a celery stalk, so I guess that explained hers.

I soon learned that the Haviland sisters were keen on photography—when the camera was pointed at them. At such times their usual somewhat blank expressions changed so suddenly to smiles of unfettered joy that I wondered if I had missed something. They licked their lips, posed, and grinned as though a jury of future husbands might evaluate their images. I was pleased to know that whatever happened under Luke's and my guidance, the girls' photos were likely to portray an exceptionally happy experience.

The visitors from Japan carried more serious photo equipment, with tripods and long lenses suitable for capturing wildlife in minute detail. Their English was heavy on courtesy and light on everything else, which might be why Jackson assigned Kiki and Newsom to them and gave the British family to Luke and me.

Minutes after we welcomed the Havilands, Luke put me in charge of the daughters. "Girl duty," he whispered. "All yours." I figured he had met enough visitors to anticipate something unusual, but I had no idea what that might be. I was about to learn that some guests required more effort than others.

While the newcomers settled in their tents, Luke and I headed for the parking area to ready our Land Cruiser for the afternoon game drive. We would guide the guests on two outings a day, the first from just after dawn until late morning and the second following afternoon tea, until dinner around eight. During the heat of midday, when all wise animals took shelter from the sun, everyone would remain in camp.

Luke handed me a list of supplies to check: fuel, oil, water, spanner, and other automotive necessities, plus a first aid kit and freshly provisioned camp box. He reminded me to bring my new rifle and long-range radio. Optional but useful items, he said, were a personal canteen and my journal for recording animal sightings and other field notes. The last item made me smile. I doubted Mr. Kitwick had ever imagined such an outdoorsy, adventurous future for his gift.

Inside the camp box I found another checklist specifying the items needed for "sundowners," which meant drinks. Based on the Havilands' preferences, today's sundowners required gin, tonic, and Diet Coke, an unfamiliar variety of my favorite beverage. I checked the labels on two cans and ticked "Diet Coke" off the list. A dozen bottles of water and a snack from Nate's kitchen, roasted groundnuts, completed the inventory.

We had been at work less than thirty minutes when a shrill whistle pierced the air. "Tent five," Luke said with a knowing look. "You won't need your rifle, but take it anyway."

I grabbed my firearm and ran. I found Lacey and Slim huddled together on the king-size bed I had built, shrouded in mosquito netting. A heap of delicate clothing on the hardwood floor resembled a pile of fruit bats. On the coffee table, the girls had arranged brightly colored leaves and random bits of foliage they must have collected outside. A quick survey told me that none of the species caused blisters, infection, or death. Less indigenous doodads crowded the nightstands: pink nail polish, a hair band, sunglasses, tiny bottles of lotion and perfume, and a diary with a cat on the cover. I had never imagined so many foreign objects, much less colorful girlie clutter, in the tents Stash and I had furnished with so much care.

Slim still had the alarm whistle pinched between her lips. Lacey was gripping a can of insect repellant aimed at the canvas wall. "Tarantula!" she shouted, pointing to a large, harmless spider.

I put down the rifle. Under the girls' watchful stare, I eyed the blameless, cowering arachnid. "This is a black house spider. Quite timid. He's far more interested in small insects than in you."

The girls gasped and mewled as I coaxed the creature into a drinking glass. It was a burly specimen, but nothing compared to the palm-sized spiders Zola regularly shooed from our house. I covered the glass with a tissue and carried it outside, thinking how different these girls were from the females I knew at home. I had once watched Mima flick away a scorpion without a blink.

Less than an hour later, the whistle blew again. This time, Slim had fried her "travel" hair dryer—an appliance designed for 110 to 120 volts—by plugging it into the camp's higher-voltage outlet. Apparently, no one had told her that the current in Africa was the same as at home in Great Britain. The ensuing smoke and sparks appeared to worry her less than the loss of an essential grooming tool.

"Now what do we do?" She turned to me, sodden and forlorn.

Both girls were dabbing towels at their long, wet hair. They wore bathrobes with not much on underneath, as far as I could tell. I tried to avert my eyes. Although the situation seemed ridiculous to me, the sisters appeared quite undone by the crisis.

I cleared my throat. "If you sit in the chairs on the deck, the hot breeze will dry your hair quite reliably," I said, managing to keep a straight face.

"What about the lions?" Lacey asked, peering through the door.

"At this time of day, the animals are all asleep," I replied, stretching the truth only a little. This seemed to reassure them.

Afternoon tea brought the camp together again a couple of hours later. Teaspoon had laid the buffet with tea paraphernalia and one of Nate's generously iced layer cakes. The Japanese guests arrived at precisely three thirty, all eight carrying their excellent cameras and bulging camera bags. They bowed and smiled. Jaleen must have noticed their polite confusion about local tea-serving customs because she quickly stepped in to pour.

The group settled together in a corner of the seating area, chatting softly in Japanese. In lieu of speaking, Jaleen did a good job of returning their smiles and head bobs. Kiki and Newsom lingered nearby in case anyone wanted to ask a question or otherwise engage in conversation. With this congenial but self-contained group, conversation in English seemed unlikely.

Margaret and George Haviland hurried in next. They looked fresh and eager. It crossed my mind that the couple might be happy to have discovered a thick stand of trees between their tent and their daughters'. Serious-looking binoculars hung from their necks. George carried a *Birds of Africa* guidebook bristling with bookmarks. When they had settled at a table with tea and cake, Luke complimented them on their gear.

"You're interested in birds, I see."

"We are," Margaret answered. "I hope to spot a carmine bee eater, a Marabou stork, and …" She stopped, flushed. "So many, really." She shared a look with her husband. "Our daughters are less keen, I'm afraid."

George cast an annoyed look toward the path. "Where *are* they?"

"Bones will fetch them," Luke said, checking his watch. A little over two hours of daylight remained. After that the game drive would continue in the dark with a handheld spotlight. Birding would be finished until the following morning.

I was turning to go when Lacey and Slim sauntered up the path, fluffing their shiny, dry hair.

"*Dios mío*," Luke said under his breath.

The girls were dressed in skimpy tops and short shorts. They both wore flip-flops that resembled platters of pink-tipped marzipan toes. Lacey had pinned a thick mess of curls on top of her head with a bright red clip. Slim wore what looked like a stretchy yellow bandage around her chest. Below the bandage was an acre of pale midriff and a blue butterfly tattoo.

I must have been staring because Luke palmed my cheek to turn my face toward his. "Go get sunblock, insect repellant, extra ponchos, extra hats, and a blanket. Put them in the Cruiser."

I rushed off, wondering why he hadn't told the girls to go back to their tents and dress more appropriately. Didn't Lacey and Slim understand they were going for a four-hour, open-air drive through the African bush? Apparently, correcting guests was prohibited, even when they acted like morons. I realized I had a lot to learn about the finer points of guiding.

* * *

Straight out of camp, a cheetah stepped across our path. Luke pressed on the brake. Seeing a cheetah up close was an uncommon experience, rarely accomplished without an impressive show of bushcraft by a persevering guide. I suspected Luke felt irritated by the almost zoo-like ease of the encounter.

Behind me, Slim uttered little bat-like squeals of excitement. Lacey shouted, "Ooh! A baby leopard!" and jumped to her feet.

Luke killed the engine. "It's a cheetah. Please sit down."

I noted the command, polite yet firm. Lacey lowered herself to the edge of the seat she shared with Slim. On the upper bench, Margaret and George had raised their binoculars and quickly dropped them. Now they sat forward, studying the cheetah with rapt attention. Their focus and demeanor suggested a captivating interest, the exact response guides hoped to inspire. I couldn't believe our luck, minutes out of camp.

"This is a male," Luke said. He had shifted his body a half turn toward the passengers and casually rested an elbow on the seat back. But his eyes never left the cheetah. His rifle was mounted under the dashboard, inches from his hands. His voice stayed low and even. "He has a full stomach. Can you see? He won't be hunting today."

As Luke spoke, the cheetah paused and took note of the large, diesel-smelling object that had interrupted his walk.

The girls squealed almost in unison. "It's looking at us!" Lacey slid sideways into Slim, putting a few more centimeters between herself and the fastest cat on the planet, now about three meters off our right front tire.

"If we sit still and stay quiet, he'll lose interest," Luke said.

The girls froze—a commendable response. I hoped they remembered to breathe.

Luke's posture, his steady voice, and everything about him projected the calm he hoped to instill in our passengers. Shouting, standing, and gesturing broadly not only ruined the serenity of the setting but also alerted and scattered the wildlife we wanted to observe. Worse, attention-getting behavior so close to an unpredictable creature could spark its curiosity or even its hunting instinct.

"See the black marks beneath his eyes? A leopard doesn't have those. It has a band of spots around the neck. So we say 'the cheetah weeps for the leopard's necklace.'"

I noted the way Luke took in and corrected Lacey's misperception without implying she was stupid or ignorant. Actually, cheetahs and leopards possessed entirely different head shapes, body types, and markings. But to an unschooled eye, I supposed they could look alike. My admiration for Luke was growing by the minute.

The cheetah soon had had enough of us and disappeared in the grass. Luke drove on, pointing out a fish eagle cruising overhead and a hornbill pecking in the dust. Margaret got busy checking birds off a list.

"Is that a Bradfield's hornbill or a crowned?" she called from the back.

Luke slowed the Cruiser and nodded toward me.

I cleared my throat. "A Bradfield's. The head is paler brown, and it has a smaller, orangier beak."

"I see," she answered, studying the guidebook George was holding open. "There are, um …" She paused. "Seven different hornbills. Are they all found here?"

"The gray and the yellow-billed are most common here."

"What about Damaras?" she asked, studying the book. "Might we see those?"

Behind me Slim let out a loud, exasperated sigh.

I shook my head. "Damaras live in drier regions."

Luke rewarded me with a nod and a polite revving of the engine that ended the inquiries. I remembered Marks's admonition to keep in mind the interests of everyone in the group. Avid birders could easily monopolize the commentary because bird species were abundant in Africa, and they were everywhere.

Luke shifted into first gear and stepped on the gas. The Cruiser shot forward. For the next several minutes we bounced and heaved across the chalky hardpan, nosing into dried-out rivulets and up steep, tilting dune slopes. I glanced back to see Lacey and Slim sitting forward, gripping the rail, boredom cured as we rocketed along. The butterfly on Slim's midsection hovered an arm's length from my face. She flashed me a grin and pushed up the little round sunglasses that had slipped down her nose.

I felt the heat of a blush rise in my cheeks. I turned to face the front, mortified, hoping she hadn't noticed. At that moment, Luke sped up a rise that dropped off suddenly, sending us airborne for a fraction of a second. High-pitched whoops accompanied our landing on flat, grassy turf. Although I doubted liftoff was a sanctioned driving technique, I silently thanked Luke for the timely distraction.

20

WHILE FENDING OFF TEENAGE BOREDOM, Luke also put a good distance between us and the other vehicles. At a little after four o'clock, Newsom, Kiki, and we had headed in different directions in three Cruisers, four guests to a ride. The guides long ago had divvied up the reserve into three sectors, each measuring in the tens of thousands of acres. By keeping to one sector and rotating each time out, we introduced guests to new terrain and, frequently, different species on every foray. Equally important, we avoided the sight and sounds of other vehicles.

I learned right away that solo tracking was a point of pride at Motembo. Unlike guides at many camps, ours worked independently. They tracked and spotted on their own and never radioed colleagues to join a sighting, not even a five-star one such as lions at a kill or the increasingly rare phenomenon of two nearly extinct rhinos jousting for dominance.

The practice required the skill to find and follow spoor in all conditions, sometimes over great distances. The best guides turned the hunt into an adventure by pointing out the basics of tracking—how to distinguish old and recent prints, read scat and broken branches, and figure out an animal's direction of travel and likely whereabouts. Some guests found the hunt even more thrilling than the sighting at its end.

On most days the herbivores—elephants, giraffes, zebras, a dozen species of antelope, and more—could be found quite easily on the open plain. Crocodiles and hippos occupied known stretches of the river. A guide's familiarity with the terrain and its animal residents came into play here. No elephants in sight? Let's try the water hole. None there? The marula grove. Has the herd moved to another sector? Let's look for tracks. And so on. The guides had given names to familiar stretches of wilderness: Little Serengeti, Grassy Reach, RIP Gulch.

For our first outing with the Havilands, Luke's and my sector included territory I had crossed while driving to camp six months earlier. We passed a familiar thornberry thicket and a pair of pointy termite mounds I recognized. I thought we might be going toward Three Flat Rocks and the lion pride that hung out there. But Luke skirted the boxy boulders and headed straight for the river.

"You're skipping the Rocks?" If I leaned toward him, we could talk over the noise of the engine with little chance of being understood by the passengers in back.

"We've already seen a cheetah, so let's save the lion hunt for later. We need to manage expectations, Bones. If we find lions now, the guests will expect a bloodthirsty cat every five minutes." He gestured toward the river. "We'll go look for waterbirds while it's still light."

I sat back in my seat. Margaret and George, at least, would be thrilled.

The sun was descending, but its heat and burn potential remained intense. I retrieved hats and a tube of sunblock from the trough next to my seat. Holding them out for Lacey and Slim, I was careful where I looked. The blue butterfly took up a monstrous portion of my peripheral vision. Slim accepted the sunblock and a hat. Lacey declined the hat but put out her hand for a generous squirt of lotion.

Behind them, Margaret looked my way and shrugged as if to say, *They don't listen to me.* She mouthed the words "thank you." I suspected she had given up trying to direct her daughters or at least decided to choose her battles. George apparently avoided family dramas as much as possible. He sat back in his seat, squinting through his binoculars at who knows what.

In the side mirror I discovered a pretty good view of the girls behind me. Slim had perched the hat on her head at a jaunty angle without using the chin strap. Lacey's head remained bare except for the shiny crimson clip. They were rubbing sunblock into their pasty skin, unaware of my gaze. Observing such an intimate, unguarded moment felt embarrassing and wrong, so I picked up my binoculars, George-like, as a diversion. A moment later we crested a grassy berm and came upon a trio of warthogs rooting in the soil.

"Pigs!" Lacey jumped up and sat down again.

"Warthogs," Luke responded, stepping on the brake. "The only pig species adapted to grazing. These three are digging for tubers and roots, the occasional delicious worm. Subterranean delicacies."

"Ewww."

"Blech."

The sighting was brief because the warthogs preferred to dine alone. They raised their heads to glare at us, turned heel, and trotted off with their shoestring tails pointed skyward.

"Cuuuuute!" Slim aimed her camera at the three round black bottoms rapidly receding in the distance. Not a great shot, she must have decided, because she swung around to photograph Lacey instead. "Say cheetah!"

"Cheetah!"

Luke turned the key in the ignition, looking grim.

"Cheetah!"

"Oops! We hit a bump. Say it again."

"Cheetah!"

The girls fell into fits of laughter. The hilarity continued as we pitched over the rough terrain. George told them to pipe down. They did, for a minute or two, until the hat I had given Slim flew off and sailed into the grass.

"Stop! The hat!" she yelled.

Luke hit the brake. I leapt to the ground, checking right and left for man-eating predators. When I jogged back with the hat in my hand, Luke shot me a look that said, *Isn't this fun?*

We were approaching the river when a tall black ostrich wandered out from behind a bush. Seeing us, the giant bird froze midstride. Luke drew within a Cruiser length. The girls, eye-to-eye with an eight-foot creature standing stiff as a fencepost, at last fell silent.

"The common ostrich. Male." Luke looked past the girls to address Margaret and George. "This bird is not particularly intelligent. He thinks he's invisible."

"Because he's not moving?" Lacey was sliding into Slim again, wary of a dark, glassy eye fixed on her.

Luke shrugged. "His brain is smaller than his eyeball."

"Ridic!" Slim exclaimed.

"How come he doesn't get eaten?" Margaret asked.

"He has excellent vision." Luke pointed toward a distant copse of marulas. "This ostrich could spot a lion in those trees, or even a snake on a branch. Plenty of time to run away."

"Snake?" Lacey shrieked. "Gack! I hate snakes. Keep me away from there."

"Will do," Luke said, starting the engine. The odds were good that we were within a stone's throw of a snake at that very moment—in fact, at almost all times. Luke would not mention this, I was pretty sure.

A few minutes later, we reached the fringe of trees that marked the river. Luke steered under a dense roof of intertwining strangler figs and down a gentle slope. After the heat on the plain, the deep, moist shade felt like a dip in spring water. The Cruiser crashed through thickets of foliage that made everyone duck and lean toward the center. The girls shrieked a few times at the novelty of knocking over bushes and slender trees that then sprang up behind us. Before long we nosed into an opening that gave way to a panoramic view of the main channel and its slow-moving current. The wide, sandy shore I had previously used as a road stretched before us. But on my initial visit I had failed to appreciate the vibrant birdlife.

Margaret quickly checked off black-winged stilt, glossy ibis, and curlew sandpiper. A flock of chittering red-billed queleas swooped in for a drink. We saw a number of waders, gulls, and terns. In a few minutes we had identified a dozen different species.

Even Lacey and Slim were paying attention now. When Lacey asked to borrow Margaret's binoculars, I handed her mine. She adjusted the focus and surveyed the scene. "I'm looking for snakes," she finally said. "I hope I don't see one."

I hoped so too. Most particularly, I hoped she never laid eyes on a certain long, green reptile that made its home in the thatched roof at Motembo.

When we had spotted and named every bird on the scene, we relocated to a new vantage point, one I recognized from my adventure in the mud. Caper bushes fringed the riverbanks. Date palms dense with fronds leaned toward the water. Luke parked the Cruiser and wasted no time identifying a saddle-billed stork and a pair of little grebes.

I scanned the foliage lining the banks, hoping to spot animals of greater interest to Lacey and Slim. A short distance upstream, I spied a structure that took me by surprise: a hunting blind partially covered in vines. Surprise quickly gave way to gratitude as I recalled my rescue at the hands of Good Sam and his sons. Jackson had said the men maintained a blind on the river.

They hunted to feed their families, he had told me—for the pot only and only when visitors were absent.

A troop of vervet monkeys erupted in excited chatter. I looked up to see a dozen monkeys vaulting toward us.

"Chimps!" Lacey announced, pointing her camera skyward.

"Monkeys," Luke said. "Vervet monkeys."

In short order, the cheekiest ones among them leapt into the date palm leaning over the Cruiser. They jumped and swung, jockeying for a good view of the humans parked below. A quick, bright-eyed juvenile achieved a perch directly over Lacey's head. The monkey appeared particularly interested in the shiny red clip in her hair.

"Time to go," I said, pointing upward. Luke, whose hand was already on the ignition, had come to the same conclusion. Then two things happened at once: the engine roared to life, and the monkey urinated. It was only a slight dribble, but as I turned in my seat, I braced for all hell to break loose.

Slim's eyes went as wide as the O of her mouth. Margaret, admirably calm, pulled a tissue from her pocket. George sat back and bit his lip.

But Lacey appeared unaware of the droplets glistening in her crown of hair. Looking at Slim, she said, "What's wrong with you?"

A loud, snorting guffaw rendered Slim momentarily speechless. She waved a finger at the top of Lacey's head. Choking with laughter, she finally managed, "He got you."

Baffled, Lacey touched her hair. Her expression shaded from confusion to disgust to horror as she examined her fingers and brought them to her nose. "What …?" She cast a look back at the spot we had hastily vacated. "Monkey pee? Flipping *monkey pee?*"

"Don't worry," I said. "Only a trickle. From a very small monkey."

"Ewww! Ebola!" Tears pooled in her wide, frightened eyes. With her contaminated hand suspended in the air, she sat rigidly upright, paralyzed by the possible consequence of tilting her head.

"She's totally skeeved out," Slim informed me, patting her sister's knee.

"Really, Lacey, you'll be fine." I had never addressed any of the Havilands by their given name. This seemed to get her attention. She blinked.

"In a minute we'll stop for sundowners and clean it off. You'll be good as new." I was making this up, of course. I had no experience with monkey pee on the hair or skin. But it was probably not a death sentence. Luke seemed cool about it, so I guessed I was on the right track.

While Margaret patted Lacey's head with a tissue, we sped toward the baobab tree, the same one I had explored on my way to Motembo. This struck me as an excellent choice for drinks at sunset and maybe a soothing antidote to Lacey's unfortunate experience.

The tree itself was phenomenal—gigantic, ancient, rare. Its huge trunk offered privacy to guests who might need to pick a flower or kick a tire, with the added surprise of a hollow interior. The Havilands, three of them at least, could relax with their beverages while taking in a panoramic view of the sunset. If luck came our way, a Technicolor horizon might silhouette an elephant family or a pair of giraffes ambling across the plain.

As we made our approach, Lacey still hadn't moved except to perfect the downward curve of her frown. Her attitude required adjusting, in my opinion. So I tried a diversion. "The baobab tree is the *world's largest succulent*," I said, puffing up the modifiers as if I were imparting the world's most amazing fact. "The tree before you is at least *a hundred years old.*"

Margaret and George looked suitably impressed. Even Slim sat up and squinted at the behemoth rising from the plain. Lacey leaned stiffly toward me, so close I could feel her breath on my ear. "I don't give a rat's butt about the tree. What about the freakload of pee on my head?"

I bit the inside of my cheek to keep from laughing. The girl had backbone, after all. I gestured for her to come closer. "Some people think monkey pee is good luck. Good luck in love and, uh, school."

She looked at me.

I nodded. "You can buy it in bottles, like perfume. Very expensive." I put a finger to my lips—our little secret. In the rearview mirror I watched her peer at her hand. Whether or not she believed me, the frown had disappeared.

A moment later we rolled to a halt beneath the baobab's weirdly branching limbs. Luke made a show of scanning the boughs overhead. Then he killed the engine and stepped out. "Wait here."

While he made his way around the tree, scouting for animals, I retrieved a handful of disinfectant wipes from the first aid kit and handed them to Lacey. "Monkey pee erasers. We always carry these."

Her face softened, as if a smile might be forthcoming.

I leaned in. "They don't erase the good luck."

As expected, the temperature plunged along with the setting sun. And as expected, the girls' clothing proved wholly inadequate. Unlike their more suitably dressed parents, Lacey and Slim never left the Cruiser during sundowners. They did not go to pick a flower or view the opening in the hollow tree, not even after Margaret returned proclaiming its wonders. They sat like two brown lumps bundled in ponchos and a blanket, peering at the flaming sky. Occasionally, a pale hand snaked out to lift a can of Diet Coke to thin, bluish lips. Faced with a new way to die, Lacey shivered noisily, tapping her flip-flops against the metal floorboard. By the time darkness fell, Luke had decided the fun was over. With permission from Margaret and George, he cut the drive short and headed straight back to camp.

21

As planned, the Havilands departed after four nights, a fairly typical length of stay. Thinking back, I felt grateful to the British family for their excellent introduction to guiding. In Margaret and George I had met engaged, inquisitive travelers whose special interest in birds sharpened my own avian skills and my comfort using a guidebook as backup. In Lacey and Slim I had met distracted, fearful, hapless adolescents who required extra attention, patience, and diplomacy.

I recorded in my journal the animals we spotted during the Havilands' visit. Fortunately, Motembo's green boomslang was not among them. The list included close to a hundred bird species. To Luke's credit, we also racked up the Big Five: elephant, Cape buffalo, leopard, lion, and rhinoceros. His tracking skills plus his knowledge of every hectare in our vicinity had never failed to result in the sighting we wanted. Slim, unimpressed, grumbled that we hadn't seen a tiger. I informed her that seeing a tiger would require a very long drive, all the way to Asia.

Four days in charge of Lacey and Slim had required me to call upon a storehouse of wit and practical skill. I got to practice shower drain routing, poisonous plant identification, first aid, and card tricks. Most important, girl duty taught me that foreigners, just like the people I had known at home, respond gratefully to kindness and respect—at all hours of the day and night. (A hippo honk plus a skeeved-out girl had equaled a whistle call at 3:00 a.m.) After a particularly harrowing encounter with a monitor lizard, Lacey had thrown her arms around me and pressed her lips to my cheek. This felt more like an assault than a kiss, but I wasn't complaining.

On the morning of the Havilands' departure, the girls took numerous photos of themselves snuggled up against Luke and me. Smiling along with them wasn't difficult. The girls could be exasperating, but they were harmless and predictable. I felt great relief that I had made it through my first guiding experience without any major goof-ups. I had managed to identify all the birds Margaret and George spotted, sometimes before Luke did. The gin and tonics I mixed for sundowners won special cheers. (I unknowingly poured in twice as much gin as required.) I learned to maintain guide-like cool in the face of girlie transgressions, bare skin, and a butterfly tattoo. Khaki fever never broke out of the temperate zone.

My final duty was to accompany Luke and the Havilands on the drive to the airstrip. As the family climbed aboard a Cessna for the flight to their next camp, Luke and I stood next to the Cruiser, waving goodbye. "Well done, Bones," he said. "Now you can handle anything."

His approval boosted my confidence, as he knew it would. But I would soon learn that girl duty barely cracked the surface of things a guide needed to handle.

The Japanese left that day too. When the entire camp emptied all at once, a frenzy of activity erupted in every quarter. As soon as the guests vacated their tents, Jaleen and her helper moved in to ready the accommodations for the next occupants. Extra-thick towels and silky cotton sheets thudded in the dryers. Nate turned up the volume in the kitchen. His voice and laughter rang out amid the clang of metal, the rattle of glassware, and the groaning and thumping that accompanied weighty deliveries. Teaspoon got busy scrubbing the pavilion and polishing the already gleaming lacquer that armored the bar. Kiki caught up with paperwork and the scheduling of future guests. I joined the other guides in vehicle maintenance and forays into the bush to clear brush, scout for animals, and plan promising routes for the game drives ahead. The camp turned over at a hectic pace—cleaned, resupplied, and ready for new visitors in less than a day.

Over the next several weeks, a steady stream of guests flowed in and out of camp. We hosted singles, couples, and groups; English speakers and non-English speakers; ecotourists, journalists, honeymooners, families, and everyday travelers from all over the world.

Many of our guests were glossy with wealth and accomplishment, as solid and self-contained as planets. Yet they often surprised me with their friendliness and approachability. Others, strenuously rumpled and outdoorsy, proved skittish and difficult to please. We welcomed barrel-sized individuals whose bellies spilled over their belts, as well as the intensely aerobicized who missed their daily runs. These latter guests usually worked off excess energy on yoga mats in the pavilion. Some of our visitors had unhealthy relationships with alcohol or drugs, some with each other.

The ditzy-looking woman who couldn't find her tent turned out to be a renowned theoretical mathematician. The white-haired gent who walked with a limp was a mountaineer who had summited Annapurna. As they poured out of the vehicles that delivered them, occasionally wearing baseball caps emblazoned with the name of a tour company, we never knew what to expect.

At first I felt shy around these visitors—people so worldly, with college degrees and passports stamped at borders all over the globe. Gradually, I came to realize that the visitors found me equally interesting and exotic. Though I learned the value of listening well, I also learned to hold my own in conversations, drawing upon knowledge and experiences they seemed eager to hear. With every passing week as a guide trainee, I grew more self-assured.

Local people visited the camp too. I formally met Good Sam's sons, a modest lot who shrugged off my gratitude for winching me out of the mud. Newsom's wife came by, white-haired and smiley, with elegant, upright posture that suggested a history of balancing burdens on her head. The most surprising person I met was a friend of Jackson's, a professional wildlife photographer who stopped at Motembo on his way to photograph game. The man was small and wiry, with slicked-back hair and a gravelly voice. He was dressed from head to toe in denim except for the flashy red jewel that sparkled on his pinky finger.

Jackson made the introduction. "Bones, this is Ruby."

I blinked. "Ruby? Of Ruby's Amazing Safaris?"

"The same," Ruby said, pumping my hand. "You've seen my calendars?"

* * *

My days as a guide trainee began before dawn and ended after we escorted the last guests from the campfire to their tents, often well past midnight. The work absorbed, exhilarated, and exhausted me. I slept as hard as I worked, frequently falling into bed fully clothed.

Thoughts of home and my family, even my worries about Zola and Skinner, seldom penetrated the more immediate priorities that crowded my head. Mima's image frequently flashed before me, though—her heart-stopping smile, the shine of her hair, the two of us entwined and breathless. In the press of work, those sweet memories flared and died like fireworks melting in the sky.

But Zola and Skinner had vanished almost completely from my mind. In the brief moments they reappeared, I felt a rush of guilt mixed with something akin to disbelief. How could I so abruptly put aside concerns that had consumed me only a few weeks earlier, concerns that could still overwhelm me if I let them?

Baba must have guessed that the dramas playing out at home would recede in the face of my training at Motembo, at least in the beginning. "Become the best guide you can be," he had said. I was working hard to follow his advice. But I hadn't realized how thoroughly guide training would refocus my attention.

In one way, though, I remained fully involved with my family's current entanglements. Not a day went by that I didn't think about animal poachers and the devastation they caused. The crushing reality of poaching rode in the Cruiser with Luke and me on every game drive, every day.

Only three rhinoceroses were known to exist in the vast reserve surrounding Motembo. They were black rhinos, coveted for their horns and in grave danger of extinction. A concerted effort to save and breed their white rhino cousins in heavily guarded reserves had rescued that species from annihilation. A similar concern for black rhinos had yet to ensure the animals' survival. As Luke and I toured Motembo's sectors, we considered ourselves lucky to see even one. When we did, we usually spotted a pair of armed rangers, Marks's men, standing in the shadows.

Most of the rhino bodyguards were local residents dressed in various combinations of official and unofficial ranger clothing, looking the worse for wear. They gripped assorted, humble weapons that could do little to deter paramilitaries armed with grenades and automatic rifles. At best, the rangers might keep away desperate locals—impoverished men not unlike themselves, looking to lift their families from a tenuous, barebones existence. Each time I saw the rangers posed watchfully near an animal, I was struck anew by the difficulty of their jobs, the paltry funds supporting them, and the exceptional courage the work required.

Magnificent elephant herds still roamed our reserve, although Luke said fewer came through than in the past. We were acutely attuned to the fact that ivory poaching claimed tens of thousands of African elephants every year, hundreds a day. Countless elephants that once might have crossed our territory had been erased from the face of the earth. All that remained of them was ivory. Ivory stacked like firewood in warehouses. Ivory fashioned into trinkets, whatnots, and doodads. Ivory carved into intricate works of art and sold for millions in legal and black markets across the globe.

The ongoing depletion of African elephants made Motembo's herds all the more precious and wonderful. The elephant families Luke and I encountered included enough old tuskers to excite an army of ivory traffickers. Fortunately, the ravages of the trade had so far spared our bonded groups—the families, herds, and affiliated elephant kin that awed and enchanted our guests. With no recollection of hunters or poachers seared into their memory-rich souls, the herds were wary but approachable. They tolerated humans to a remarkable degree, provided we demonstrated the proper respect.

On nearly every outing, Luke and I treated our passengers to a lengthy, hushed elephant visitation. We were careful to maintain a decorous distance between the Cruiser and the herd, particularly when calves were present. We always approached the animals at an angle and turned the vehicle politely broadside before stopping. We cautioned our passengers to sit quietly in place, which was rarely a problem with at least one six-ton goliath eyeballing us at close range. At the first sign of agitation or displeasure among the animals, we fired the engine and backed away. A stomped foot, bugle call, or mock charge with flared ears all meant "time to go!"

I came to know the elephants we met day after day, just as I had identified individual elephants near my village—the watchful matriarch with the ragged tail; the rowdy juvenile, already with a cracked tusk; the curious auntie; the nervous cousin with her eyes fixed on us as she pretended to feed, grass trailing from her mouth. Each herd had its individual characters, yet all herds were similar in the familial behaviors that knit them together.

I never tired of introducing guests to these intelligent, social, closely bonded creatures. At first, conscious of my role as trainee, I commented sparingly. But soon Luke's nod became routine, and I evolved into the guide who talked about elephants.

"Here you see an older female, her sisters, their adult daughters, and all their offspring. They live together and share infant care and child rearing."

I spoke just above a whisper. If I sensed the guests wanted more, I would continue. "The oldest female carries a deep store of knowledge essential for the herd's survival. She decides where the family will go and how long they will stay. She's the chief protector, the prime holder of memory, the navigator …"

I knew when to shut up too because the elephants themselves held us in thrall. Their beguiling ways, their gentle nudges and low rumblings, their layered networks and special affinities never failed to captivate. Frequently, an inquisitive or rascally individual ventured almost within reach. The matriarch would notice, of course, and, depending on her assessment of the situation, intervene or not. If she felt comfortable with us, she might even participate in a closer inspection. Often enough, a sniffing, exploring elephant trunk touched one of us on the head or shoulder, light as a wisp.

As much as I loved lingering near the herds, I always worried when the lead elephant showed a relaxed attitude toward humans. Aged matriarchs with exceptionally long tusks were prime targets for poaching. Throughout Africa, these crucial females were being killed off at earlier and earlier ages, leaving the next female in line, if she survived, too young and unprepared to step into the leadership role.

The severe disorientation that follows the death of a matriarch can lead to the collapse of an entire herd. Calves become orphans. Young females are too traumatized to nurture or breed. No one remembers the location of the water hole or where to find the marula trees and their delicious fruit. Surviving elephants carry horrific memories that render them fearful and sometimes aggressive toward humans and their crops. Retaliatory hunting begins, and the cycle starts again.

Echoes of my mother's death made the plight of the elephants all the more poignant. My own family had been lucky. We hadn't collapsed without Mama because Zola, still in her teens, had stepped up quite capably to care for us.

As I studied the lives of elephants, Marks, too, was never far from my mind. Antipoaching efforts and the dangers they entailed formed a subtext in my life as a guide. I frequently wondered where Marks might be at a given moment. I worried for his safety. At the same time, I wished to hear he was closing in on the ruthless overseers who controlled the ivory trade. I kept my radio close at hand in case his patrol ventured within range of camp or our vehicle out in the bush. But so far I had heard nothing.

I learned that radio protocol in the bush discouraged nonessential communications, especially between the alpha ranger and a guide trainee. Jackson and Luke occasionally heard from Marks. They passed on what he said, mostly official business concerning tire tracks, campfires, or other signs of unusual activity in our area. From time to time, he reported the capture of a poacher or a group of poachers working together some distance from us—small-scale, unaffiliated opportunists for the most part. The oddly sober high fives and campfire toasts that followed told me a lot about my colleagues' concern for Marks and the risks even a minor success represented. I imagined they had reacted with similar gravity to news of poachers caught by their late hero, Bongani Baas.

As the weeks flew by, Motembo felt increasingly like home. The camp's tightly bonded community had welcomed me warmly, and now its members had become as familiar and important to me as people I had known for years. My relationship with Luke differed little from my long friendship with Roop. I sorely missed Mima but found consolation in the thriving partnerships I saw between Jackson and Kiki and between Luke and Jaleen. I couldn't wait to share a life and a tent with the woman who had already set up camp in the reaches of my heart. As much as I loved Motembo, Mima's absence was a privation I felt every day.

One afternoon, Chiddy arrived with deliveries for the kitchen and a letter. "Helloooooooo, Bonesy," he called, rushing his great weight toward me. With a flourish he handed over a thick envelope.

My heart did backflips when I saw the handwriting on the front.

"I bring you love and kisses from your fine, fine girlfriend." The sparkle in his eye almost outshone the diamond in his earlobe. "She is looking very well, you know." He quickly added, "For someone who is lonesome and achy."

The camp had emptied of guests that morning. My assignment for the day was to drive tools and lengths of wood to the bridge at Motembo's entrance and make repairs as needed. I stuck the letter in my shirt pocket and almost ran to the Cruiser, glad for the chance to be alone. I set off, and once I was near the bridge, I parked in the shade and opened the envelope.

Dear Bonesy,

Surprise! Chiddy came by for supplies and offered to deliver a letter to you. He's leaving for Motembo in the morning. I wish I could go too! I think about you all the time—how your training is going, whether you're happy and well. Do you still like the people there? Are you meeting visitors from all over the world? You must have so many stories! Chiddy said he plans to stay overnight in camp. Maybe you'll have time to write back? I hope so.

Everyone here misses you. Especially me.

Roop and Granny Nobbs came into the store this week. Granny was using a new walker with wheels and a basket for groceries. Roop told me Mrs. Dubin at the bank managed the legal process for Granny to take possession of Grandpa Nobbs's safe-deposit box. When Granny opened the box, she found the will he had written leaving everything to her, plus some money. Roop didn't say how much, but he did say Grandpa Nobbs won more at the cockfights than anyone ever guessed. He looked pretty happy—Roop, that is. His chicken business is growing. Mother and I are thinking about selling chicken parts in the store as soon as we get a new fridge.

Oh, Roop said fishing has been lousy without you.

I've seen Zola a few times. Unfortunately, she's always with Skinner. After what you told Mother and me, I don't like him at all. Did you know he wears a lucky bean seed bracelet like yours, only thicker? At least eight strands, wide as a cuff. Maybe he's your sister's project, like she's trying to reform him or something. Good luck with that is all I can say.

Donovan and Drew still go to your uncle's shop most afternoons after school. They work in the store on Saturdays. Stash has taken on a few more carpentry students. The workshop is buzzing. When your Aunt Letty came in one day and asked how I was, I told her very busy! I must have mentioned something about needing more help in the store because, much to my surprise, she returned the next morning and said "when can I start?" Now she sits at the cash register, and I'm free to do everything else. The customers love her, of course. I'm very grateful for her help. (Between you and me, I think she has another motive—making sure the twins aren't pressed into service before they finish high school.)

By the way, we keep the Temik behind the counter now. That way we can see who buys it, and how much. Our new doors and locks should help prevent thieves from breaking in. I'm still haunted by the thought of poisoned water holes and poisoned animals. Are you seeing herds of elephants, alive and well? I hope you are.

I've saved the not-so-good news for last. I'm sorry to tell you my mother isn't well. She tires easily and gets winded doing the slightest thing. When she comes to the store, she only lasts a couple of hours, and even that's a struggle. You can see why I'm so grateful to your aunt. I'm really worried about my mother. We're going to see another doctor next week.

I hope you won't be too disappointed if you and I have to delay our plans. Maybe the doctors will know what to do, and Mother will be back to normal soon. That's what I'm hoping, of course. But I think we both should be prepared in case my family needs me here and I can't join you at Motembo for a while.

When are you coming home for a visit? Soon, I hope. In the meantime, please remember we all love you and miss you. Me most of all.

Your Mima

I reread the part about Mrs. Swale as if the words might hold a different meaning the second time around. They didn't, of course. Yet the truth of them remained inert on the page, unprocessed. I couldn't believe Mima's mother was ill. She had always seemed so sturdy and dependable, a fixture in the grocery store. I wondered if Mima could be mistaken about the symptoms or their severity. Mrs. Swale worked hard; maybe she needed a vacation.

I shifted in my seat and swatted away a fly, resisting the tendrils of despair that threatened to creep in and overtake my mood. If Mima was correct, her mother's illness held implications I didn't want to think about, at least not yet.

I found only slightly better news in Skinner's continued ignorance of the deceptions simmering around him. Zola's deceit still clenched my stomach with worry. My sister's confidence in her exit strategy struck me as foolhardy, even if she had managed to convince Marks the plan would work. Clearly, she had recruited Marks as a coconspirator. Or had he recruited her? The details were nebulous, but the peril remained the same.

For relief, I thought about Granny's windfall, Roop's chickens, Stash's busy workshop, and Aunt Letty's new job. The people I cared about at home intersected like threads in a fabric, crossing and recrossing in a tightly woven pattern. I didn't mind at all that I hung off like a loose button. I remained attached to my loved ones, and that was all that mattered.

A beetle thwacked against the windscreen, jolting me back to the Cruiser, the bridge, the tools, and the lumber piled around me. I rotated my arms to ease the knot between my shoulder blades. A furl of hot air brushed against my skin. The surprising thing was how calm I felt, how I had taken in and tucked away the unavoidable reality that Mima and I might not be together for a long, long time.

I fingered the strand of lucky bean seeds circling my wrist. Good fortune in work had little to do with luck, it seemed to me. My journey from Bonesy the kid to Bones the guide trainee had taken industry, diligence, and the support of caring people. Without the effort I had put in and plenty of help from others, I would probably be coaxing cassava out of a dusty patch in the shadow of my boyhood home.

In love, though, my lucky bean seeds had more than lived up to their name. Mima embodied everything I wanted in a girlfriend, life partner, and wife. At times I was still astonished she had chosen me. Her devotion to her family and her sense of responsibility concerning the store threw a big, fat wrench into our tender plans. Yet I viewed those loyalties as another reason to love and admire her. I was the one who had gone away, after all, expecting her to follow. Had I assumed too much?

That disturbing thought had rippled between my ears more than once. Once again, I quashed it. I slid the letter into my pocket and reached for the hammer. Mima and I were solid, committed, working toward a future we both could share. Our good fortune seemed so assured and complete that I almost felt sorry for Skinner and his malevolent, duplicitous, doomed existence. Skinner would never be as lucky as me, or as lucky as Zola and Marks for that matter.

A row of nails had popped up from a dried plank in the middle of the bridge. I hammered them in, barely registering the racket that sent a brace of guinea fowl rushing for cover. My sister, her future husband, and the scam they were running on Skinner overtook my mind like a dense cloud of dust. As much as I loathed Skinner and his ludicrous, eight-strand lucky bean seed bracelet, I dreaded the day he would discover just how unlucky he was.

That night, I skipped the campfire and Jackson's hospitable Amarula to retreat to my tent and answer Mima's letter. I carefully cut a page of creamy paper from the back of my journal to use as stationery and borrowed a good pen from Teaspoon. In flickering lantern light I wrote for over an hour.

I told Mima I shared her concern for her mother and assured her I would support any decisions she felt necessary. I asked her to greet my family, the Dirty Dees, Roop, and Granny. I said the days were flying by. I explained how we divvied up the responsibilities in camp so that everyone contributed something important and worthwhile. As I wrote, I thought about roles that might one day interest her. She was more than capable of handling any job, even guiding if she wanted to train. I told her I saw many elephants and other interesting wildlife, including the guests! I said I didn't know when I would be home. I wrote that I loved her and missed her, that life wasn't complete without her. I assured her there would be a place for her at Motembo whenever she was able to join me. I folded the pages and put them in an envelope, dropping in a single lucky bean seed I had found on a trail near camp.

22

As the weeks passed by, my status as a trainee faded from everyone's mind, including my own. My responsibilities differed little from Luke's. During one three-day period when camp was full and Newsom had been called away on a family matter, Jackson assigned me to guide four Australians while Luke and Kiki took other foursomes. This put me in sole charge of the Aussies' wildlife-viewing experience, covering all three sectors, the Big Five, and any special interests the guests might declare. Although Jackson's confidence in me boosted my own, a case of the jitters almost overshadowed my excitement. I had learned enough to know that much could go wrong on a game drive: a flat tire, a dead end in mud or water, an unwell, injured, or misbehaving guest, a too-close encounter with the animal kingdom, or worse, animals that refused to show themselves.

The men, four brothers celebrating a fiftieth birthday without their wives, were relaxed and jokey. All four had been on safari before. They knew and respected the drill. To my relief, they weren't too particular about seeing every species in Africa but responded with gratitude at every decent sighting. Sundowners brought them special pleasure (double gin and tonics, my specialty), and the men were good company around the campfire. After they departed, Jackson handed me a fat envelope containing a generous tip and a note that read, "Eight thumbs up for our guide, Bones!"

The next day, Jackson came after me holding a clipboard. "It's about time we tied up the loose ends and got you certified. Meet me in the Cruiser."

I drove us to the trees bordering the river, where he directed me down a trampled gash in the foliage. When I stopped at the edge of a glistening, silt-clogged bog, he gestured for me to drive straight in. I looked at him, eyebrows raised. *Really?*

He nodded. I swallowed, gripped the wheel, and rolled forward.

We had moved less than a Cruiser's length when the mud sucked and held us like a living, grasping thing. For a moment, all four tires whirled in place, kicking up a viscous spray that I knew I would have to scrub off the sides of the vehicle later that day—if we ever got out. I shifted into reverse but succeeded only in digging us in deeper. Then I tried rocking forward, reverse, and forward, also without success. Finally, I took my foot off the accelerator, defeated. The Cruiser came to rest in the mud. It was my first test, and I had failed.

"Good," Jackson said, grinning. "Now winch us out."

Oh. Apparently, I hadn't failed yet. I silently thanked Chiddy for teaching me how to use a winch. I had also studied the procedure in my guide manual and watched Good Sam's sons winch my van from the mud. But I had never pulled a vehicle out alone. I rolled up the legs of my khakis and, saying goodbye to the newish sheen on my boots, stepped into the ooze.

Slogging my way to the front, I kept an eye out for snakes. I remembered to slip on a pair of leather gloves, step one. Steps two, three, four, and five were taking shape in my mind as I scanned the opposite bank. A sturdy tree located straight ahead looked like a worthy anchor. I gripped the hook and the winch strap and walked out the cable. Jackson was reading, apparently going over the list of skills I needed to prove. He appeared relaxed and patient. If this had been a game drive, four passengers in various states of alarm would be sitting up with their eyes fixed on me. I practiced acting more confident than I felt.

With only a modest amount of fumbling and backtracking, I got the Cruiser hooked up and ready to go. I slid in behind the steering wheel and used just enough engine power to help the winch roll the tires forward. When we reached solid ground, I hopped out again, jubilant, trying not to show how relieved I felt. I quickly respooled the cable and stowed the strap. When I climbed back in and turned the key, the engine sprang back to life. I said silent thank-yous to the Cruiser, to the excellent winch, and to the hardworking battery.

Jackson made a note on the report card, or whatever he had clipped to the board. "Well done. Now drive that way," he said, pointing.

We entered a small clearing, where he told me to turn around and drive back the way we had come.

"Toward the river?"

He nodded.

At the edge of the muddy flats, I stepped on the brake and looked at him, uncertain. "What now?"

"Drive in."

"Again?" I couldn't hide my dismay.

He tilted his head toward the abyss. "Drive in."

I sighed and plunged us back into the muck. I tried every strategy I could think of to maneuver the vehicle across the sucking mess without getting stuck. But once again the tires spun, the mud flew up, and we came to a dead stop in a nightmare of sludgy ooze. I eyed Jackson, wondering if he was such a nice guy after all.

"Now get us out without using the winch."

"Without using the winch," I repeated, letting the words sink in. *How the fuck am I supposed to do that?* I nodded. "Okay."

I got out, my mud-encrusted boots too far gone to worry about. High-stepping from tire to tire, I muscled my way forward. The strain on my calves and thighs felt like a hot iron. Each wheel had sunk about halfway down. A semiputrid algae smell wafted up from the mire. A company of insects flew in for a look. The vehicle had come to rest more than three meters from firm ground on the opposite shore.

Vegetation lined the riverbank, much of it broken and flattened by the hooves of animals coming to drink. I spent the next half hour gathering dry limbs to use for traction. Jackson sat back in his seat with his hat tilted down over his eyes. Was he asleep? Evidently, he expected this to take a while.

My job would have been easier if I could have used the jack to raise the front tires. But with no firm surface on which to rest the frame, the jack was useless. I wedged as much material under the tires as I could wrestle down and under through the mud. Dark sludge coated my forearms and shins. I peeled off a leech. Sweat soaked my spattered shirt. I thought about Jaleen and the sorry job of laundering she was going to face.

When I had done all I could to shore up the tires, I made a few more trips to gather wood and laid a thick mat of interlocking branches from the Cruiser to the shore. A small flock of blacksmith plovers moved in to peck invertebrates from the displaced mud. Downstream, a magnificently horned sable ankled into clear water for a drink. When I returned to the driver's seat and cranked the engine, the sable and the birds startled and fled.

"Looks good so far." Jackson had lifted his hat and leaned forward to inspect my work. "What else could you do to improve traction?"

"Reduce the air pressure in the tires?"

"Right. Let's try without that first."

I pressed lightly on the accelerator, rocking my body forward, willing the tires to grab. They spun. I let up and then pressed again. Something underneath took hold, and the Cruiser lurched forward a foot or two. I gave it more gas, and we shot ahead, rocking and rolling across the branches and sticks all the way to solid ground.

I'd had about enough of the river for one day, so I was glad when Jackson directed me toward camp. We took our time getting there, though. On the way, he made me stop and change a tire. Then he made me change the spare tire back to the original. He opened the hood and drilled me on basic mechanics. Then he got out the first aid kit and asked about the uses for each item inside. By the time we trundled across the bridge to Motembo, I was covered in dried mud and ready to drop from fatigue. The good news: Jackson had ticked off an entire column of items on his list.

Over the next several days, he took me out and tested me on tracking, birding, wildlife photography, navigation, and survival skills. In the evenings, we left the campfire for a good look at the night sky. I identified constellations, planets, and satellites. One night he asked, "How much gin goes into a gin and tonic?"

I was about to answer when he grinned. "That's a joke, Bones." He waved a sheaf of papers marked with checks and comments. "We've covered all the requirements, and you passed every test. As your on-job trainer, I am authorized to pronounce you qualified. The paperwork will take a few weeks, but for now, congratulations. You are a certified professional safari guide."

⋀ ⋀ ⋀

We were entering peak season when Jackson assigned me four guests from the United States: an orthopedist, his wife, and a younger couple. By then I was familiar with the casual ways of Americans, so I tried to remember and use their first names. Out of respect for his age and position, I addressed the physician as "Dr. Griff." The others were Nina, Todd, and Abby. I learned the four had previously traveled together to professional conferences on sports medicine. Todd was a distance runner with expertise in physiology and the engineering of high-performance athletic shoes. All four appeared physically able, comfortable with each other and the outdoors, and excited about their first African adventure. I anticipated a smooth and enjoyable three days.

Our first game drives took us far from the river, to the sectors that included Little Serengeti and RIP Gulch. Game viewing was spectacular on the dry, open grassland. The guests gave me too much credit for tracking animals that simply lived there, out in the open. Dr. Griff, the most avid photographer in the group, captured interesting images of giraffes, zebras, and Cape buffalos. Impalas were so numerous that he soon ignored them.

Nina, Griff's wife, was a good spotter even without binoculars. She pointed out several varieties of raptors circling overhead and was the first to see a distant bushbuck and a small herd of tsessebe grazing on the fringes. Of the four, Nina seemed the most reflective and the most attuned to the sensory pleasures of the bush—the sounds, sights, and smells. She brought to mind a researcher cataloging the feel of intense solar heat or the taste of the dust and microscopic vegetable matter that salted the open air. While Dr. Griff scrambled to take photos, she sat very still, watchful and contemplative, carried away on the back of a galloping intellect.

The other female was an un-self-conscious beauty who taught middle school and must have dealt with numerous crushes akin to khaki fever. For a knockout, Abby was remarkably natural and unaffected. She struck me as a paragon of organization too, the mother lode of preparedness. Every day she showed up looking as if she had consulted a very thorough list and confirmed her readiness with checkmarks. Wide-brim hat with chin strap, check. Polarized sunglasses, check. Multipocketed vest bulging with essential tubes and packets, check. Binoculars, water, long sleeves, long pants, sturdy boots, and socks, check, check, check, check, check, check.

What was on her mind, admirably, was safety—and, as I soon discovered, the potential for danger in just about every creature she saw. She leaned into Todd for protection when we slowed to view baboons, warthogs, and even a lone waterbuck. When RIP Gulch yielded a leopard lounging on a tree limb, I felt a tap on my shoulder. "This is close enough," she whispered.

I stepped on the brake, thankful that Dr. Griff's long lens would be sufficient for a close-up.

Abby's caution stood in stark contrast to the barely contained energy of her boyfriend, Todd, the long-distance runner. I had guided his type before—a superbly conditioned athlete who chafed at the restrictions imposed for safety's sake on all guests in the bush. A body accustomed to exercise suffers in its absence. I knew this and encouraged Todd to use the jump rope, mats, and weights we stored in a chest behind the bar. He took a look at them. But during the hot midday hours in camp, instead of working out in the pavilion, he retreated with Abby to their tent and wasn't seen again until afternoon tea. I really didn't blame him. In Todd's shoes, I would have stayed with Abby too.

On their third and final night at Motembo, the staff surprised the Americans with a private bush dinner in a clearing under the night sky. A previous bush dinner with the full complement of visitors had been a surprise too. But no one in this group had expected a second, intimate version of that exceptional experience. Although tonight's location was a short walk from the pavilion, dense foliage, a small hill, and a canopy of darkness shielded the clearing from any hint of civilization. I drove the unsuspecting foursome there on a circuitous route at the end of our evening game drive, adding to the illusion that we remained deep in the untamed wilderness.

When we arrived, the campfire cast a warm, dancing circle of light. Teaspoon had set up a makeshift bar and was pouring flutes of sparkling wine. A dining table covered in white seemed weightless, an apparition afloat in the glow of a dozen candles. While the guests oohed and exclaimed, I noticed Good Sam and his sons quietly patrolling the shadowy fringes, rifles in hand. There would be no party crashers here, human or otherwise.

Nate presented another excellent, multicourse meal. I sat at one end of the table, with Nina and Dr. Griff on my right and Abby and Todd on my left. They were all chatty and in good spirits, excited about their final game drive the following morning. We had saved the riverine corridor for last.

Dr. Griff said he wanted a good photo of a hippo with its mouth wide-open. Nina hoped to spot a crocodile and a monitor lizard. I made a pitch for the rich variety of waterbirds we were likely to see. Casting aside caution about managing expectations, I added that we might encounter the ornery bachelor Cape buffalo that hung out in the ravine.

Teaspoon was pouring coffee in my cup when he leaned forward and whispered, "Jackson wants a word."

I excused myself and left the table. My boss was standing behind the bar, holding a long-range radio. "I just heard from Marks," he said in a low voice. "He's on poacher patrol across the river. Spotters have seen campfires and tire tracks over there. They're checking it out."

"How far away?"

"For now, far enough west not to alter your plans. I know you're headed to the river tomorrow. Before you get too close, I want you to check with Good Sam. He'll be at the blind, keeping an eye on the ravine. He doesn't use a radio, you know, because the signal there is poor. You'll have to walk in to see him. If he gives the all clear, you can go back and complete your drive as planned."

"Otherwise?"

"Choose another sector." He tipped his head toward the table. "Best not to share too much with them about armed criminals."

I took in his words and his reasoning. But I recoiled at the idea of disappointing guests who were so eager to visit the river. Even leaving them alone while I checked with Good Sam would violate my training, wouldn't it? I wanted to question Jackson and protest, but he had already turned away and was walking toward camp. Surely he knew poachers weren't interested in us. On the contrary, they would take great pains not to be seen.

I was building up a head of steamy umbrage when my thoughts shifted to Marks, my future brother-in-law, out in the dark with a backpack, a rifle, and two or three sketchily trained rangers. He could be facing men who wouldn't think twice about shooting him, poachers who would do anything for tusk or horn. With shame I realized how warped my thinking had become. Marks was risking his life to protect Motembo's wildlife while I worried about leaving guests alone for ten minutes and about the possibility of *disappointing* them.

I glanced toward the four at the table. They were laughing at something Nina had said. In our two days together I had come to know this group rather well. They were intelligent and cooperative, experienced travelers capable of withstanding a change in plan. Abby could be skittish, but more than once she had revealed deep reservoirs of self-control and common sense. I believed she could withstand a few minutes in the Cruiser without a guide. I worried most about Todd, a tight coil of energy who could become a handful. My hike to the river and back would have to be quick. If Good Sam discerned signs of trouble and advised me not to drive there, I would think up an interesting detour, something new and photogenic. It wouldn't be the end of the world.

I cast a squint at Good Sam standing deep in the shadows. As always, he was being careful to remain out of sight. It seemed unfair, a serious screwup by Mother Nature, that such a caring man was burdened by such an off-putting appearance. I smiled and nodded. He grinned and raised a hand. I saw a flash of disorderly teeth and biceps like shredded chicken. In spite of his age and wear, Good Sam possessed the vision of a fish eagle. I waved back, hoping those steely, bloodshot eyes would spot nothing out of the ordinary anytime soon.

23

The air held a bite as we drove out of camp the following morning. The sun had barely edged into view. Like a starter's pistol, the first ray of light set off a chorus of birdcalls competing for notice against the bluing sky. I leaned out to read the morning news: fresh tracks that crisscrossed the earth in all directions. Lucid, muddled, or violently scrambled, new prints at dawn told the story of a nocturnal world churning with life.

Abby and Todd sat in the seat behind me. Nina and Dr. Griff huddled on the higher bench. They all wore zipped-up jackets they would shed within the hour. I could feel their anticipation, the excitement that rides on every game drive heading out of camp. Whatever happened on my final morning with them, I would do my best not to disappoint.

Jackson had heard nothing from Marks since the previous evening. He told me he had radioed for an update but had failed to make contact. "He probably followed the poachers out of range, into a canyon or beyond the hills over there," he said, tilting his head. "Either scenario bodes well for your trip to the river." With a stern look he added, "But they also could have moved closer, into the ravine. Anything is possible. Don't drive in without checking first with Sam."

I nodded my assent.

"Luke, Kiki, and I are going to meet twelve new guests at the airstrip. We're taking them on a tour of the village and a school. We'll be out of contact most of the day. Newsom's off, so you're on your own. Your guests' luggage will be delivered to the plane, due at noon. Give them a good sendoff."

"No problem."

Considering the uncertainties ahead, I planned to engineer something thrilling prior to my recon with Good Sam—lions, if possible. The females and cubs that frequented Three Flat Rocks would do. Even better would be the coalition of males Luke had spotted roaming the sector—three magnificently maned subadults. The trio had arrived to hunt and bulk up before competing to mate with the local pride. Judging by the clarity of the morning news, the lions wouldn't be difficult to find.

After a good look at the tracks around camp, I drove away fast, speeding over flats and rises, brambles and rocks. A speedy getaway, I had learned, added to the sense of excitement and purpose. The guests hung on, ready for anything. As we approached Three Flat Rocks, I slowed to steer the Cruiser in a wide, deliberate arc. When I leaned out to examine new prints in the dust, no one said a word. By then they knew what tracking looked like and the likely reward at its end.

The male lions turned up about half a kilometer south of the rocks. We found them resting in the grass, panting, their muzzles stained dark with the blood of a recent kill. Two of them raised their heads to look at us. The third didn't bother. They all appeared weighted down, hypermetabolic, pinned in place by hugely swollen bellies.

I parked about six meters from the lions and turned off the engine. I heard rapid, nervous breathing from Abby behind me. I imitated the posture I had learned from Luke, swinging one arm over the back of my seat to convey relaxed confidence while keeping a close eye on the kings of beasts. Nina and Todd sounded appropriately awed. Dr. Griff's camera clicked several times. I said a few words about male coalitions. Abby grew so quiet that I turned to make sure she was conscious. She darted a frantic glance from me to the lions, as though they might pounce the second I looked away. Guessing she'd had enough, I fired the engine and backed off. Lions were an excellent start. So far, no one had even mentioned the river.

I knew where I was going to abandon the Cruiser and the guests—at the baobab tree, a notable attraction this foursome had yet to see. I chose the tree for the same reasons we often picked it for sundowners. The giant trunk provided a sense of protection, privacy if needed, and an intriguingly hollow interior. It stood alone on the plain, with wide-angle views in all directions. Even better for today's purpose, the guests would have an unimpeded and, I hoped, reassuring sightline to me as I walked to and from the river.

On the way there, I dawdled a time or two to deliver pertinent facts about the world's largest succulent. The tree loomed like an ancient citadel.

I still hadn't worked out how much to reveal about the hiatus ahead. Did a somewhat routine scouting mission by a certified professional safari guide require an explanation? A guide the four had trusted from the moment they arrived at Motembo? I could make up a story about scouting for dangerous wildlife. But that seemed ridiculous after our intentional, up-close encounter with a coalition of lions. My real purpose, scouting for dangerous humans, implied a far more worrisome threat. Jackson had been correct in cautioning me to say little.

I parked the Cruiser under a mess of crazily forked baobab branches, facing the green scrim that marked the river. The sun at low angle cast a rosy glow westward. Griff got busy snapping photos. Nina and Abby commented on an alien plant that had sprouted from a crease in the tree bark. Todd stretched and rotated his shoulders, peering up at limbs the circumference of oil drums. While the novelty of the location diverted their attention, I clipped the radio to my belt, slid my rifle from the rack beneath the dashboard, and stood.

"Wait here," I said. Then I stepped down and walked away.

* * *

I took long, purposeful strides to escape as fast as I could. Each footfall detonated a cloud of dust. I stifled a sneeze and regretted not bringing my canteen. Then I saluted myself for having left it behind, a sure sign to the guests that I would return without delay. I could almost feel four pairs of eyes drilling holes into the back of my shirt.

As a matter of course, I scanned the landscape for telling shapes, colors, or movements. The only animals I saw were the usual impalas and a distant herd of zebras. Normally, a walk in the bush would provide a wealth of interesting distractions—things as small as a column of ants or a thistle on a bush. Nothing diverted me now. I hurried past the three termite mounds and the thicket of feverberry bushes. Near the marula grove, a baboon sentry spotted me and sounded a warning. *Yak! Yak! Yak!*

I skirted the trees. Crossing the last stretch of plane, I said a silent goodbye to the four people waiting in the Cruiser. In a few more strides, I dropped out of sight.

Good Sam's blind stood a short distance upstream from the trail I descended into the ravine. The water level was low, in a few places little more than a shiny coating on the mud. A mokoro had been grounded and hauled up near Good Sam's blind. Motembo's ever-vigilant lookout saw me coming and was already climbing down the ladder.

I hurried toward him. "I didn't know you had a mokoro."

"I don't. It belongs to the hunter who showed up a while ago."

My heart sank. "A poacher?"

"No. At least not the kind you worry about. He has a shotgun, only good for small game."

Small-scale poaching was a problem we encountered frequently in the reserve. As long as the hunting was intended for the pot, to feed local families, and the hunters stayed away from our vehicles, we looked the other way. Jackson even encouraged Good Sam and his sons to quietly bag a sustainable supply of game in return for their services to the camp. I felt cautiously optimistic.

"Which way did he go?"

"That way," Sam said, pointing. "Over the rocks to the other side. I haven't seen or heard anything from the people Jackson's worried about."

My shoulders relaxed as if unscrewed from heavy armor. "Good. We'll drive south and enter the ravine downstream. If he comes back, he'll be out of our sight. Thanks, Sam."

I was turning away when he must have gotten a look at my wrist. "He has on a bracelet like yours."

"What?"

"The hunter. This many seeds." He placed thumb and forefinger against his wrist a few inches apart.

"A lucky bean seed bracelet?"

He nodded.

My breath caught in my throat. "What else about him did you notice?"

"He's tall, with plenty of muscle. Looked straight at me. He has a scar here." He ran a finger across the bridge of his nose.

The news had barely detonated before I started backing away, in a rush to relay the message. "His name is Skinner. He's trouble, Sam. I'll try to let Marks know he's here."

Caper bushes grabbed and scraped my shins as I scrambled back up the trail, oblivious to every sensation except the chokehold of alarm. Skinner hadn't paddled this far to hunt birds or hares. He was connecting with poachers via the river, just as Baba had guessed. I stumbled past the leadwood tree, which was aquiver with chattering monkeys. What if Skinner had come to deliver more poison to his underworld partners, the same men Marks was after? The possibility of a second break-in at Swales unnerved me almost as much as the thought of more poisoned wildlife. I was breathing hard when I emerged from the ravine. Before I could unclip my radio, the receiver buzzed.

"Jackson?" I said.

The radio crackled in my ear. "Bonesy, it's me. A ranger patched me in." A strangled, gasping sound came through the static. "Something terrible has happened."

It took me a moment to recognize the voice. "Baba?" Was he crying?

"We found Zola. She's alive."

"What? You *found* her?"

"By the river." He took a deep, ragged breath. "A few days ago, Skinner told her about a cartel of poachers—well armed, with a web of paid lookouts. He boasted about his own involvement and tried to recruit her. Later, he overheard her repeating everything over the radio to Marks. He heard her say she loved him. She told me he was wild with rage." I heard a wrenching sob. "She could barely talk, Bonesy. He beat her. He beat her almost to death. Then he left her, bleeding and unconscious."

I was unsure whether the next sob came from him or me.

"He told her he was going to kill Marks—find him and kill him. That was early yesterday. She thought he left in a mokoro. He could be there by now."

"He is here. He was seen leaving the river some time ago. Does Marks know?"

"We couldn't reach him."

"I'll find him, Baba. Tell Zola I'll find him."

Exactly whom I was going to find, I hadn't specified. Was I going to stop Skinner or warn Marks? Either way, every minute mattered. Skinner was hurt and furious and running on rage. And he was dangerously unconcerned about his own safety, judging from the mokoro left in the open and his face-to-face encounter with Sam. I imagined he was half crazy yet also ferociously single-minded in his quest for revenge.

All I knew of Marks's location was that he had gone out of radio contact, probably because of distance or a barrier such as a hill or a dense growth of trees. Picking up his days-old tracks without additional information would take time and more luck than I could hope for. Worse, Skinner already knew where Marks was. He had traveled here, landed his mokoro, and gone off in the correct direction. I shuddered to think about the network of informants pitted against Marks and the other rangers, a network that included Skinner.

Stopping him from getting to Marks before I did became my all-consuming, fire-in-the-belly objective. I ran, slid, fell, got up, and clambered down the same trail I had followed to the river minutes earlier. Good Sam had gone out of sight, perhaps back inside the blind, but the mokoro sat where I had seen it before. I willed myself to focus, to slow the pistons pounding in my chest so that I could calmly, methodically track down Zola's attacker. I tried not to picture Zola lying injured, bleeding, and left to the hyenas or whatever scavenger sniffed her out first. I couldn't imagine my father's anguish when he found her—anguish coupled with profound relief that Skinner hadn't dragged her off, never to be seen again.

Skinner's waffle-soled boots had stamped clear imprints in the shelf of mud supporting the mokoro. The spacing and depth of the prints fit his stride and weight. I followed the tracks over the same stones he had stepped on, across the river and up the bank on the other side. He had made no effort to conceal his movements. At the top of the ridge, broken branches and trampled, fresh-smelling grass marked the path forward. A buffalo would have done less damage. Either Skinner didn't think he would be followed, or he didn't care. Tracking him would be straightforward if I kept my wits about me.

I followed the trail at a fast clip, jogging from one easily visible marker to the next without a pause. Minutes ticked by, maybe an hour, maybe more. Sweat ran like fingers down my back. My determination to move fast almost equaled the stomach-churning dismay I felt with every step that took me farther from the guests I had abandoned at the baobab tree. Leaving them alone in the wild was an unimaginable breach of guide protocol and ethics. I blinked away a hot, furious pool of moisture in my eyes. In addition to his other crimes, Skinner had endangered four tourists and possibly ruined my career.

I consoled myself with the thought that Nina, Griff, Abby, and Todd would cope perfectly well in my absence. Unlike me, they had water. They would be safe in the fortress of the Cruiser, buttressed by an almost full tank of gas and a key in the ignition. When they realized something was amiss, they would simply drive back to camp. They probably had gone already.

This line of thought comforted me. With the other guides away, I imagined the Americans arriving in camp to a warm, impromptu welcome by Jaleen, Teaspoon, and Nate, who were no strangers to the unexpected. The staff would provide an early brunch and drive the four to the airstrip in time for their flight. Then someone would go to the river to ask Good Sam where I was. He would tell them I was chasing a bad guy named Skinner. Questions about that could wait. With twelve new guests due in camp that afternoon, no one would have time to worry about me.

At least that's the story I told myself. The encyclopedia of alternate outcomes, things that could go horribly wrong, I shoved into a small, dark wrinkle of my brain. Thinking about lost guests, injured guests, or even dead guests was a futile, nonproductive, ridiculous exercise. The priority now, the undeniably more urgent life-or-death matter, was preventing Skinner from carrying out his mission. The man was an evil blight, a sociopath who massacred animals, who had beaten my sister nearly to death, and who was at that very moment hell-bent on murder.

My loaded rifle hung from my shoulder. I gripped the strap as I trotted through the grass, aware of the elephant-stopping firepower pressed against my back. The thought of using the rifle to kill a man was so foreign to me that my mind resisted the puzzle of what I was going to do when I found Skinner. How did I expect to rein him in? What was my plan? Could I find my way to the calculating, cold-blooded zone I knew from hunting—the icy calm that enabled me to aim, fire, and kill? The prospect filled me with revulsion even as I vowed to stop Skinner, whatever it took.

I ran, jogged, or walked, depending on the clarity or obscurity of the prints leading me forward. The land was new to me, beyond Motembo's borders. A few times, I lost the trail and circled to find it again. As the morning drifted into afternoon, my most immediate concern became the sun hanging like a lantern over my head. Searing, nearly vertical rays broiled the top of my hat and produced a dazzle on the crabbed, bleached earth. Skinner's tracks lost definition in the glare. I slowed my pace to pay closer attention to the powdery topsoil and crispy vegetation. My mouth was gummy with thirst.

The tracks led to the shade of a mahogany tree where Skinner must have stopped for a rest. His prints formed a few tight circles, and I saw a butt-sized dent where he had sat. As much as I welcomed the cool of the shade, I welcomed even more the chance to make up time. Marks and his patrol had covered an impressive stretch of hinterland since his call to Jackson the previous night. I was beginning to worry the chase might not end before dark.

The plain rose up to a rumple of dun-colored hills. Radio contact would be sketchy from there even if I dared chance a call. I didn't. If Skinner happened to be closing in on Marks, the sound of the radio could lead him directly to his target. In any event, Marks had probably turned off his radio to avoid detection by the poachers he was tracking. As a precaution, I turned mine off too.

I had crested a gentle slope when I registered the first faint whiff of wood smoke. The scent brought me to a halt. I sniffed the impacted air, hoping I was wrong. Fire was a monstrous, terrifying prospect on a day so hot that it seemed a snap of the fingers could ignite a person's hand. Smoke rose above the western horizon, pale and almost invisible against the exhausted afternoon sky. But there was no mistaking the dusky perfume of burning wood. Either an abandoned campfire had roared back to life, or poachers had set the earth ablaze to flush out animals they wanted to kill. Neither possibility suggested a controlled and harmless burn. Fire on the drought-baked savannah almost always spelled chaos and disaster, an inferno of heat and death that sent every creature running in fear.

The dead calm offered some hope. Without a wisp of breeze to fan the flames, fire would take its time advancing up and down the hills. This was the only good news in the entire ghastly nightmare. I had no choice but to press forward, toward the burn. A whiff of smoke wasn't stopping Skinner. His prints had gotten farther apart, heavier at the toe. He was running.

I matched his pace, step for step, gasping for breath in the suffocating atmosphere. He was closing in on Marks, I was sure—rushing to exact revenge before fire scattered the patrol and forced him to retreat. Caution slowed my feet whenever the tracks led over a rise or around a bend. My rifle had a greater range than Skinner's shotgun, but surprise was an advantage I did not want to lose.

The sun had crossed its zenith when I summited a slope ribbed in granite. In quick succession three things happened. A furl of desiccating wind blasted me in the face. A herd of frightened impalas raced by, pronking and wheezing. And a gunshot rang out, followed by two more in quick succession. The shots had come from somewhere ahead of me, beyond the next stack of hills.

In a panic, I ran, slipped, fell, got up, and ran again toward the sound, toward the fire, toward Skinner, Marks, and the animal slaughterers Marks was determined to stop. It sickened me to hope that the shots I had heard were from poachers killing animals fleeing the fire and not from Skinner's gun. A Noah's Ark of easy targets was headed in the opposite direction. Rodents, birds, and creatures large and small rushed past me, caught up in the climate of fear. In their haste, they seemed oblivious to the human swimming upstream. A springbok nearly charged into me before darting to the side. I could only hope no buffalos would thunder my way. A wrenching thought snaked into my head: if ivory poachers had started the fire, I needn't worry about oncoming elephants.

Smoke stung my eyes and throat. I coughed and squinted into the haze. Flames had crowned a hill a kilometer or two away. A sounder of warthogs raced down the slope. Then, at last, I spotted what I had come for. In a copse of old-growth hardwood between the fire and me, I saw movement. Not animals, but a man.

I crouched low and moved closer. Unshouldering my rifle, I crept in for a better look. I blinked, taking in the scene before me. The man wasn't Skinner. He was a ranger I recognized from the village. And there was another ranger with him. The men stood next to a third person sprawled on the ground. I straightened up and ran. The fallen man was Marks.

Shock and disbelief distorted the rangers' faces. They recognized me right away and stepped to the side. I knelt next to Marks's lifeless body while they told me what had happened. The assassin had surprised them, they said—a man with a shotgun. He yelled, "Your precious Zola is dead. I killed her." Then he fired once at close range and ran.

The rangers said they fired back. They might have wounded him. They gave chase, but not for long because the wind came up, and they feared the flames would engulf them all. So they had rushed back to claim Marks's body before making a run for safety.

One of the men handed me a canteen. I drank my fill and handed it back, speechless, numb with grief and defeat. My tears fell on Marks's bloody shirt. Ash drifted through the acrid air and landed on his ruined face. The fire was closing in, but I almost didn't care. The metallic scent of blood rose up as I helped the men wrap the corpse in a tarp, which we then roped to a pole. The men hoisted the pole to their shoulders, one man on each end. Marks's body swayed heavily between them.

"Our Jeep isn't far, over those hills," one of them said, pointing. A hot gust of wind pushed at the knotted tarp. "Follow us."

"No. I'm going after him."

They stared at me with raised eyebrows but didn't try to change my mind. The one who had offered water gave me his canteen and a few sticks of biltong. The other clenched my fist in his. He held my eyes in a look so solemn that I knew he thought he might be the last person to see me alive. A hundred meters away, a tree exploded like a flare. Pockets of flame dotted the landscape. A bushbuck raced past, its singed coat trailing smoke. The rangers were turning to leave when I remembered to tell them the most important thing.

"His name is Skinner. The killer's name is Skinner."

* * *

Skinner had taken a route perpendicular to the path of the fire, like a swimmer trying to escape a riptide by swimming parallel to shore. Not a bad strategy if he went fast enough and the direction of the wind could be trusted. The sky to the west was flushed an angry orange. The air to the north looked brighter, a sun-washed backdrop to the smoky haze.

I tied a bandana over my nose and mouth, shouldering the canteen and my rifle. Dusty hardpan several meters ahead revealed a clear set of waffle-soled imprints. The prints indicated short strides with the left foot coming down hard. The right print was barely visible, evidence of a limp. If the rangers had wounded Skinner as the prints suggested, he wouldn't be difficult to catch.

The image of Marks's ravaged body swam before me, still unthinkable yet seared into my brain. I was painfully aware that I had failed a man I revered. I had failed my sister, my father, and every guide and ranger who lionized Marks's dedication and courage. I had even failed my beloved elephants. I had failed them all because Skinner had gotten to Marks first.

The next few moments became my inauguration into the dark art of tracking a person I intended to kill. My earlier revulsion had vanished. I sprinted like a man possessed, past the heat and soot of the fire, past the choking smoke. In time I raced into a bright stretch of grassland the wind had seen fit to spare. Even as I outpaced the flames, my all-consuming purpose was to run down Skinner and end his sorry life.

My goal was a puny thing next to the mighty, unstoppable march of the sun. I emerged from the haze to encounter the long shadows and peachy sky of a day nearing sunset. Skinner had led me out of the fire and into the coming abyss of night. Even with the help of a full-faced moon and the blood spatters that had begun to mark the trail, tracking him after dark would be difficult, if not impossible. *Let him live to see one more sunrise*, I thought. *Tonight we will rest.*

I searched for a place to shelter before the sun cast its last fan of light. I harbored little doubt Skinner was doing the same. His wound would make him vulnerable to nocturnal predators, especially if he limped half-blind and bleeding through the patchy lunar glow. He had accomplished his purpose. He likely knew the rangers had given up chasing him, and he was unaware of my pursuit. The fire burned far away now, moving another direction. I didn't credit Skinner with remorse for killing Marks or even depression over revelations of Zola's treachery. But he must have felt immense fatigue after his long, hate-fueled trek across the bush. His lawless colleagues weren't coming to his rescue, as far as I could tell. Chances were good he would pick a spot in a thicket or a copse of trees, tend his wound, and settle down until dawn.

The landscape offered little in the way of cushioning, no moss or springy groundcover to ease a night's rest. The place I chose backed against a north-facing boulder that radiated the heat of the day. The warmth wouldn't last long, but it was something. I was rationing the biltong. Even though I had eaten most of it, hunger sank its teeth in me. I remembered the raw, empty feeling from the lean years at home, a state I had hoped never to experience again.

As night closed in, the crushing reality of Marks's death settled on me, a blanket of pain. Tears ponded in my eyes, spilled, and ran unchecked. I wept for Marks and Zola, for my shameful, forced desertion of the Americans, for the career I had probably ruined, for all the dead and mutilated elephants that criminals like Skinner had massacred, and for the terrified orphans and leaderless elephant relatives left behind. I tried and failed to think more positive thoughts, about Mima and Roop and my family at home. But those people did not belong in the dark scenario I was plotting now. I wanted no loved ones with me on the hunt to murder Skinner. I put them all in a closed compartment, a mental safe-deposit box where they would stay until this was finished.

The moon cast a phantasmal light. I anticipated a long, cold night poisoned with grief, anger, and hatred. Exhaustion trumped it all, though. I leaned back against the bed of rock with my rifle resting across my outstretched legs and closed my eyes. The next thing I heard was the predawn *kook-coo-coo* of a red-eyed dove.

I was on the move before the sun cleared the horizon. Skinner's day-old footprints had lost their crisp edges, and the droplets of blood had darkened. Still, the trail wasn't difficult to follow. In about a hundred meters, the tracks turned east, back toward the river. I considered skipping the methodical job of tracking Skinner and instead racing straight to his mokoro, to wait and surprise him there. But on the off chance he had another destination in mind, I stuck to the trail.

Now the prints and trampled grass led over a complicated landscape of granite-laced grassland, barren hardpan, and gently rolling dune slopes. The wall of smoke to the south told me the fire had burned all the way to the ravine, where it would likely fizzle and die. The wide, muddy flats there formed a barrier that would protect Sam's blind on the far bank. I could only imagine the stampede of animals Sam must have seen from his high outpost.

A few minutes later, I found the place where Skinner had rested for the night. He had chosen a spot next to a nearly dry stream where a mess of wild creepers competing for moisture strangled their own kin. Footprints led into the shallow water, where he had probably tried to clean his wound. He had peed against a tree and stretched out flat on the tangle of vines. The tracks that led away from his resting spot were recent, sharp-edged, and neatly compressed. Next to every right footprint was a deep, round hole the circumference of a coin. He was leaning heavily on a walking stick. I knew the end of the hunt was near.

My preparations became studied and methodical. Already, I was steadying myself for the job of aiming, firing, and killing. I crouched at the edge of the stream and splashed water on my head and face. I ate a stick of biltong and took a small sip from the canteen, rationing its contents to fuel the grim task ahead. I checked the cartridges in my rifle. I peed in an arc against the same tree Skinner had used. I was turning to go when the sound of gunshots cracked through the air—first one shot and then another.

The reverberations and the tracks led me in the same direction. I had walked only a short way when more shots rang out. I guessed Skinner was firing at easy targets, francolins or guinea fowl, driven by hunger and the realization he had nowhere to go. Would an ill-advised campfire be next? He had no training in outdoor survival as far as I knew. Marks's killer would be as reckless and disdainful of his surroundings as any ivory mercenary. The thought pushed me to run faster.

I came to a broad plain thick with whippy grass. A barely discernable, rapidly closing part in the grass marked Skinner's passage. The plain hosted a herd of zebras, the usual scattering of impalas, and several giraffes currently ambling across the trail I wanted to follow. The ever-skittish impalas had moved to the far right side of the field. Most of the zebras were drifting that way too. Clearly, Skinner had stayed to the left. The less easily impressed giraffes took several minutes to clear the area. When they did, I hurried past a mess of trampled grass, picking up Skinner's trail farther on. The lost time didn't worry me. I knew I was closing in.

I found him close to an hour later. The tracks had brought me to a densely wooded zone thick with underbrush. I heard him before I saw him. He was beating the ground with his walking stick: *thump-thump-thump*. I crept to a tree trunk and peered around it. What I saw then, I will never forget.

Skinner had stepped into the jaws of a gin trap, one of the merciless devices poachers used to disable random animals. The jagged metal teeth had clamped down with a force that snapped his left leg to an unnatural angle and cut deep into his calf. Blood poured from the wound. His other leg, where he had been shot, was streaked with dried and fresh blood. He was propped on an elbow, brandishing his walking stick at something out of my view. A wounded hyena lay panting a couple of meters in front of him. Behind a scrim of bushes, another hyena paced back and forth, slinging drool. A third sat under a tree, waiting patiently. The pack had sniffed him out, looking for an easy meal. Skinner must have shot at them until he ran out of ammunition and then flung the weapon at his boldest tormentor. The gun lay in the dirt near the mortally wounded animal.

My lifelong adversary did not intend to let the hyenas or anyone else end his life. His jaws were working hard, chewing. Even crouched behind the tree a distance away, I could hear the crunching and grinding of his teeth. Red saliva ran down his chin. I watched him put down his stick and quickly raise another handful of lucky bean seeds to his mouth. He had unstrung enough beads from his bracelet to empty almost a meter of black cord, now draped across his knee. The poison could take hours to kill him.

I rose and stepped out from behind the tree. He must have been too weak or too far gone to register surprise. He looked at me with narrowed eyes, chewing faster. Staring at my face, he closed his fingers around the walking stick. Something crackled in the underbrush. I unshouldered my rifle, took aim, and ended the suffering of the wounded hyena lying at my feet. Then I turned my back and headed for the river.

24

THE MEMORIAL FOR MARKS DREW a crowd that filled every table, chair, and stool at Captain Biggie's. People spilled out the door and stood or sat on the dusty sidewalk, smoking and talking in low voices. Guides and rangers came from camps all over the region. Villagers crowded in, blank-faced with disbelief. Everyone I knew and loved was there.

After the tributes, there were toasts—many toasts, with laughter as well as tears. Captain Biggie kept the glasses full. No one was in a hurry to leave.

I commandeered a table for Jackson, Kiki, Luke, and Jaleen. They had closed Motembo for the week, leaving Teaspoon and Nate in charge. In the absence of guests, Good Sam and his sons were on the job, cutting back overgrowth and tidying the paths between the tents. Apparently, they had work to do at the river too, clearing a crush of logs that had turned up overnight. Jackson told me that Sam's sons had gone to the place where Skinner met his end. They found the gin trap, the shotgun, a few bones wound in shredded khaki, and one waffle-soled boot. Sadly, three of the hyenas that feasted there had died of secondary poisoning.

The Americans I had abandoned at the baobab tree had driven themselves back to camp as I predicted. But—and this was the astonishing part—they had not returned until the next morning, *twenty-four hours* after I left them. I couldn't imagine any of those guests, least of all Abby, voting to spend the night in the open air, under the stars in the African bush. An entire day *and night*? No one filled me in on how they spent those long, blazing daylight hours and even longer, bone-chilling midnight hours. I wasn't sure anyone at Motembo knew the whole story, but it must have been a whopper. The Land Cruiser, tidy, polished, and in peak condition when we drove out of camp in the morning, had come back a dented, mud-caked, half-demolished heap, as though a herd of Cape buffalos had kicked it into the river and horned a gash in the front seat for good measure. One look at the wreckage, and Jackson had ordered the vehicle driven out of sight of the other guests. Fortunately, the Americans had returned in somewhat better condition.

No one in camp had spent too much time worrying about me. Jackson had assumed I had driven the guests to their plane as planned and then taken a few hours to scout the sectors and enjoy my time with no assigned duties. When the Americans showed up without me the following morning, twelve new guests had settled into camp and were getting ready for their first game drive. The question of where I was took a back seat to more immediate concerns—most urgently, the pressing needs of the four guests who had experienced far more of the African bush than they had expected to. After a feverish morning in which Kiki managed to arrange connecting first-class flights to the United States, the Americans departed for home, more or less satisfied with the outcome. Shortly after they left, I walked into camp.

Upon my return, I was relieved to find my journal in the Cruiser where I had left it. With a heavy heart, I turned back the cover. Under the name "Bongani Baas," I printed a new memorial entry: "Marks." Then I thumbed through the worn pages, reading jottings that traced what I believed to be my now-finished, short-lived career as a guide. Near the back I discovered a note from Abby:

> Bones, we all hope you're alive and well enough to read this. Please write to us about what happened after you went away. Everyone is worried and wants to know. I trust you don't mind that I read parts of your journal, looking for guidance. Your notes and writing inspired me. I've started journaling myself. I plan to encourage my students to do so too. Wishing you well, Abby.

She closed with her address and a little drawing of a girl wearing a vest with many pockets.

Now, at home in the village, I had already started writing my response. The letter was going to be lengthy because I wanted to explain why I had abandoned her and her friends at the baobab tree, not just what had happened afterward. I felt they needed to know everything about Skinner, maybe as far back as the cobra and the washtub, to fully understand the forces at work on that fateful morning. In return, I hoped Abby would write back to tell me all that had happened after I said, "Wait here," and walked away.

I hadn't reached Marks in time to save him, but no one questioned my decision to try. Instead of firing me for abandoning the guests, Jackson had handed me my official guide certification papers, which had finally come through, and awarded me four weeks of home leave. I found out the ivory poachers Marks had been following slaughtered at least one big male tusker as the terrified animal fled the same fire that threatened us. After sawing away the tusks, they carved "Warlords/Stay Away" in the side of the carcass. Tragically, despite heroic efforts by men like Marks, the war against the ivory trade was far from over.

The first thing I did during my home leave was build ramps for Zola next to the stairs at Baba's house, Rotting House, and Swale's Grocery. My sister's wheelchair was helping her get around while she healed from multiple fractures and internal injuries. The doctors said the chair was a temporary aid. She was young and resilient, they said. In time, with therapy and support, she was likely to make a full recovery.

I had been shocked when I first saw her. She peered at me out of swollen, blackened eyes with the expression of a person bludgeoned by despair. Her arm rested in a sling. A long, shapeless robe concealed bruises and bandages I could only guess at. When I leaned in to kiss her cheek, I saw on her neck rows of purple bruises the size of lucky bean seeds. As fast as I could, I slipped off my bracelet, unstrung the seeds, and threw them to the wind.

Zola's condition tapped a deep reservoir of compassion in my friend Rooper Nobbs. He became my sister's devoted helpmate, asking nothing in return. On most afternoons he pushed her chair to Rotting House, where she sat quietly on the newly painted porch with Granny, who understood that conversation was not required. Even as the Ovambos clucked and stirred up dust, grief claimed my sister's full attention.

At the gathering to honor Marks, Roop positioned Zola's chair next to a table with Granny, my father, and Mrs. Swale. I had been intensely relieved to find Mima's mother pink-cheeked and vigorous—the image

The Story of Bones

of good health. Mima told me what had happened. On short notice, after her mother experienced chest pains and fainting, the doctor sent her to a specialized medical center for a new procedure to replace her narrowed aortic valve. Instead of opening her chest, the surgeon delivered the valve through a catheter, a less invasive operation that within days got her on her feet and breathing normally again. Mima had brought her back to the village shortly before I arrived, delighted to surprise me with the good news.

Already, Mrs. Swale was back at work, negotiating new hours and responsibilities with Aunt Letty. Apparently, my aunt had become a little territorial behind the counter. Mrs. Swale said she guarded the Temik like a bulldog. Customers with rat problems were forced to choose between the rats and my aunt's sharp-eyed surveillance. Some actually chose the rats.

I was helping Captain Biggie serve drinks at the memorial when I noticed that Chiddy and Uncle Stash had taken their chairs outside. They sat in the shade, with Hannie and the twins at their feet. The children's frequent bursts of laughter came as a tonic on that mostly sober afternoon. I carried out a tray of lemonade and got an earful of Stash's latest trove of interesting facts.

"They're flammable," he was saying. "Did you know that, Donovan and Drew? It's true! Because of the hydrogen and methane." He glanced up at me. "Oh, hi, Bonesy. We're discussing flatology."

"Where is your fine, fine girlfriend?" Chiddy asked, changing the subject. "She has been missing you these many, many weeks."

I tilted my head toward the door. "Inside. I've missed her too."

I didn't add that I hoped my separation from Mima would soon come to an end. Jackson had pulled an extra chair to his table and invited Mima to join him and the Motembo crew. She had been sitting there now for at least an hour, talking, listening, and taking the measure of people I had come to know well. They were learning about her too, of course. I glanced through the door to see Jaleen and Kiki lean toward her to share something that made them all laugh.

The two rangers who had carried Marks's body out of the path of the fire had sat quietly on stools next to the bar for most of the afternoon. They were local men, unused to large groups of people and too shy to speak during the tributes. I went inside and stood next to them, not expecting to talk. I just wanted to recognize the men, to say with my presence that I respected them, honored their work, and appreciated their loyalty to Marks. I was startled when one of them spoke. His voice was so soft I had to move in closer.

"We buried him deep." His eyes were not on me but somewhere else, remembering. "When we finished, we placed rocks on the disturbed soil, a blanket of rocks and stones. That night we slept by the side of the grave. I woke up at sunrise. Even before I opened my eyes, I felt them there. Elephants. A herd of elephants stood about ten meters away, on the other side. They were very quiet. The biggest female stepped forward first. She wanded her trunk over the stones and gently toed one of the rocks. After a moment she moved on. The rest of the elephants filed slowly past the grave, one by one."

Author's Note

The Story of Bones is a companion to my previous novel, *Waiting for Bones*, which focuses on the four Americans Bones abandons at the baobab tree. The account of what happened to Abby, Todd, Nina, and Griff during their harrowing day and night in the bush ends with unanswered questions about their guide.

Although my intention in *Waiting for Bones* was to illustrate the precarious nature of life in the bush—animals and people can and do simply disappear—in hindsight, the mystery of what had happened to Bones was too intriguing to ignore. Did he go off to smoke a cigarette? Be sick? Scout for animals? Did a lion get him? Did he twist an ankle and encounter hyenas? Was it snake bite? Sunstroke?

We knew Bones kept a journal. When he walked away, leaving the foursome parked under a baobab tree, he took his rifle and long-range radio but not the journal or his canteen. He went toward the river past a stand of trees, where a baboon barked a warning. When he reached the river, he dropped out of sight. Although he abandoned them, the Americans thought he was an excellent guide. That was all we knew about the man named Bones.

I decided to flesh out Bones's story in the voice of Bones himself, starting with his life as a ten-year-old boy and following him as he grows to manhood in a sub-Saharan village. My own travels to southern Africa supplied background, including templates for the fictional camp, Motembo, and the general routines of an African safari. Although the scourge of wildlife poaching is all too real, *The Story of Bones*, including locations, characters, and events, is fiction—an imaginative work anchored in research and insights gained from people I consulted, leaned on, and pestered.

Daniel Karn walked me through the world of hunters, firearms, and ammunition, answering countless inquiries with patience and wonderful detail. His response to the question "What do you carry when you go hunting?" was a list of forty-nine specific items.

Brian Cousins, a master angler, supplied all I needed to know about fishermen and fishing, including the phenomenon of birds stealing a catch.

John Cousins, whose breadth of interests and knowledge is legendary, answered questions about vehicles, jacks, winches, mud, rifles, guns, solid lead projectiles, river currents and cut banks, water temperatures, and the adventures of small boys.

Tim Sanborn, MD, and his colleague Ted Feldman, MD, supplied Kate Swale's symptoms, diagnosis, and cure.

Judith Barnard interrupted her own writing to offer cogent insights and wordsmithing.

Shelly Bell Hetner crafted a striking cover and provided guidance on all things digital.

Readers who previewed the entire manuscript reminded me how essential fresh, discerning eyes are to the quality of a final draft. These previewers gave generously of their time and enthusiasm and showed eagle-eyed attention to detail: David H. Colton, Reven Fellars, Susan Garrett, Marianne Devries Horrell, Julia M. Nowicki, and Frani O'Toole.

My profound thanks to each and every one.

My husband, Dirk Vos, has been an unfailing source of encouragement since the day the screen was blank. I am deeply grateful for his love and support every step of the way.

An excerpt from *Waiting for Bones*

by

Donna Cousins

Chapter 1

"Wait here," the guide said.

Then he stepped down from the Land Cruiser and set off on a path so sketchy it might not have been a path at all. The four passengers seated two-by-two in ascending rows behind the front seat watched puffs of dust explode behind his boots as he stalked away. Bones, the guide, had never left them alone out there—not for a minute.

They were parked beneath a colossal baobab tree that thrust itself up from parched sub-Saharan earth. The sun had only moments before breached the horizon and begun its assault on the cold morning air. Sitting in the roofless, wide-open vehicle in zipped-up jackets they would soon fling away, they stared at their leader's back, alert for any clue to his unexplained departure.

The land around them appeared spare and endless. Random clusters of flat-topped vegetation measured a foot in height or twenty and stood a few yards away or a mile, perspective being the first casualty of a vast, alien wilderness. To gaze into the distant dawn was to feel as small as an insect. Yet a short drive in any direction could change the landscape entirely, from wide-open bushveld to dense, riverine woodland or muddy, croc-infested delta.

"He's going for a smoke," Todd said, squinting into the middle range. He was leaning forward, with his kneecaps hard against the back of the vacated driver's seat. "Bones smokes, you know."

Abby was resting her hand on the plank of Todd's thigh, one variation of the bodily contact that was as characteristic of this pair as their fair-haired good looks. They were always touching, if not like this then with Todd's arm around Abby or her head tilted against his shoulder, as though physical contact formed the bond that made them a couple. But as she watched Bones shrink into the landscape, Abby's fingers gripped more forcefully than before the rock-hard quadriceps of the man she would most likely marry.

"No, I think he wants a better look, up there," she said. She released Todd's thigh to point a crescent of varnished fingernail at a rise spiked with termite mounds the size of tepees. "See? He's walking that way."

In her other hand Abby cradled a pair of binoculars so powerful she could spot the ticks on a distant rhino. She held the lenses against her cheekbones and dialed down on a bouncing black cavern that turned out to be the barrel of the rifle slung over Bones's shoulder. Bones took the rifle? She hadn't noticed until now.

A glance across the seat in front of her confirmed that the gun rack was indeed empty, a long, dark void. Bones's canteen was still there, so old and battered it might have watered Ernest Hemingway on his way to shoot a lion. The ignition held a key attached to a fob that hung in the air like a spider lowering itself for a glance at Bones's guidebooks: *The Birds of Southern Africa*, *Reptile Encyclopedia*. Next to the books sat Bones's journal, a rain-swelled volume with curling ivory pages.

"I've seen him smoke," Todd insisted, nodding his head. "More than once." He had watched Bones light up after dinner, the flame of the matchstick a tiny comet next to the campfire that warmed them each night under a bright swath of stars. The guide had stood unblinking in the amber glow of the fire, exhaling tusks of smoke that curled upward and vanished into the night. A young man who had seen everything.

Abby rubbed the lenses of her binoculars with a silken square, then folded the cloth in a neat rectangle and tucked it inside her multipocketed travel vest. Simple tasks that tidied and organized steadied her in untamed surroundings. A careful traveler, she looked for adventure modified by first-class provisions for comfort and safety. She would go almost anywhere with a guide as capable as Bones, and she planned and packed with attention to the smallest detail, ticking from a list the clothes, hardware, and pharmaceuticals suggested for every possible contingency.

"He took the rifle," she announced, in case anyone had failed to notice. "And the radio."

Behind Abby and Todd their friends Nina and Griff occupied the uppermost seat and a marginally superior vantage point for taking in the great sweep of the African bush. At the moment no parts of Nina and Griff happened to be pressed together, but the two shared the nearly telepathic bandwidth that comes with almost three decades of marriage. Now they exchanged a bewildered look that said, *Bones is walking away?*

None of them needed reminding that Bones was more than their driver. He was a bush-savvy scout, navigator, and tracker—the unquestioned leader. Safari guides interpreted roars, snorts, and cackles. They were repositories of essential wilderness skills and lifesaving wisdom. Most of all, they stood between the tourists perched high in unenclosed safari vehicles and the hard realities of the African bush.

In the middle seat, Todd shifted his legs to a new acute angle. His tall, angular body appeared devoid of fat, and he had recently worked his storkish stride the entire length of the Chicago marathon. Immobility chafed at him like a tether. Hands that spanned two and a half octaves on the piano now fingered a riff across the tops of his khaki-clad thighs. As he watched Bones stride away, his head bobbed on his long neck as if keeping time to music, and the toes of his shoes rose and fell against the metal floorboard. He was the image of uncontained energy, a man who had spent a lifetime fidgeting and training, every muscle primed for the long haul.

He visored his hand to stare at Bones's retreating form, hoping to prove his own astute grasp of the situation. "He's probably got a Dunhill going already."

"Why couldn't he smoke right here?" Abby wanted to know. "We wouldn't report him or anything." Her voice had grown testy. She needed the wide, reassuring moat formed by expert guides and camp staffs who kept luxury inside and everything that was harsh and dangerous out. For her, Bones's departure changed everything.

"He doesn't know that," Todd answered. "And he's not going to break a rule in front of us."

"Leaving us here isn't breaking a rule?" She lifted her binoculars. "Look how far he's gone." She paused, watching. "Maybe he wants to see what's behind that hill."

"You mean the dagga boy?" A hint of a smile played on Todd's lips.

Abby twirled the focus. "A buffalo?" The pitch of her voice had risen. "There's no buffalo."

Bones had warned them about dagga boys, the bachelor Cape buffalos infamous for aggression. Ornery and persevering, a dagga boy would charge any intruder, even stalk a person on foot for miles.

"Maybe he wants to shoot our supper," Griff said, joking, hoping to ease her discomfort. "Buffalo burgers."

Nina gave him a look. "Bones would rather shoot a poacher than almost any animal. Whatever he's doing, he'll be right back." She said this with her usual unshakable assurance. It suited Nina to believe that life was controllable and that she was in charge of her own roomy universe, but of course this was as untrue for her as it was for everyone else.

She tipped her face to search the forked thicket of baobab that canopied above their heads and wondered uneasily what wild creatures might be attracted to that stout, sheltering leviathan of a tree. Without guidance from Bones, she was not sure exactly what to look at or listen for. Now every twig and mote, every toot and whistle seemed equally significant. She picked out the network of veins in a translucent leaf. A tiny gecko stared back at her. The natural world seemed to be projecting itself with unusual clarity.

Todd locked his fingers and placed both hands flat on top of his head. He twisted around to look at Griff. "This is fun. Just sitting here."

"Relax, Todd," Griff said. "Watch for birds."

Abby pointed at a small one poised like a jewel on the tip of a thistle. "Look. A lilac-breasted roller."

Todd looked, unimpressed. He was okay during game drives, when the excitement of the hunt sucked up every joule of excess energy. Stopped dead under a tree, however, the urge to move tormented him like an itch. Now he squirmed, drummed his fingers, and eyed their guide's diminishing backside.

Abby, too, was watching Bones. He had walked past the termite mounds, hurried right past them. "Now where's he going?" she said, exasperated.

Todd stood and reached for the side rail. "I'll go find out."

"You're not serious." The expression on Abby's face said she knew he was.

"Forget it, Todd," Griff said. "He's only been out there a few minutes."

"Less than ten," Nina put in.

"Less than ten? Who's wearing a watch?" Todd's eyes traveled from wrist to wrist.

Griff reached over and tugged on Todd's sleeve. "Sit. Please. No one walks around here unarmed. He'll come back any minute."

The expression on Todd's face said, *You are so lame.* But before he could shape his disgust into words, the jarring *yak-yak-yak* of a frantic baboon rang across the grassland. *Yak! Yak! Yak!* An unmistakable warning to head for the trees.

About the Author

Donna Cousins earned a master's degree from the Medill School of Journalism before becoming a fiction writer. She has worked in Europe and Asia, where her articles on local culture have appeared in the *Courier*, the *Singapore American* newspaper, *Orientations*, and *Asia Magazine*, among other publications. In the United States, she was a founding editor of *Career World* magazine. Her previous novels include *Landscape* and *Waiting for Bones*, for which she won awards from *Writer's Digest*, *ForeWord Review*, *ForeWord Magazine*, and the Midwest Independent Publishers Association. She lives in Chicago.

www.donnacousins.com
donna@donnacousins.com

Made in the USA
San Bernardino, CA
01 July 2019